THE CASE OF THE
CURIOUS COOK

THE CASE OF THE CURIOUS COOK

A WISE Enquiries Agency mystery

Cathy Ace

severn
House

This first world edition published 2016
in Great Britain and 2017 in the USA by
SEVERN HOUSE PUBLISHERS LTD of
19 Cedar Road, Sutton, Surrey, England, SM2 5DA.
Trade paperback edition first published
in Great Britain and the USA 2017 by
SEVERN HOUSE PUBLISHERS LTD

British Library Cataloguing in Publication Data
A CIP catalogue record for this title is available from the British Library.

ISBN-13: 978-0-7278-8668-2 (cased)
ISBN-13: 978-1-84751-771-5 (trade paper)
ISBN-13: 978-1-78010-838-4 (e-book)

All Severn House titles are printed on acid-free paper.

Severn House Publishers support the Forest Stewardship Council™ [FSC™],
the leading international forest certification organisation.
All our titles that are printed on FSC certified paper carry the FSC logo.

Typeset by Palimpsest Book Production Ltd.,
Falkirk, Stirlingshire, Scotland.
Printed and bound in Great Britain by
TJ International, Padstow, Cornwall.

For my mother and sister, and in memory of my father . . .
and every one of those ninety-nine green bottles
hanging on the wall

ACKNOWLEDGEMENTS

With thanks to my agent, Priya Doraswamy, of Lotus Lane Literary Agency, and the entire team at Severn House Publishers who allow the women of the WISE Enquiries Agency to tackle their cases and get into (and out of) many dreadful pickles. Also to Mum and Dad, who engendered a passion for books in both their daughters, to all the librarians and booksellers who have stoked those flames over the decades and have now played their part in allowing this book to find its way into your hands.

ONE

Henry Devereaux Twyst, eighteenth Duke of Chellingworth, was terribly worried about the books in the lower library. Following his marriage to Stephanie Timbers, some three months earlier, the couple had moved into the bedchamber and apartment on the second floor of Chellingworth Hall formerly used by Henry's grandparents. Having been mothballed for decades, the bathroom where he and his bride performed their daily ablutions in a carefree manner had been harboring a dangerous secret; a rubber ring inside one of the art deco taps had perished. This small failure had allowed water to seep, unheeded, along a meandering pathway until it arrived at the bookshelves in a corner of the ground floor library. What might have been no more than an unfortunate inconvenience had assumed the proportions of a potential tragedy, because the shelves in question were reserved for the Twyst's impressive – and priceless – collection of ancient bibles and sacred books.

It had cost a pound – *just one pound!* – to purchase a replacement for the offending rubber washer; the cost to remediate the damage to the irreplaceable books, if remediation were indeed possible, was yet to be determined. Beneath the watchful gaze of his mother, Henry paced the morning room muttering under his breath as he awaited a verdict. The Chellingworth Bible was of particular concern; one of only two known volumes of its type, it had been created by Dominican monks in the mid-fourteenth century, probably around the time Geoffrey Chaucer himself was born, and was now under a terrible threat. It was over six hundred and fifty years old, and Henry was keenly aware it had come to harm on his watch.

'Any news yet, Henry?' Stephanie entered the room silently, startling her husband.

'Not a dickie bird. He's been in there for over an hour.' Despite his impatience, Henry's spirits lifted a little at the sight of his wife. *His wife.* How wonderful that knowledge made him feel.

His mother Althea smiled at her daughter-in-law's arrival, and patted the spot beside her on the sofa with an encouraging smile.

Stephanie hovered uncertainly and checked her watch. 'The doors will open to allow public admittance in forty-five minutes. I think I'd better get the lower library roped off for today. We don't want to disturb him.'

Henry's spirits plummeted again. 'You're right, of course,' he acknowledged with a sigh. 'I'll just pop my head in and tell the chap he can find us in the estate offices when he's finished.'

Their conversation was interrupted by the arrival of Edward, the Twyst's butler.

'Mr Bryn Jenkins is asking to see you, Your Grace. Should I tell him to join you here?'

Henry turned and pulled down the points of his waistcoat beneath his jacket. 'Absolutely. Bring him in immediately.' He smiled nervously at his wife and mother. 'Now for the moment of truth.' The tremor in his voice betrayed his anxiety, which made him cross.

A head taller than the duke, and a decade older than Henry's fifty-five years, Bryn Jenkins carried himself erect, and with dignity; his wiry, birdlike frame was upright. His bony, slightly hooked nose twitched as he crossed the spacious room and his hands fluttered as he cleaned his spectacles then replaced them upon their perch.

Finally facing each other, Henry waved an outstretched arm toward a chair, and Bryn Jenkins took a seat.

Henry also sat, and asked, 'Is it bad?' It was the best he could muster.

The lenses of his eyeglasses glittering in the morning sun, the book-restorer's expression was impossible to read. Henry hardly dared breathe.

Bryn Jenkins replied, 'Not as bad as it could be, Your Grace. Thank heavens. I believe I could have everything returned to good order pretty quickly, relatively speaking. Patience and experience should do it. And it'll cost a bit, too, of course.'

Henry had expected the topic of money to raise its ugly head, but was at least relieved to discover he wouldn't forever be known as the duke who'd allowed a piece of internationally-renowned art to be ruined. 'The Chellingworth Bible can be saved?' He finally dared say the words.

Bryn smiled toothily. 'It can be, Your Grace. Though, of course, as I am sure Your Grace is aware, it shouldn't really be called a "bible" because it's a book of biblical stories, designed to allow holy teachings to be delivered in such a way that fourteenth-century, illiterate peasants could understand them. The Twyst Bible on the other hand, now that's a *real* bible, of course. I'm sorry to say it's in slightly worse condition. While it's not as old as your other volumes, it's still quite something for me to get to work on a copy of the 1611 King James Bible presented by King James himself to your forebears, Your Grace. Your family tree and the accompanying signatures inside its back cover must be very precious to you. That part is undamaged I'm happy to say, though there's some damp in a portion of the front binding and the spine. A lot of work, that'll be, but I can get it shipshape, sure enough.'

Henry beamed. 'That's not as bad as I'd feared.'

The dowager put down her cup and saucer and clapped her hands. 'I am so relieved, Mr Jenkins. I'll admit I've always been more fond of the Twyst Bible than the Chellingworth Bible. It has a long-lived connection with the family – though I know the world beyond these walls would disagree about the relative value of the two volumes. What about the William Morgan Bible? That's older than the King James, and, being the original Welsh translation, probably more culturally sensitive in these parts.'

Bryn tilted his head. 'That's a very thoughtful thing to say, Your Grace. And you're quite right – means a lot to we Welsh, does that one. Not as valuable as the King James, but, as you say, a culturally sensitive work. That one's fine, funnily enough. Not a bit of damage. It was saved by its box. Good Welsh oak. Well-oiled and polished. Almost as good as waterproof. Stopped the seeping in its tracks.'

'That is a relief,' chimed in Stephanie. 'Any other volumes damaged?'

Bryn stood, holding out a piece of paper. 'A few, yes. Here's a list. I've written up what I propose to do, and what it'll cost.' He handed the paper to the duke, incorrectly judging he'd be in charge of the work ahead. 'There's just one thing I haven't said there,' he added.

Scanning the notes, and focusing on the worryingly large amount of money involved, Henry answered absently. 'And that is?'

Bryn shifted his weight. 'Usually I'd do the work at my own shop. I've got a little place in the attic where I do my restoration work. But for these? I don't think I could afford the insurance. Besides, there's some sort of strange shenanigans going on at the moment, so I'd rather the items didn't spend any time there at all. If there was somewhere here, at Chellingworth Hall, where I could bring my tools of the trade, so to speak, I could do it all without any of the pieces having to leave the premises.'

'Of course we can arrange that, can't we, dear?' said the duchess.

Henry lifted his head. 'Pardon? Oh, absolutely. Whatever you say, my dear.'

Stephanie smiled. 'When would you like to begin, Mr Jenkins?'

Straightening his shoulders the tall man rubbed his chin. 'The first thing to do is to clear all the volumes away to a safer environment, and I think that should be done immediately. For that we'd just need a secure place. Then I'll need a dry, well-lit room – no direct sunlight, mind you – with some good, solid, flat tabletops, no drafts, and quite a few power outlets. The room shouldn't be dusty. Wherever it is, it'll need a thorough vacuuming. And, of course, you'd probably prefer there to be effective locks on the door.'

Henry panicked. With 268 rooms, Chellingworth Hall was bound to offer something of the type Bryn Jenkins had just described, but he was dashed if he could think of it.

Stephanie stood. 'I know exactly the place, Mr Jenkins.' She looked at her watch. 'If you would return at, say, nine o'clock tomorrow, with any supplies and equipment you might need to bring, you will be able to inspect the room to ensure it meets your needs. Will that suit?'

Bryn nodded eagerly. 'Sounds spot on, thank you, Your Grace. I'll be back and forth here over the next few weeks. I'll make arrangements with my daughter to schedule proper cover for me at the shop.'

'But of course,' replied Stephanie, moving to pull the bell-rope beside the fireplace. 'You have that lovely place Crooks and Cooks, don't you?'

Bryn preened himself. 'You've heard of it?'

'Indeed I have, Mr Jenkins. I've been there on many an occasion myself. You might not remember me, because I spent most of my time upstairs in your cookery books' section with your lovely daughter, Val.'

Bryn Jenkins looked stunned. 'You know my Val?' was the man's first remark. 'Well, I never,' he added.

His awestruck blubbering was curtailed when Stephanie turned to Edward, who had appeared at the door in response to her ringing for him. 'Close off the lower library for today, please, Edward, and arrange for Mr Jenkins to have all the help he needs to take a number of volumes from the lower library to His Grace's old bedroom. Then ask Mrs Davies to dust, vacuum, and polish the old nursery. Not His Grace's old nursery, but the sixteenth duke's, please. Thank you.' Turning to Bryn she added, 'The sixteenth duke's old nursery is spacious and has large, barred windows, facing north. It was wired for power when it was used by the seventeenth duke during his photography-loving phase. I think it'll meet your needs.'

Bryn glowed with delight. 'Absolutely, Your Grace . . . Your Graces,' he stammered as he walked out of the room almost backwards, and almost bowing.

As the door closed behind the bookseller Althea asked, 'Is there something else, Edward?'

Henry looked up. His mother's tone was odd. He could see that Edward, unusually, was shifting his weight from one foot to another. Indeed, he was almost hopping. He looked extremely uncomfortable.

Edward cleared his throat. 'It's Lady Clementine, Your Graces. She's fired her nurse – again – and is insisting a replacement is found within the hour. Nurse Thomas is packing as I speak. I wondered how Your Graces would like me to proceed. It would appear the situation is rather urgent.'

Henry rolled his eyes in his mother's direction. Althea sighed. 'She must have sacked the poor woman at least half a dozen times in the past few months. I'll go to Lady Clementine shortly, Edward. If you'll ask Nurse Thomas to stop packing, that would be helpful. Thank you.'

'Thank *you*, Your Grace.' Edward vanished through the door.

Once they were alone, Henry allowed himself to sag a little. 'Thank you for offering to intercede with Clemmie, Mother. She can be a terrible bother, I know. When she arrived with her leg in that plaster cast, months ago, I thought we'd be shot of her by now.'

'So did I,' agreed Althea. 'As children go, she's a challenge. If only she could find her soul mate, as you have, Henry.' Winking at her daughter-in-law the dowager added, 'Thank you for taking him off my hands, dear.'

Henry's wife's gaze toward him was both loving and sympathetic as she said, 'Clemmie would have been back in London weeks ago,

had she not taken that tumble down the steps to the croquet lawn.
I don't know why she thought she could manage all on her own
and without her crutches.'

'I'd better get along and see your sister right away,' said Althea,
kissing her son on the cheek. 'And I want to catch Mr Jenkins before
he leaves. I'm rather intrigued to find out what he meant by "strange
shenanigans" at his bookshop. Sounds like that might be just my
cup of tea.'

'Mother . . .' called Henry with a warning tone as Althea left the
room, ignoring him.

In the hallway, Althea caught up with the bookseller. 'Mr
Jenkins, I wonder if I could have a word before you leave about
the unusual goings-on at your bookshop?' Her eyes twinkled with
anticipation.

Bryn blushed. 'It's nothing that needs to concern Your Grace,
I'm sure,' he replied.

Althea winked. 'Oh go on – tell me. I adore the sound of "strange
shenanigans".'

Bryn sighed. 'It's nothing, really. Honestly. Just the sort of thing
a person who runs a shop should – well, I don't know I would say
"expect", but I'm sure stranger things have happened.'

Althea licked her lips. 'So, something unusual then? Not just
books going missing? That's the sort of thing one would expect,
I'd have thought.'

Bryn's eyes lit up. 'Exactly; Your Grace is very perceptive.
Pilferage is something a person might expect. But this? Well, it's
the exact opposite, you see.'

'The opposite?'

Bryn looked over his shoulder, as though to make sure the pair
couldn't be overheard, and leaned in. 'Yes,' he whispered. 'It's a
real puzzle.'

'Oh, I do so love a puzzle,' said Althea brightly as she took the
man's arm and steered him toward the empty dining room. 'Now
why don't you tell me all about it?'

TWO

'Annie's late, again,' noted Mavis MacDonald, consulting the watch pinned to her chest. 'Does that girl have no idea at all of time? It was only last night we agreed on meeting here at the office at ten o'clock.'

'I think you're stretching the use of the word "girl", Mavis. In fact, given that Annie's fifty-six, I think you've snapped it,' said Carol Hill wiping the mouth of her infant son, who was perched on her lap. Her head popped up as she heard excited yapping outside the open windows of the converted barn; the WISE Enquiries Agency had been using it as their office base for about six months. 'That'll be her now. And it sounds like she's brought Gertie with her.' She held up her son so she could look into his cherubic face. 'You like Annie's puppy Gertie, don't you, Albert? Yes, you do. And Gertie likes licking your feet, doesn't she? Yes, she does. Gertie's a very cute little thing – just like you. She's still a baby, just like you.'

'The wee bairn'll grow up sounding like an idiot if you keep speaking to him like that, Carol,' chided Mavis with a kind glint in her eye. 'Children don't need to be cooed at. Just treat him like a small human being. Use your normal tone. It's what I did with my two boys, and they turned out to be fine young men.'

Carol sighed quietly, and forced a smile. She was discovering that being a new mother meant anyone and everyone felt they had the right to dole out parenting advice – whether she wanted it or not – and she was beginning to find it rather wearing.

The door flew open and a scrambling puppy dragged a skidding human into the room. 'Hold on there!' cried Annie at Gertie, to no effect. Spotting the wriggling, squealing baby, the young black Labrador began to strain in her harness, all four of her gangly legs sprawling in different directions, and both of Annie's doing the same thing. Annie struggled to shut the door behind her and released her grip on the dog's lead at the same time. 'Look out, Car, incoming. Gertie'll be after Bertie's feet!'

Carol stood, lifting her wriggling son's legs out of the dog's frantic reach. 'He's not Bertie, he's Albert, Annie. *Please* don't call him that.'

'Alright, doll,' said Annie, collapsing onto the sofa in a heap. Gertie decided to give up on trying to reach Albert's tasty toes and launched herself at Annie's lap instead.

'Ach, a babe and a pup – we'll never get anything done today,' snapped Mavis, retiring to the cubbyhole beneath the stairs to pour herself a cup of tea.

'Where's Chrissy?' called Annie, wrangling her puppy's eager pink tongue away from her face.

'Driving down from Nottingham where she's been doing some work for a pig farmer who suspected his estate manager was fiddling the books,' said Carol, burping Albert on her shoulder. 'She had to slum it in an eighteenth-century farmhouse with only six bedrooms for a few days.' She winked at Annie. 'Won't be back until tonight. I'm to email her the minutes of the meeting.'

With Gertie finally settled at her feet, Annie thanked Mavis with her eyes as she took a mug of coffee from her friend and colleague. 'Is Chrissy being escorted by the enigmatic Mr Alexander Bright?'

'Not this past week, though they're usually joined at the hip,' replied Carol, knowingly.

'I bet they are,' replied Annie with a wicked grin, but too quietly for Mavis to hear. 'And Althea?' she added more loudly.

'On her way,' replied Mavis. 'She had a meeting up at the hall and will be delivered here in her car by Ian Cottesloe.'

'Oh, the perks of being a dowager duchess.' Annie snorted out tea as Gertie pawed her leg, squeaking with excitement. Even at the tender age of six months she'd learned the connection between the scent of coffee and the likelihood of biscuit crumbs to come.

'So let's begin,' said Mavis, calling the meeting to order in a quieter-than-usual voice. 'We missed our Monday meeting this week because you were working on that case in Cardiff, Annie; you had a hospital appointment, Carol; and Christine was in Nottingham. We've all had a copy of Christine's report on her case, so let's consolidate yours, Annie.'

Annie placed her mug on the table, and dropped a tiny piece of a Rich Tea biscuit onto the floor for Gertie, who lunged forward, inhaled it, and wagged her tail furiously.

'I can tell you that The Case of the Cheapskate Chip Shop Manager has been successfully concluded.' Annie beamed, proud she'd coined another alliterative title for her endeavors in the field. Mavis tutted. 'I learned a thing or two about battering and deep fat frying, I can tell you, and I used my unfailing abilities as an investigative superstar to gain entry to the office at the back of the chip shop, and take photos of the orders and receipts. Turns out the halibut wasn't halibut and the so-called "vegetarian" frying oil wasn't vegetarian at all. The manager was cutting corners all over the place and charging for stuff he wasn't providing. I've sent all the paperwork on to the owner.' She swelled with pride.

'Everything copied to Carol so she can send the invoice?' asked Mavis.

'Yes, and I sent it first thing this morning,' replied Carol.

'Well done, ladies,' praised Mavis. Annie reached down to pet the wriggling Gertie. 'I'll follow up with the client. If she's happy with your undercover work in Cardiff, Annie, it could be very good for us; she owns a chain of seventeen chip shops across South Wales. Who knows where this might lead.'

Annie sat back in the sofa and sighed. 'Probably to another placement where a woman in her fifties with dark, St Lucian skin and an accent straight out of the East End of London won't stick out like a sore thumb. So something low paid, working class and 'orrible, I shouldn't wonder.'

Annie noticed Mavis's eyes soften. 'Ach, come along with you. You know we value your efforts; this was a case where Carol couldn't do it because of Albert, Christine's plummy accent – or even her natural Irish brogue – would have made her unlikely to blend into the workforce of a chip shop in Cardiff, and me?' Mavis hooked her gray bobbed hair behind her ears. 'They'd take one look at me and think I was too old for the job, even though I could jump over the heads of most youngsters. You were the ideal choice; you're a real asset to this firm, and don't you forget it.'

Annie took the compliments and smiled. She looked proud when she said, 'Ta, Mave.'

At that moment, Althea Twyst and her trusty Jack Russell, McFli, arrived at the office. It took a good five minutes before the dogs had finished greeting each other. Finally Gertie and McFli were paw to paw on the floor, contemplating their next moves.

Mavis began, 'I have a case for you in Swansea, Annie, which means you'll have to stay there for a couple of nights at least, or maybe up to a week. That's as far as the client's budget will extend.

It begins on Sunday, when Carol will start a leave of absence from the office.'

Annie was confused. 'What's wrong with Car? Car? Is somethin' up with Bertie?'

Carol shook her head. 'Car*ol* is just fine, thank you, as is A.L.B.E.R.T. It's David. His mam's suffered a mini-stroke and he's off to see her for a few days now that she's out of hospital. He won't be able to look after Albert at all, so I'll be working from home. Thanks Mavis, I'll take you up on your offer. You OK with that, Annie?'

''Course, doll,' said Annie with a grin. 'What's the job for me, Mave? Frying fish again, back working behind a bar – or something more exotic?'

'A manufacturer of sweets – sour lemon gobstoppers, that sort of thing – on an industrial estate just outside Swansea. Night shift,' said Mavis.

Annie couldn't resist. 'What, they reckon someone's got sticky fingers? Ha!' She laughed at her own joke, and the three other women joined in, Albert smiling and burping along with them.

Althea raised her hand. 'I think I might have a new client for us too.'

All eyes turned toward the compact little woman who was sitting very upright on the sofa, sporting an early-summer outfit that, surprisingly, combined pale blue, vivid green and puce.

Mavis straightened her shoulders. 'Aye? Go on then. Tell us about it.'

Althea looked coy. 'I don't know if it will come to anything, but I met a very nice man at the hall who mentioned he has a bit of a problem at his bookshop, so I took the opportunity to press him on the matter. I think he's got something that could be right up our street. He'll be here in five minutes.'

Annie's tummy turned. Althea's ideas about the sort of matter a professional firm of enquiry agents should look into sometimes didn't quite tally with those of the other four members of the company. Mavis had often suggested Althea didn't seem to be able to differentiate between amateur sleuthing and professional investigating.

'Go on,' urged Mavis.

'He's the man working on the bibles and so forth that were damaged by the water that leaked into the lower library from Henry and

Stephanie's bathroom. He also has a bookshop in Hay-on-Wye, and mentioned some "strange shenanigans" going on there. I said we might be able to help and he seemed interested.' Althea smiled, her bright eyes twinkling with delight.

Mavis started pacing. Annie reckoned she was working out how to let the dowager down gently. Finally Mavis said, 'If it's shoplifting, he should get in touch with the local police. They have all sorts of free services to help retailers come up with the type of surveillance they need to utilize to be able to protect their merchandise. Of course we could advise on the same topic too, but we'd have to charge for our services, and that might be beyond the wallet of a bookshop owner.'

'Oh no, that's not it at all,' said Althea. 'No one's stealing his books, it's quite the opposite. He's already been to the police, and they've said they can't help, so I said we could.'

Three pairs of puzzled eyes stared at Althea. It was Mavis who spoke. 'I'm sorry, dear, what exactly do you mean?'

The dowager looked excited. 'He's got more books at the end of the month than at the beginning. They just seem to materialize. Out of thin air. And they aren't even the type of books he sells. He reckons someone's sneaking into his shop and depositing books there without his knowledge. He has no idea why anyone would do such a thing. He's completely baffled.' Althea had the same look about her as a cat that's dropped a mouse at the feet of its human. 'He said he'd be happy to hear how we can help him out. This could be the first paying client I've brought to the business. Isn't it thrilling?'

'The Case of the Baffled Bookseller? Brilliant!' said Annie with a chuckle.

Mavis tutted. 'You mean he sells books, but he ends up with more than he started with?' Althea nodded. 'And this has been going on for a while?' More nodding.

'Cor, that sounds a lot more interesting than working the night shift in a sweet factory,' said Annie, her eyes glowing.

Mavis shot Annie a warning glance. 'The sweet factory is a real case. With a paying client. That's our priority.'

A polite cough drew everyone's attention. 'Hello there. I'm Bryn Jenkins. Am I in the right place for the detectives?'

'Mr Jenkins, there you are. Do come in. Mavis, shall we take tea while Mr Jenkins tells us about his curious case?' asked Althea.

It was Mavis's turn to clear her throat. 'Aye, tea's a good idea while we all listen and try to decide if there's anything our firm of enquiry agents can do to help Mr Jenkins.'

'Please, it's Bryn,' said the bookseller as he somewhat cautiously took the seat the dowager duchess was patting, a welcoming smile on her face.

By the time he'd told his tale, everyone had finished their tea, and all eyes turned toward Mavis.

'And you have no idea where these books come from?' Mavis was trying to work out if Bryn Jenkins was imagining things, or if there really was a puzzling case to be investigated.

Bryn Jenkins removed his spectacles and cleaned them absent-mindedly. 'It's as I've told you. I have a specific way of marking the books I have for sale. Color-coded stickers allow me to price them easily and I know every volume I have on offer. Each one has passed through my hands; I know my stock inside and out. Besides, some of the books that have shown up aren't anything to do with crime. Nor are they cook books. The only "crime" is that they are on my shelves and tables, and have no business being there at all.'

Mavis silently admitted the man seemed quite sure of himself. Sensible, too. She'd listened as he'd explained his well-organized systems for shelving, stocktaking, and promoting. She'd learned a good deal about the strange things people had tried to sell him, and was still grappling with the list of bizarre items he'd told them he'd found inside second-hand books over the years. He was all business, this Bryn Jenkins. Mavis warmed to him.

'I cannae agree it's a crime that books arrive in your shop, unheralded, but I accept it's curious,' said Mavis thoughtfully.

'Can't you pass them to someone else in Hay-on-Wye who owns the sort of shop that sells that particular type of book and be done with it? I know the town has dozens of bookshops, and I can only imagine someone, somewhere, would be happy to take them off your hands and sell them on,' said Carol.

Bryn rose from his seat and re-polished his already gleaming spectacles, something he didn't seem to know he was doing. 'I see what you mean, but that's not the point. Yes, I could divvie them up and dole them out around my fellow booksellers, but I want to know where they come from. What if they're stolen? I'd be acting as a fence for crooks if I sold them, and I can't be doing that. And even if they aren't stolen, I still don't like it. I know it's not as bad as someone removing books from my shelves and running off with them but . . .' The man paused, flapping his elbows as he ground the corner of his handkerchief around the lenses of his glasses, 'I realize it sounds a bit odd. Indeed, my daughter Val, who runs our cookery-themed area, has told me I'm being a stupid old so-and-so on more than one occasion. But, you see, I can't help it. I feel like I've been violated in some way. They might as well have *taken* books instead of *bringing* them; I feel the same way about it. Something's going on in my shop, and I don't know what it is. It's been months now, and I don't like it. It's affecting the way I look at everyone who comes in to browse. It's sucking all the pleasure out of being in the shop for me. So, yes, it is something I would be prepared to invest in. What could you do for me, and how much would it cost?'

Carol and Mavis exchanged a glance. Carol spoke. 'I believe what you need is a good, old-fashioned surveillance job. We'd be looking for people who deposit books rather than removing them, but the principle remains the same. It could take some time, so I'd suggest an installation of cameras.'

'I thought I'd already mentioned I've got one of those, and mirrors too.' Bryn Jenkins sounded a little exasperated as he pushed his spectacles onto his nose.

'Yes, you said you have a camera, signs announcing its presence, and some mirrors so you can watch people in hidden corners,' said Carol. 'We could ascertain the best positions for viewing points, possibly install some extra equipment, and we could also review recordings of comings and goings, saving you the time and effort of doing so. We'd study the recordings on a daily basis, reporting back to you on our findings. That's not something you've been able to do, as I understand it.'

'You're right there,' said Bryn with a sigh. 'With the shop, the sort of work I'm doing up at the hall and my responsibilities as the Chair of the Hay Booksellers' Association this year, it's all a bit much for me, I must admit. I had no idea that latter post would involve so much work – especially organizing the book tent for the Chellingworth Summer Fete. In previous years I've merely turned up with stock on the morning of the event; I didn't have an inkling about how much went on behind the scenes by way of preparation. The meetings are frequent now. The duchess is very . . . detailed in her approach.' He peered over his wire rims at Althea.

'The young duchess is taking her new responsibilities seriously,' replied the dowager cautiously, 'as is quite proper. I haven't overseen the fete for some years, the task falling to a self-governing committee.'

Bryn's shoulders relaxed. 'I was at one of the meetings yesterday. There's a bloke called Tudor Evans – he runs the Lamb and Flag pub in Anwen-by-Wye, I understand, and some woman named Marjorie Pritchard – who's got quite a voice on her. They both seemed to be vying for control all the time. But the duchess? Well, I know she's only in her early thirties, and, of course, wasn't born with a title, but my word, she's giving them a run for their money. She looks like such a meek little thing, you'd never expect her to have so much gumption.'

Annie smiled at the mental picture she was conjuring. 'I bet Tudor gives as good as he gets,' she noted.

'That he does. Some of the meetings run for hours and hours. The duchess doesn't leave anyone in any doubt about who's in charge,' added Bryn growing in confidence by the minute. 'Does it quietly, too. And, can you imagine, she used to come to my shop? Said she knew my daughter when I met her earlier. I mentioned it when I phoned Val to let her know I was coming here and she said, yes, she used to come in to the shop all the time. Before she was the duchess – when she was just Stephanie Timbers. Quite pally they were, says Val. Never thought my girl would be friends with a duchess.' His cheeks flushed when he noticed Althea giggling.

Mavis noted the pride and wonder in the man's voice. She silently admitted to herself she'd never envisaged a personal future where she would be sharing a home with a dowager. Dismissing such thoughts she said, 'It's nice to chat, of course, Bryn, but I'm sure we all need to get on. I propose we prepare a written quote. Carol can email it to you, along with a contract, and you can read them at your leisure. Would that suit?'

'Admirable plan,' said Bryn with gusto.

THREE

Carol Hill wished Albert would nap for more than twenty minutes at a time. It was something she felt guilty about wishing, but she wished it nonetheless. She hated to admit it, but her mother had been right when she'd warned her pregnant daughter she'd only understand the true nature of exhaustion when she became a mother herself.

Albert was, by all standards, a 'good' baby, but Carol needed more sleep than she was getting. She was cross with herself that she'd agreed to go to Bryn Jenkins's shop in Hay-on-Wye that afternoon to come up with a surveillance plan for his premises, but it had seemed like a good idea at the time. Her 'it'll be good for Albert and me to get out and about for a bit,' comment to Mavis rang in her ears, along with Albert's bawling from the back of the car.

'Not long now,' she cooed over her shoulder at her son, then she pressed the 'play' button on the CD unit and Tom Jones's Greatest Hits began. *Again.* She'd discovered to her delight – at first – that the voice she'd grown up loving also soothed her infant son. She was relieved to hear happy gurgling replace distressed squealing behind her as the now overly-familiar introduction to 'It's Not Unusual' struck up. She settled herself to another twenty minutes of listening to Jones the Voice as she and Albert followed a caravan being pulled along at a snail's pace by a driver who seemed partial to unexpectedly using his brakes. The school holidays hadn't even begun, but Carol got the impression everyone in Britain who owned a caravan had decided to tow it along the narrow roads of Powys that day.

Finally arriving at the large car park in Hay, Carol attached Albert to the front of her body in his carrying-sling, and set off to find the bookshop where she hoped she'd be able to come up with a plan of action pretty quickly. The sunny day had encouraged hundreds of holidaymakers to visit the pretty market town and its internationally-renowned selection of bookshops, so Carol took her time negotiating the pavements which were hardly wide enough for two people to pass each other.

Her progress was further slowed by the interactions she had to bear with complete strangers; a surprising discovery she'd made since Albert had arrived was how transfixed with babies many people were. They'd comment on the device she used to transport him, his clothes, his unusually thick, curly, blonde hair – just like her own – and his vivid blue eyes. It felt to Carol as though she'd disappeared. She'd become no more than an adjunct to her son; his means of transportation, rather than a person in her own right. 'I'm more than a feeding, cleaning and carrying unit,' she wanted to say. Instead, she gazed at her beautiful son looking up at her from her bosom, in awe of the power he seemed to possess to draw the attention and delight of all ages and types of passers-by. Eventually she found the Crooks and Cooks Bookshop, and allowed herself a few moments to stand opposite it to study the place.

It was on a corner where a steeply descending road intersected a more level one at right angles. It was a good location; those simply wandering all the little streets of Hay would not be able to avoid it, whereas those with more purpose would be easily able to locate it. A red-painted door stood open between two large bay windows, which also had red-painted woodwork. A massive sign above the door bore the word 'CROOKS', with a painting of a mackintoshed sleuth holding a magnifying glass to its left, and a masked bandit wearing a striped jersey and carrying a bag marked 'SWAG' on his shoulder to its right. Below that – beneath a friendly-looking, fat '&' – the word 'COOKS' had a man in chef-whites wielding a giant whisk to the left, and a woman in a flowery apron bearing a mixing bowl and spoon to the right. Carol felt it was just the sort of place she'd be happy to browse for hours, her two favorite occupations of investigating and baking being equally represented.

Carol waited for a gap in the traffic then carefully stepped down from the kerb to cross the road.

The person sitting behind the high counter just inside the door of the bookshop was reading. Pallid skin, less-than-clean, obviously-dyed, blue-black hair scraped up in a topknot – *or was it one of those man-buns*? Carol wondered – and a long-sleeved charcoal hoodie all looked out of place on a summer's day among the shelves bearing thousands of brightly-colored spines and eye-catching enlarged book jackets. Carol couldn't immediately decide if the person was male or female, but guessed the assistant's age to be somewhere in their thirties. She decided to begin on a positive note.

'How lucky you are to be able to read all these books whenever you want,' she said, feeling a little jealous. She hadn't so much as picked up a book since Albert's arrival.

The bored-sounding response of 'I s'pose', could have been uttered by either a man with a high voice or a woman with a low one, Carol just couldn't tell, which annoyed her, because she reck-oned any professional enquirer worth their salt should be able to tell a man from a woman.

'I'm looking for Mr Jenkins,' said Carol affably. 'My name's Carol Hill.'

'Need him especially, do you?'

Carol nodded.

'Upstairs.'

Carol suspected she wouldn't get much more out of the assistant, whatever its gender, so headed to the top floor of the shop where Bryn and a woman of about forty were huddled over a box on the floor.

At that very moment, Albert decided to bawl his head off for no apparent reason, so all three adults gave him their attention, and, when he had settled, Carol greeted the couple properly. Both Bryn and the woman who turned out to be Val, his daughter, were tall, for Welsh people; Carol's five feet three inches and considerable girth and bosom were pretty much the norm among her fellow country-women, but both Jenkinses were at least five-eleven and they were thin to the point of emaciation. Carol felt her baby-weight dragging her down.

Having clarified she would only need to be shown around the premises once, and then she'd be able to come up with a costed plan for the installation of equipment and the reviewing of record-ings, Bryn descended to his realm downstairs leaving his daughter to deal with the investigator. Once he'd gone, Carol took the chance to sit down and adjust her son in his harness, and tried to work out why the woman looked so familiar. She was sure she'd seen her somewhere before, but couldn't put her finger on it. Carol struggled with a recollection on the edge of her memory as she fussed with the straps of her baby-sling. Expecting the conversation with Val to open with some sort of discussion about Albert – something she'd noted was now invariably the case – she was surprised when the woman did no such thing. Instead, she went right to business.

'I know Dad's had books turn up unannounced downstairs, but I haven't had anything like that happen up here. Of course, you're welcome to put up some cameras, or whatever, but I already have one up there.' She pointed at a sign that said 'Smile please – you're on camera' beside a small, obvious-looking unit fitted to the wall just below the ceiling. 'There's only one spot where it can't see what's going on, and I have mirrors up here—' she pointed toward the ceiling above her – 'so I can watch the reflection from the counter. It's the same sort of set-up Dad has downstairs. To be honest, we don't have a lot of stuff go missing. There's bound to be some, and I don't think we'll ever stop it all. But I keep the high-priced stuff here beside the counter where I can see it, so there are only very low-cost items over there. If they get lifted, I'm not losing more than a few pence each time.'

Carol glanced around the shop, taking in the array of items on offer and spotted a prominent display of books with Val's face on the cover. Turning to face the woman she said, 'Of course, you're "The Curious Cook" from BBC Wales. I knew I'd seen you somewhere before, but you look a little different in real life. I really enjoyed that series.'

Val's cheeks colored. 'Yes, that was me, but quite a few years back, now. The connection helps with the business, but I can't use the name to promote the shop, because the BBC owns the rights to it. Like you, when people get up here and put two and two together, they often remember me. The recipe book helps, and it still sells pretty well, I'm pleased to say.'

'So it should,' replied Carol, beaming. 'I gave copies to my mam and all my aunties for Christmas the year it came out. Loved it, they did. The TV series too. It was such a good premise – travelling Wales, hunting down ingredients, recipes and the traditions behind them, then cooking all the food and serving it to deserving groups. You did a lot for the reputation of Welsh cooking. Didn't you used to have a restaurant too?'

Carol noted a shift in Val's demeanor. Shrugging, the cook-turned-shop-owner spoke quietly. 'Mam was diagnosed with cancer, and Dad couldn't cope. First of all I packed in the restaurant, and kept going with the TV recordings, but even that was too much. I was away such a lot, and I found I really needed to be here, in Hay, with Mam and Dad, so I told the show's director I'd have to take a break. To be fair to them, the BBC people were very nice about it, but it wasn't easy, in so many ways.' She looked down at Carol with sad eyes. 'Everyone who worked on that series was out of a job, essentially, because of me. They decided to not recast it with another person doing the research and cooking, so they all had to find work on other projects. Mam needed a lot of support for a couple of years, until she died, and by then the opportunity had passed. Like Mam.' She shook her head with a wry smile.

Carol's heart went out to the woman. 'I'm sorry to hear that,' she said quietly. She smoothed Albert's head to comfort him, and herself. Attempting to lighten the mood she added, 'This seems like a great way for you to still be connected with what was obviously your passion. Your love of cooking came through loud and clear on TV.'

Carol judged her changing of the topic had worked when Val perked up and replied, 'Yes, it's not a bad way to make a living. I can stay connected with recipes, food and cooking, without any of the deadlines or stresses. And I still cook at home, of course. Dad's pretty understanding when I try out recipes on him. Sometimes it can take a few attempts before it all turns out alright.' The women shared a grin, then Carol decided it was time to get back to business.

She stood and wandered the shoulder-level book- and cooking accessory-laden shelf units in the empty store. 'What's it like when it gets busy in here? Bodies would create more blind spots, I'd have thought.'

Val nodded. 'It can get full. When coach trips come to town people tend to walk about in groups. I get dozens of women in here at a time, sometimes. It is mainly women up here, because of the cooking theme. Dad gets more of a mixture down below – though, as I'm sure he'll tell you, a lot of his customers are also women. About sixty percent, for him he reckons. For me up here it's about ninety-five percent. It's why this is a good pairing, see? Crooks and cooks together.'

'Two of my favorite things,' said Carol with a smile.

'Are you a baker?' asked Val with enthusiasm.

'That's my passion. I enjoy the precision of it. Of course, I also cook our main meals, but my husband helps a good deal with that. He likes to sling things together and you can't do that with baking.'

'True, that's why getting baking recipes correct takes such a lot of trial and error.'

'Mind if I take some photos?'

'Help yourself,' replied Val pleasantly enough, and turned her attention to sticking price labels on the little boxes she was pulling from a package beside the till.

Carol took in her surroundings from a professional point of view. Clicking photographs around the place she smiled as she thought of her own mother holding items for which she hadn't paid above her head in an effort to dissuade people in shops from getting the idea she was about to pocket them. Rubbing Albert's head she told herself to get on with what she was doing, and to stop missing her mother.

'I think that's enough for now, thanks,' said Carol heading for the top of the stairs. 'I'll see your dad down below, then get back to him with a quote. OK?'

Carol could tell Val was hovering on the edge of saying something. She waited.

'There is something else,' said Val, her head disappearing beneath the counter. She reemerged holding two large volumes. 'These are a couple of the books Dad found downstairs. I've hung onto them because I like some of the photos. Look.'

Carol leafed through the books which were modern publications showing photographs of Swansea through the years.

'My mam has some of those. There are quite a lot of them, aren't there?' said Carol. Val nodded. 'She likes them. The chap who puts them together uses photos from the city archives, the old *Swansea Evening Post* and people send him stuff, I believe.'

Val nodded again. 'I went to Swansea University and they've got some shots of when they were building bits of it. That's why I kept them. But then I saw these . . .' She turned to pages marked with sticky notes. 'These miniatures.'

Carol peered as best she could with Albert attached to her front.

'Try this,' said Val, handing Carol a large, round magnifying glass. She grinned wickedly and added, 'I'm surprised you haven't got one of those in your handbag, what with you being a detective.'

Carol returned Val's smile, and focused on the tiny drawing. 'It's a butcher shop,' she said sounding as surprised as she was. 'That's an odd thing for an artist to draw, isn't it?'

'Flick through some more,' urged Val.

Carol did so and became more puzzled by the moment. 'I know I sound like an old fuddy duddy, but these just aren't the sorts of things I'd expect someone, who's clearly talented, to take the time to depict,' she said, finally raising her head. 'There are a few of grand vistas and buildings, but a lot of them are of pubs and even construction sites. Even this one of Swansea Bay is full of oil tankers. Surely there are more picturesque views an artist could recreate? What are those big round things rolling down this hill beside a castle in this one, for example? I get why an artist would want to portray a castle but are those supposed to be something?'

Val grinned. 'I wondered that too. They're "zorbing" balls; giant inflatable balls into which a person is harnessed and then they roll and bounce down a hill inside them. Goodness knows how they come up with the names for these things. My fifteen-year-old niece informs me they are great fun. They look like deathtraps to me, but she says they're all the rage. Seems we have a lot of what they need to work out well in Wales.'

Carol gave the matter some thought. 'People with strong stomachs, and hills?' Val nodded. 'I can only imagine how many people have been sick inside them, which even for a mother of an infant who has to deal with all sorts isn't a pleasant thought.' The women shared a grimace, and a laugh. 'A bit of an odd thing for a miniaturist to depict, wouldn't you say?'

'It's what she's known for,' said Val quietly, 'well, not the zorbing things, but portraying what's going on in everyday modern life. That's why I think she did them.'

'Who?'

'Lizzie Llewellyn.'

'*The* Lizzie Llewellyn? The one who was murdered?'

Val nodded. 'I'm not an expert, but they look very much like her work to me. I wondered if . . . well, I wondered if you WISE women could do a bit of digging about to see if they really are by her. If they were . . .'

'They'd be worth a fortune,' said Carol in awe. 'There was a bit on the news on the telly a few weeks ago about how much her work increased in value after she went missing, and how it's just gone up again now they've found her brother guilty of her murder.'

Both women allowed a moment of silence to pass.

'It's terrible, I know,' said Val shaking her head. 'So sad.'

Carol suspected Val was trying to not look excited. 'How many are there?'

'Twenty-seven,' said Val quickly, then she blushed. 'About that many,' she added sheepishly.

Carol gave the matter some thought. 'Any of them signed?' Val shook her head. 'So we'd need to dig up an expert or two to authenticate them. What about provenance?' She flicked to the front of the books. 'Both of these say Daisy Dickens, in pencil. Any idea who that is?'

'I've Googled it and I can't find anyone with that name. They're not very old books, one was published ten years ago, the other seven.'

'And these were among the books that have just appeared on your father's shelves, downstairs?'

Val nodded. 'I've been storing some of the offending volumes up here in that cupboard over there, and I spotted these.'

Carol dared a raised eyebrow as she looked again at the tiny little people in balls rolling around what appeared to be the grounds of a castle. 'And your niece says this is "zorbing"?' She pointed at the balls.

'Yes, "zorbing." Kids these days, eh? But there, I expect I sound ancient now. It's like me having to ask Sam downstairs to not wear rings in all those piercings. They can be so off-putting.'

Drat! thought Carol, *the person downstairs might as well be called Pat or Chris. I still don't know if it's male or female.*

Carol ventured, 'Does Sam ever manage to sell anything for you?'

Val grinned. 'Yes, surprisingly, she does. She's quite knowledge-able about crime fiction, which you might not think, to look at her. When she arrived I was the one who spoke up for her. Dad didn't think she'd go down well with the customers because of how she presents herself, but I think most people accept her as some sort of curiosity. Which probably isn't how she wants to be thought of, but there you go. But the rings in her piercings? Even I thought they had to go.'

Delighted she finally knew how to speak about Sam, Carol asked, 'Has she been here long?'

'About two months. A bloke Dad knows who runs a bookshop in Haverfordwest rang up and said she was looking for a job for the summer. He told Dad she did well at his place, so we took her on.' Val lowered her voice. 'Cash in hand, you know. We need a bit of cover now and again, and it's been good for me to be able to get a few hours off midweek. Just as well now that Dad's going to be up at Chellingworth Hall working on those bibles.'

Carol realized she needed to press on. 'Tell you what, Val, I'll get a set of our standard terms and conditions to you so you can look them over regarding the agency taking on your case, as well as your dad's, then I can draw up a quote for you, the same way I'm doing one for him.'

Val sat down. 'Ah, now there's the problem; I haven't really got much money. Bless them, the BBC never did pay well, and the restaurant ate money – pardon the pun. Even so, I'd managed to set myself up with a little cottage just outside Hay. About a year after Mam died I sold it so Dad and I could buy this shop. I had to do something to get him going again, or he'd have withered away. I moved back in with him. Into my old room, in fact.' Her expression told Carol it was an arrangement which left a lot to be desired. 'I only take a pittance out of this place, a bit of spending money rather than a salary. All the money we make goes back into stock. So I'm a bit short of cash.'

Carol immediately wondered what Val's father was planning to use to pay for the services he'd already asked the agency to quote against.

'Could you work on some sort of percentage basis?' ventured Val. 'Whatever we sell the miniatures for, you get a cut?'

Carol knew she was on shaky ground; if anyone's time but her own were to be used on this case, she'd have to get an unusual arrangement agreed by her colleagues. 'We've never done that before. I'll have to talk about it with the rest of my group.'

'Of course.'

'I'm sure you want to keep these safe—' Carol nodded at the books – 'but do you have any photocopies?'

Val beamed. 'An entire set, and I even did enlargements, though they're a bit blurry.' She handed over a folder full of papers. 'I'll hear from you, then?'

'You will,' said Carol. 'Meanwhile, I'd better get some photos of the set-up downstairs, and get back to the office.' The women hugged – around Albert – and Carol carefully descended the stairs.

Carol left the shop about fifteen minutes later, just after Bryn had rushed out saying he'd forgotten he had an appointment with a potential client. She crossed the road to snap shots of the front of the building. As she did so, her attention was taken by an elderly man pushing a bicycle down the hill toward the shop. Turning onto the street in front of the shop's door, he leaned his cycle against the wall, pulled a parcel of books from inside its basket and plonked them on the end of the table outside the shop. Carol snapped furiously, right up until the man had cycled past her and out of sight.

'Your mam's done very well today, Albert,' she informed her infant son. 'I think I've caught the book-depositor red-handed. Let's go and see what he put on that table, shall we?' Albert blew spit-bubbles by way of a reply, and Carol took the photographs she needed of the books the man had delivered, then headed back to her car.

A few hours later, having had the chance to update Mavis on her progress on the telephone, she was feeling less chuffed: Mavis had pointed out how solving a case the agency hadn't even been commissioned to take, and where there was certainly no contract in place to allow them to charge for their services, was not the best way to go about business. Carol had to agree with her colleague as they spoke, but she mentally took the moral high-ground as she sipped her warm milk before bedtime.

FOUR

With Albert's two a.m. feeding over, and him finally asleep, Carol found herself annoyingly alert. She decided the best thing to do was apply herself to discovering all she could about the possible creator of the mysterious miniatures, firstly because she was genuinely curious and, secondly, because she'd warmed to Val but felt her colleagues might need some convincing when it came to taking on her case.

Half an hour later she was in her element, her fingers tapping at keys as skillfully as those of a concert pianist, the output being, to her mind in any case, more melodious than any music ever composed. She didn't miss living and working in London, but she did miss the relative freedom of the hours she used to spend at her desk connecting with the world through the wonders of modern technology. Left to her own devices she'd have spent her entire life like that without even noticing the lack of real human companionship. David's arrival in her department at work had saved her from existing in a techno-bubble, and with Albert's birth had come a depth of love and true, primordial connectivity. She was bound to her son forever, which was something she considered as she delved into the facts surrounding the death of Lizzie Llewellyn which centered on the killing of one sibling by another – something she, as a new mother, couldn't imagine.

Having decided she'd begin by trying to find out about Lizzie Llewellyn, the artist, she quickly realized she'd left behind the representations of the dead woman's art and seemed to be getting drawn into the coverage of her brother's trial for her murder. The more 'news' she read, the more she came to the belief it was all just one big swirl of regurgitated hearsay. Online sources seemed to feed off each other, and even the big-name newspapers and TV channels with journalists dedicated to the Llewellyn case didn't seem to do much more than restate what had been said in court. Carol began to wonder if the creature once known as 'the investigative journalist' was as dead as the proverbial dodo.

From the aggregation of all the various reports she unearthed, it became clear to Carol that two critical factors had led to the highly unusual, but not unheard of, situation where Nathaniel Llewellyn, the brother of Lizzie, had been convicted of her murder without her body ever being found: the large amount of blood found at his cottage in Gower, and the testimony of a neighbor, one Mrs Wynne Thomas, that she'd seen Nathaniel bundling something large and bulky into the hatchback of his car on the same day as the discovery of said blood.

Carol considered what she'd discovered. Unlike the jury, Carol didn't have the chance to see photos of Nathaniel's cottage where the blood had been discovered, but she read enough descriptions of the place and the scene witnessed by the police upon their arrival to be able to work out for herself that any such photos would have been likely to turn the stomachs of most people.

The pathologist called by the Crown had testified it was unlikely anyone who'd lost the amount of blood she judged to be present at the scene could have survived. She'd further confirmed it was definitely Lizzie Llewellyn's blood – DNA testing had proved this beyond doubt. Carol noted the pathologist had grudgingly accepted, under cross-examination, that it was possible for a woman of Lizzie Llewellyn's age, size and level of fitness to survive even after losing a couple of pints of blood, though Carol spotted the Crown had leaped upon that acceptance and the pathologist had stated likely disorientation and possible unconsciousness, if not immediate death, ensuing.

The lack of a body, a murder weapon and even a credible time of death meant the jury had been subjected to a great deal of evidence about the coagulation rates of blood, as well as contradictory evidence from witnesses about their interpretations of the patterns of blood at the scene.

She read various reports of the testimony of several witnesses all of whom agreed the brother and sister had been arguing loudly and aggressively when they ate a meal together at The Bay Bistro in Rhossili on the afternoon of the day before the grisly scene had been discovered. No one had seen Lizzie Llewellyn alive after she got into her brother's car in the car park at Rhossili.

Nathaniel claimed the siblings were having one of their usual run-ins about art, and their own interpretations of it, and that their so-called argument was nothing out of the ordinary, for them. He said the siblings enjoyed a good dinner together at his cottage, and he went to bed that night, with his sister using the spare room, and slept heavily. He admitted to being drunk. He claimed he didn't wake until early the next afternoon, whereupon he discovered his cottage was covered with blood and his sister was nowhere to be found. He'd phoned the police immediately, which, he claimed, proved his innocence.

He had no explanation for his neighbor's sighting of him wrangling something bulky into the back of his car that morning, affirming he hadn't woken until around two p.m. With his sister's blood and hair having been found in his vehicle – a revelation one reporter noted made the jury glare at the accused – Nathaniel stuck to his story of being in a deep, alcohol-induced sleep until long after the claimed sighting of him. The same reporter also gave a highly sympathetic account of how distressed Mrs Wynne Thomas – a woman who'd lived down the hill from Nathaniel's cottage for many years, and therefore used to seeing him about and identifying him from a distance – had been when facing the man in court.

Carol paused and gave the matter some thought. Her background checks into the neighbor didn't suggest she bore Nathaniel any animosity, nor that she had an axe to grind when it came to the Llewellyns in general. In several sources Carol noted the woman had even declined to give media interviews 'out of respect for the family.'

Carol sat back and clicked the end of her pen, the rhythm helping her concentrate. It was a horrible case. Much had been made of how Nathaniel, the younger sibling but more prominent artist, had belittled his sister's work in a now-infamous BBC documentary. He'd received huge sums of money for commissions of massive, public installations, whereas she had labored in poor conditions to produce her tiny works which challenged prevailing artistic opinions. Carol noted how it was Nathaniel's high profile as an artist who'd received money from the public purse that had added fuel to the fire of publicity, with taxpayers being only too happy to demand the immediate removal of art created by a convicted killer.

As she read on, Carol's heart went out to Gwen Llewellyn,

Lizzie and Nathaniel's mother. Press photos showed her beaming proudly at the official unveilings of several of her son's works and at small-scale shows her daughter had mounted, then haggard and drawn at Nathaniel's trial. Gwen had, it seemed to Carol, taken every possible opportunity presented to her to say she believed her son to be innocent. Believing any mother would be likely to say the same thing, Carol dug around trying to find out how unusual it was for a person to be found guilty of murder when a body hadn't been discovered, and realized it was a rare, though not altogether unheard of, verdict.

Standing down from her research for a moment, Carol tried to imagine how Gwen Llewellyn must feel; her son incarcerated for killing her daughter, her life empty and in ruins. 'Would I blame myself?' Carol asked aloud in the quiet of her own home.

Unable to discover very much at all about Lizzie Llewellyn, which made Carol wonder about how much attention the media had given the killer rather than the victim, she allowed herself to watch the entire documentary the BBC had made about Nathaniel and his work some time before he'd been accused of his sister's murder.

Other than realizing she didn't much care for his style of flamboyant murals and overblown 'statement sculptures,' the thing Carol noted was the man was a good deal more successful at shedding the pounds than she'd ever been; his photographs showed him at a variety of girths over the years. It seemed his weight went up and down like a yo-yo. She rubbed her mid-section as she wondered if she'd ever lose the baby-weight she'd gained, then realized she was thirsty. A big glass of cool milk, that was what she needed, then maybe she'd sleep. At least for a couple of hours.

FIVE

Saturday 21st June

'It's the right thing to do, and that's why I've called this emergency meeting,' said Carol firmly. She felt every eye in the room boring into her – and that was quite a lot of eyes, if you counted Albert, Gertie and McFli as well as her four colleagues.

'We've never been in this situation before,' said Christine uncertainly. 'There's the business point of view, but, as Carol says, there's the moral obligation too.'

Annie stood and paced, Gertie following her like the puppy she was. 'Look, I've got to get to Hereford to get the train to Swansea, so I can't hang about. I understand why you wanted me to be here, Car, but I'll go with the flow on this one. Whatever you all decide is fine by me. I don't know why we can't just send Bryn Jenkins the proposal and the contract and, if he bites, then show him the photos you took of that bloke on the bike and tell him we did what he wanted us to do. It'll mean we can charge him somethin', even if it in't as much as we'd like. How about that?'

Mavis remained seated when she tutted. 'It's no' the point.'

Carol remained firm. 'The point *is*, we shouldn't charge him for setting up a surveillance system he doesn't need. It's a shame, because I had a bright idea about being able to borrow all the hardware so we could have done a bang-up job for him at very little cost – so long as he and we were prepared to write a testimonial for the company loaning us the equipment. It could have done us a bit of good by getting our name onto their website. But it's wrong to do it.'

'I agree,' said Althea. 'Carol was a witness to the very action we were possibly going to be hired to detect. You're always telling me we are professionals, not just amateur sleuths. Well, professionals have ethics. I'm with Carol on this.'

The look bestowed upon Althea by her housemate Mavis could have withered weeds. Althea straightened her back and petted McFli with her foot. Silence followed – not a normal state of affairs at all.

'Ach, I agree,' said Mavis petulantly. 'You're quite right, Carol, we cannae charge Bryn a fee. Send the email you've composed, with the photos of the man on the bicycle, and be done with it.'

Carol did as had been agreed, allowing other business to be discussed briefly, then stood and made it clear she wanted to address the group. She explained about the books Val had shown her, allowed the women to circulate the photocopies of the miniatures – along with a magnifying glass Carol had brought from home – and to think about the opportunity to not work for a fee, but for a percentage of any finally agreed sale price.

'I spent some time last evening scouring a selection of newspaper and TV stories, from online sources, about the Lizzie Llewellyn case, and I've just emailed the package to all of you. I know you're off to work on this other case in Swansea, Annie, but I thought it worth keeping you in the picture. I'm sure we've all heard at least something about the Lizzie Llewellyn murder, and, if these miniatures turn out to be by her, they could be worth a good deal of money.'

Annie's eyes lit up. 'She's the one who was done in by her brother, innit? Disappeared, they thought, but they found loads of blood at the brother's cottage, and someone said they saw him pushing something that looked like a body into his car. That's the one, right?'

Carol nodded. 'He was found guilty of murder just a couple of months ago, and he's serving a prison sentence in Swansea right now.'

'I recall they didnae find a body,' said Mavis.

'You're right,' replied Carol, 'but this was one of those rare cases where the jury found a person guilty despite that. The evidence suggested Lizzie would have lost far too much blood to have survived her injuries, and blood and hair found in the brother's car, plus the testimony of a neighbor from the local area, pretty much sealed his fate.'

'And this Val Jenkins reckons these tiny little drawings are by the dead woman?' asked Annie, squinting through the magnifying glass.

'She does, and I can see why. I've poked about on the Internet and have discovered images of her work. She had a reputation for completely updating the ancient art of miniatures, going far beyond the portraits they'd usually been used to depict. She produced tiny works that portray modern life – street scenes, urban landscapes, people going about their everyday life.'

'I don't see the point,' said Annie, rising to gather herself to leave. 'I mean, who would buy one of these when you can't even really see them? Makes no sense to me.'

Christine said, 'I've seen some of her works in the homes of people I know. There's a special way of displaying them, with a large magnifying glass – bigger than the one we've got here – set into a stand, so it's always in front of the piece, all used as part of the set-up.'

Annie chuckled. 'Oh I see, just another way to put art out of the reach of the masses, eh? Not only does it cost a bomb to buy the art, but then you have to shell out for an expensive piece of kit so you can see the blessed thing. Very clever.'

'It does seem like a very elaborate way of doing things,' agreed Mavis, 'but there's no accounting for taste, as I'm sure we can all agree. Are you leaving us now, Annie?'

'Yeah, best be off.'

'How do you feel about us doing some work on this case without our being paid until the owners sell the stuff?' asked Carol.

Annie paused. 'You know I'm alright for a bit with the money I made from selling my flat in London, so I can coast for a while, and there could be a big pay-off. I mean, think about how much money all those dead singers make from their records. I reckon it's got to be the same for artists. Not going to be painting any more of those, is she? So if everyone else is alright with it, I'm for it. But now I've got to get going.'

Carol said, 'I don't think we'd all need to work on it, but thanks.'

Annie dragged Gertie toward the door, pulling on a waterproof to guard against the torrential summer rain outside. 'I'm dropping this one at Tudor's, then I'll be off,' she called over Gertie's excited yelps as the puppy tried to give McFli a parting lick. 'I've got me bags packed, and I'm on the train that'll get me to Swansea in time for the client to meet me and take me to the B&B he's organized near his factory. I'll report in by email. See you all in a week, if not before. If Carol's luck is anything to go by I'll have nabbed the culprits within two hours of arriving there, and be back here before you know it!' Smiling and waving sent her on her way.

After a short discussion about the pros and cons of taking a case with no real certainty of an income balancing their effort, the decision was finally taken to proceed with Val's case and submit a proposal. Christine's empty schedule and ability to easily connect with an art expert she knew from her schooldays settled the matter, and it was agreed Carol would draw up the appropriate contract, while Christine would put out feelers to get hold of her connection.

Carol closed the conversation with: 'That's the best start we can make, Christine, to find out if the miniatures are the real thing. I'll concentrate on trying to find out more about the person who owned the books in which the drawings were made. It's an unusual name, so I might have a bit of luck. There can't be many people named Daisy Dickens about the place.'

'I once knew a Daisy Dickens,' said Althea quietly. 'When Chelly and I were embedded with the hunting set, there was a girl by that name who had an exceptionally good seat. Plain, but a very good rider. Married a chap whose name I can't recall, though I do remember it began with a "D".'

'That seems like a very odd fact to retain, dear,' said Mavis.

'Oh, I don't know about odd. I know it struck me at the time she was fortunate to marry someone with the same initial – it meant none of her monograms would have to be changed.'

Mavis shook her head. 'Ach, what it must be to live a life where changing monograms is top of the list of things you worry about.' She smiled warmly at Althea, who grinned back.

Carol said, 'The books were pretty recent volumes. Collections of photographs of Swansea over the years. Do you think they might have belonged to "your" Daisy Dickens, Althea? Mind you, if she'd married, why would she write her maiden name in a book in any case?'

Althea waved her little hand. 'You're right, why would one? I never use my maiden name on anything. Indeed, I haven't written that name for – oh, almost fifty years. I wonder how it would feel.' She reached out, took a pen and paper from the nearest desk and wrote carefully. She looked at her handiwork. 'Althea Liversedge. I wonder what became of her,' she mused.

'Liversedge?' chorused Carol, Mavis and Christine.

Althea smiled. 'I was glad when it changed to Twyst, I can tell you that. It's a place, you know. In Yorkshire. I expect one of my forebears from long ago on my father's side came from there.'

'Aye, well, whatever it might mean, I dinnae think we can take it that this person you knew years ago can be the same as the one who wrote their name in the books Carol saw.'

'I'll do some name searches,' said Carol.

'And I'll phone a few old friends to find out what happened to *my* Daisy Dickens,' said Althea huffily.

Mavis gave the dowager an indulgent sideways glance. 'That cannae hurt, I'm sure.' She stood, signaling the end of the meeting, and began to clear the table of its accumulated cups. 'With that settled, I'm off to Brecon for my meeting within the hour, so I'll walk with you back to the Dower House to pick up my wee car.'

'Hang on a mo,' called Carol as she peered at her computer screen. 'I've got a reply here from Bryn Jenkins already. Give me a second to read it.' Mavis resumed her seat. 'OK. Well now, that's interesting. He says the bloke in the photos is another bookseller he knows. One who specializes in non-fiction, it seems. Bryn has phoned the man, who tells him he put the books on the table outside Bryn's shop because they'd mysteriously turned up at *his* shop last week and he knew they were just what Bryn would want.' Carol looked up. 'So it seems it isn't only Bryn who's received books out of the blue. He said he'd asked around his mates about this, didn't he, Mavis?'

'Indeed he did, and he assured us it was something that had only happened at his shop.'

'Well, it seems that's not quite right after all,' replied Carol. 'He's delighted to find he's not alone, and impressed we sent him the photos without charging him.' Carol smiled, trying not to gloat. 'He's also asked us for a formal quote and a contract for carrying out the surveillance at his shop to spot the *real* book-depositor. Oh, wait – here's another email from Val, who's already signed our contract. What a morning!'

Albert decided to wake up from his nap as the women were hugging and congratulating each other on their success, so Carol took him into the loo to change his nappy while plans were made for Christine to get started on The Case of the Murdered Miniaturist – a title coined by Annie before she'd left to work on her own case of the Sticky-Fingered Sweet Sorter.

SIX

Alexander Bright was angry. He didn't usually allow himself the indulgence of that emotion, but, on this occasion, he felt the best thing to do was to let his feelings pour out of him into the punchbag in his home gym. Each thwack was accompanied by a choice curse, and he pictured the faces of his adversaries collapsing beneath the force of his fists. Fifteen minutes of pounding later, he sat in his steam room unwrapping his knuckles, then plunged them into ice water. He cursed himself for having given in to his baser instincts; he prided himself on having contained his angry streak back in his twenties, but it seemed it still lurked beneath his controlled exterior, ready to reassert itself when he gave it the least excuse. Even when he was cleansed, shaved, moisturized and dressed, he still felt grubby; that was how anger made him feel – as though he was rolling around in the filth where he'd been raised.

Sliding into his Aston Martin he pressed the accelerator and nosed into the weekend traffic crawling along the south bank of the Thames. He had a couple of meetings to attend in Brixton before heading over to Christine Wilson-Smythe's flat in Battersea that evening. She'd phoned him to say she'd be in London by about three o'clock, and they'd agreed to grab an early bite to eat at their favorite place on Battersea High Street.

Christine had sounded excited when she'd told him she wanted to talk to him about a new case she was working on. Alexander hoped he'd be able to help her out; he enjoyed working alongside her on her investigations when he could.

He'd missed her while she'd been away working on a case for a week. There was nothing more he wanted in life than to be close to her, to experience the pleasure he felt when he saw how her mind worked, how she approached a problem. And she wasn't just bright – he'd witnessed her courage and fearlessness on many an occasion. Indeed, he wondered if it was the fact she could sometimes be a little reckless that he found so attractive. He knew she'd accepted his own dark history as something he'd grown beyond, but he suspected it held a certain appeal for her nonetheless. High-born she might be, but, as the daughter of a cash-poor Irish viscount who'd spent all he could on her education, she'd had to make her own way in the world since then, and had done an excellent job of it. This new career of hers as a private enquiry agent was certainly keeping her interested, and Alexander saw its attraction for her sharp, butterfly-mind; a fresh case every few weeks, different people to investigate.

The fact she wanted to talk to him about a new case boded well – maybe it was something she thought he could help with. He hoped so. If she saw him as useful, maybe then she'd see she couldn't live without him – the same thing he felt about her. But for now, that was too much to hope for. He recognized she'd set up several opportunities for him to spend time with her parents, which he knew was a good sign, but he had to bite his lip every time he watched her sleep and imagined her walking down the aisle toward him. She was the daughter of a viscount – he was the son of an absent father and an alcoholic mother. However rich he'd become, however studied his newly-invented persona, he'd always be that. True, Christine had accepted his past, but he still felt it wasn't the right time to make his bid for the ultimate happiness.

However, before their planned meeting that evening, he had a tricky situation to deal with. Some developers he knew, and had run up against in the past, were trying to get their hands on several houses in south London he'd had his eye on for some time. He'd learned they'd been waging a war of attrition against the current residents of the houses in question, trying to bring them to the point where they were so miserable in their surroundings they'd sell up for a song. While Alexander knew that meant he'd be able to snap up their houses for a good price, he was concerned about the well-being of the people being terrorized by a gang of hired thugs who were making their street a no-go area after dark. He'd organized a meeting with the homeowners at a local community center, and they'd been delighted to listen to his proposals, to which they'd reacted positively. He'd won them over by offering to buy their homes, renovate them, then rent them out, either to them, or to others who needed low-cost housing.

However, he knew he also had to get the attack dogs called off by the people who'd given them their orders. He was too well acquainted with the reputations of his competitors to easily believe a civilized meeting with them would achieve his goals, but he was concerned that most of the alternatives available to him would involve some sort of violence. He was doing his best to change. Because of Christine. He owed it to what he hoped could be a future with her to not do what he'd have done a year earlier – namely hire a group of his own thugs to overthrow those of his competitors – but to try a different approach.

SEVEN

Henry Twyst crept along the largely-unused ground-floor corridor of the east wing of Chellingworth Hall, hoping his sister wouldn't hear him from inside her apartment farther along in the same direction. He finally reached the small dining room – the one the Twysts hadn't used in years for its original purpose – and opened the door just enough to see what was going on inside. He needed to talk to his wife, but knew better than to interrupt the proceedings of the committee she was chairing. As he peered through a crack, he took in the scene before him.

'Point of order, Your Grace,' said Tudor Evans, his face pink with annoyance, 'I believe the bylaws of the committee state that the responsibility for temporary lavatories falls to the logistics sub-committee.'

The eyes of the fifteen members of the Chellingworth Summer Fete Committee all turned toward Henry's wife, seated at the head of the long, highly-polished table around which the meeting was moving into its third hour. Despite the open windows, the room was warm, the air heavy with tension. Henry could almost smell the frustration.

Stephanie Twyst opened her mouth to respond, only to be interrupted by Marjorie Pritchard, which shocked Henry.

'If Your Grace will permit, I have to say Mr Evans is incorrect in his assertion. The temporary lavatories have always fallen on the Young Wives Group, and I would suggest they should do so once again.'

A flurry of throat clearing and sipping of water broke out around the table, and Henry knew his wife well enough to spot her stifling a giggle as she stood.

'We've dwelt on this topic for so long I feel a short nature-break is in order,' she said loudly, making eye contact with her husband. 'I suggest we reconvene in ten minutes, at which time I hope we can wrap this up and move on to the fourth topic on our agenda.'

Henry extended his arm through the half-open door to beckon to his wife as chairs were pushed back from the table and people stood, stretching and yawning.

Stephanie joined her husband in the corridor that led toward the great hall. He pulled her into a small reading room, and shut the door.

Once they were inside, Stephanie let rip with some choice language Henry didn't think befitting of a duchess. 'If I don't kill one of those two – Tudor or Marjorie – before this fete is over I'll deserve a medal,' she finished.

'It all sounds a little trying,' said Henry as sympathetically as possible. He was wondering about the wisdom of raising his current concerns with his wife, given the mood she was in.

'So what is it, Henry? I haven't got long, so just get to the point.'

Henry suddenly wasn't sure where to begin. He felt relieved when his wife's eyes softened and she touched his face, gently.

'I'm sorry, Henry. I have no reason to speak to you so sharply. What's up?'

'It's Clemmie . . .' he began, his heart sinking as he uttered the words.

'Has she fired Nurse Thomas again?'

'No. Not this time. Nurse Thomas has resigned. She says she's leaving this afternoon. She said she's not just resigning from this post, but from nursing altogether. I can't find Mother; they told me at the Dower House she went off to the agency's office this morning, but there's no answer there. I think your idea of getting her a mobile phone is a good one. She's always so difficult to track down these days. Maybe for her birthday? I haven't had any other ideas about what to get her.'

Stephanie sighed. 'Oh, Henry. I don't really think a mobile phone is a suitable gift for a woman who's done as much for the community, this ducal seat – and you – as your mother has when she reaches the age of eighty. But we can talk about that some other time. As for Nurse Thomas? You can see I can't do anything. But I know *you* could win her over, dearest. She likes you. She always has. Give it a go? And, if it's not working, maybe Mavis MacDonald could lend a hand.'

'If I could find Mavis, I'd find Mother,' said Henry. 'Thick as thieves the pair of them.'

Stephanie smiled. Henry couldn't work out what the expression on her face meant when she replied, 'They're good friends, that's for sure. Kindred souls. Bring out the child in each other they do, and that's not a bad thing. We might all be glad of that one day, when we've forgotten what it's like to have more ahead of us than behind.'

'I'm in my late fifties. I'm pretty sure I have less of my life ahead of me than I've lived,' said Henry. 'You're so much younger than me, you'll be a young dowager when I die. You should think about remarrying.'

Stephanie reached around her husband's ample middle and hugged him tight. Looking up at him, she smiled. 'You silly sausage. Stop talking about me needing to remarry when you're gone – we're only just starting out, you and me. Not quite four months, that's all we've had so far. Though, I have to admit the last few hours feel like that amount of time all on their own.' Henry saw her glance anxiously at her watch. 'Do what you can with Nurse Thomas, Henry dear, and I'll try to get this meeting wrapped up as quickly as possible, then I'll find you. We can sort this out together, I'm sure. But now, I must get back.'

After his wife had left him, Henry dawdled for a moment or two, putting off the confrontation with Nurse Thomas as long as he dared. When he eventually scuttled out of the reading room, he was relieved to run into Bob Fernley, his estate manager.

'Ah Bob, just the chap,' said Henry, making the man jump. 'How are things going? Everything running along smoothly? All tickety-boo?'

He thought Bob looked a bit frightened as he heartily slapped him on the back, but he couldn't imagine why that would be the case. He made an effort to smile warmly, but Bob backed away.

'Everything seems to be just about alright, Your Grace,' the man replied hesitantly.

'Jolly good. Jolly good,' said Henry loudly, and steered the man toward the back corridors which led to the estate office. The two chatted about matters of no real consequence until they were sitting at Bob's desk.

'I don't suppose you've seen the dowager this morning have you, Bob?'

'Indeed I have. Her Grace was making her way, with McFli, to see Ivor at the Orangery about an hour ago.'

'Really? Did she say why?'

Bob Fernley fiddled with the collar of his shirt. 'Her Grace said something about a beehive, and then mentioned—' he cleared his throat, loudly – 'dead women and buckets of blood.' Henry noticed the man's Adam's apple bouncing around as he swallowed hard.

'Really?' Henry paused, then leaned in toward Bob. 'Do you happen to know if that's anything to do with that Monty Python lot?'

'Not that I'm aware, Your Grace.'

'Know their work, do you, Bob?'

'Pretty well, Your Grace, yes.'

'One of them was Welsh, I understand,' added Henry, wishing to appear knowledgeable.

'Terry Jones. He still is, Your Grace,' replied Bob, standing. 'If that's all, Your Grace, I should be . . .' He moved toward the door.

Henry knew he had to let the man get on with his work, and waved him off. Unfortunately that meant he was free to try to sort out the mess with Nurse Thomas. He decided to make one final effort to reach his mother, so picked up the phone and dialed the number for the Dower House. He was confused when his mother herself answered the call.

'Mother?'

'Henry.'

'Why did you answer the phone?'

'Because it rang, dear.'

'But where's Jennifer? She usually answers.'

'Indeed she does, but she's downstairs with Cook.'

'And Ian?'

'Poking about under the bonnet of the Gilbern.'

'Has it broken down again?'

'No, but it requires maintenance, dear.'

'Oh. I see. So what's all this about, Mother? Bob Fernley tells me you've been talking to Ivor the head gardener about dead women and oodles of blood.'

'No dear. Bees. I've been talking to Ivor about bees. I've been talking about dead women on the telephone, which is why I was sitting next to it.'

'Why would you do that, Mother?' Henry was perplexed.

'I'm working on a case, dear.'

'A case that concerns dead women?' Now he was alarmed.

'Not exactly. It's art.'

'Mother, explain yourself.' Henry was feeling decidedly cross.

'My dear boy, I don't feel the necessity to explain myself to you. I am working on a case. It is a professional matter. That's all you need to know. The woman in question is dead.'

'Dead? Dead and there's blood?' Henry panicked. 'Shouldn't you telephone the police?'

He heard his mother sigh. 'My dear child, you shouldn't worry so. Now why did you telephone me? I assume you had a reason?'

Henry was torn; he needed his mother's help with Nurse Thomas, but also felt he should try to find out what his mother was mixed up in. Making a quick decision he said, 'Nurse Thomas has resigned. I wondered if you might be able to talk to her with a view to getting her to change her mind.'

There was a pause at the other end of the line, then he heard his mother talking to someone while she had what he assumed was her hand over the mouthpiece.

'Henry?'

'Mother.'

'Mavis and I will come to the hall in Mavis's car. I don't want to have to walk among the visitors. I'll go directly to Clementine's apartments. I shall meet you there in thirty minutes.' His mother hung up.

Henry collapsed onto the chair beside the desk. His watch told him it was eleven thirty. He couldn't believe it was still morning.

EIGHT

Sunday 22nd June

Christine Wilson-Smythe was enjoying being driven by Alexander Bright through south London while she listened to Mavis on the telephone, bringing her up to date with their investigation. Hanging up she explained to her companion, 'Well that's a bit of a puzzle. Carol can't find anything at all about a woman named Daisy Dickens. It seems she doesn't exist.'

'Is that the name on those books Carol saw?'

'Yes. And we know there was at least one such real person, at one time, because Althea knew a Daisy Dickens.'

'Carol's usually pretty good at that sort of thing, isn't she?'

'Absolutely. I'm sure if there's anything to find, she'll manage it. Meanwhile, here's hoping Fliss can help.'

'This is the contact you've conjured up?'

'Yes, we were at school together. She lives out in Richmond now, which is why I said we'd eat with her at the White Cross, on the river.'

Alexander beamed. 'I haven't been there for a couple of years. As I recall, it's sometimes in the river, not just beside it; it's the one that floods with the high tides, right?' Christine agreed. 'I used to watch a lot of rugby there. It's so close to Twickenham, you get the real atmosphere. Good pub grub. Just what I fancy.'

'I'm a bit peckish too,' said Christine with a grin that lit up her face.

'And Fliss is . . .?'

'Exceptionally knowledgeable about art. Always was, even at school.'

'This would be the sinfully expensive public school every young woman of good breeding attends down near the coast?'

'But of course.' Christine giggled.

'The old school tie working for the girls, not the boys this time.'

'We used to wrap our ties around our waists to hold up our skirts which we felt were far too long to be alluring to the local lads. So, yes, those ties could tell some tales, and I see nothing wrong with using good contacts.'

'No argument from me,' agreed Alexander as he pressed the accelerator as much as he dared.

Parking was a nightmare, with the result the couple walked into the little walled beer garden just in time to see a tall, willowy blonde nab the last table.

'Fliss,' called Christine and the blonde's head spun round. The woman spotted Christine, that much was clear, but she stared round-eyed at Alexander, then smiled broadly. *Or was it wickedly?*

'Alex!' called Fliss.

Christine didn't like the feeling in the pit of her stomach when she saw her old schoolfriend's arm curl around Alexander's shoulder as she kissed him on the cheek.

Alexander pulled back from the woman and turned to face Christine who'd managed to slap a smile on her face just in time. 'I was about to say Felicity Hathaway, meet Alexander Bright, but it seems you're already past requiring introductions.' She hoped she'd managed to keep any annoyance from creeping into her voice.

Fliss hugged her old chum and smiled. 'Alex and I met at a few parties given by the Thompson twins, didn't we Alex? I haven't seen you since last year's boat race. Been keeping well?' Christine noticed how Fliss's eyes sparkled when she spoke to Alexander, and she further noted that Alexander's latte-toned skin seemed unusually pink.

Trying to get away from small talk and on with the business at hand, Christine showed Fliss the photocopies she wanted her to examine. She spread a few of them on the small table, and watched as Fliss leafed through the sheets.

'Will you be eating?' A strong Irish brogue, a head of copper hair, and more freckles than one would have thought it possible to fit on the human body, accompanied the arrival of 'Siobhan, Server,' as her badge announced.

Alexander deferred to Fliss who replied, 'Fizzy water – ice, no fruit – the fish of the day, no starches, green salad, no dressing,' without taking her eyes off the photocopies of the miniatures.

Christine looked up at the server, flashed her widest smile and asked in her natural Irish accent, 'What would be your pie of the day today then?'

The server smiled wickedly. 'It's our Guinness and steak pie with our famous giant chips on the side. Guinness gravy in a boat too, if you want.'

Christine licked her lips. 'Is the gravy good?'

The girl leaned further forward. 'Got a good lot of Guinness in it, if that's what you mean. Will you have that and a pint to go with it?'

'How's the black stuff?'

The girl winked. 'They do a good job of it here, so they do. Good pipes. I drink it meself. Not from the cold tap, though.'

'Me neither. So the pie with chips and gravy for me, and a warm pint, please, Siobhan.'

Alexander added, 'I'll have the pie and all the trimmings too, but a half of Youngs' IPA for me, thanks.'

With the matter of refreshments sorted out, the trio returned to the photocopies.

Fliss began, 'These drawings were made by a hand experienced in creating miniatures.'

'Does the name Daisy Dickens mean anything in the art world?' asked Christine, wondering if a connection might emerge.

'Not that I'm aware of,' said Fliss shaking her head. She looked across the table at Christine, with warmth in her eyes. 'I know a lot, but I don't know everything. However, I think I can point you in the right direction regarding these pieces.'

'Thanks,' replied Christine, allowing her voice to relax a little. 'Does that mean this style, this technique, is ringing bells?'

Fliss sat upright – as well as she could on the backless stool – and wrinkled her forehead. She looked heavenward and she chewed her lip. 'I can't be sure, but I think they might be by Lizzie Llewellyn.'

'If they are by her, would they be valuable?' asked Christine. Fliss's steely expression encouraged her to add, 'I'm acting on behalf of a client, and they'd like to know.'

Fliss replied, 'First of all, I can't say if they are in fact by the hand of Lizzie Llewellyn. They aren't signed, as you can see, and I'm not even looking at originals here. But what I can do is suggest a line for further enquiry.' She fiddled with her phone. 'I've texted you the details of a chap with a gallery just off Bond Street. Jeremy Edgerton. He's your best bet. Knows Llewellyn's work pretty well. Put together a small exhibition of her work about three years ago. Thing is, even he'd be unlikely to say what he thinks by just looking at photocopies. He'd want to see the originals.'

'They were discovered in some books with this Daisy Dickens' name in them,' said Christine.

'Well maybe following that lead would help too. The provenance can be critical in the attribution of unsigned pieces.'

'So I understand.'

'Lizzie was from Swansea originally, studied in London, worked in France and Italy, then moved back to the Welsh coast where she lived with her brother for a time, before heading back to London again. Maybe she met this Daisy Dickens somewhere on her travels,' suggested Fliss.

'A Daisy Dickens one of my colleagues once knew was Welsh, and the drawings were in books that have photographs of Swansea through the ages in them, but that's all we know at the moment,' replied Christine glumly. Perking up she added, 'But you've given me a lead for my enquiries, so thanks for that. I wonder if the gallery will be open on a Sunday. I'll at least give him a ring and do what I can to arrange a meeting as soon as possible.' She raised her head just as Siobhan arrived with one small, and two massive platters of food, and the copies had to be placed back into their folder to allow for luncheon to be eaten.

Staring at the two plates bearing puff-pastry-topped pies Alexander rolled his eyes. 'I think the fish might have been a better choice.'

'Don't be silly,' said Christine, noticing the slightly smug look on Fliss's face, 'this'll keep us going for the rest of the day – until we have supper, in fact.' She allowed herself to stare deeply into Alexander's eyes as she made her implied point. Fliss stabbed at her fish with unnecessary vigor.

NINE

C arol woke from her nap before her infant son did, and took the chance to Skype with her absent husband. Relieved that his mother was making good progress – to the point she was insisting he returned to Anwen-by-Wye sooner than originally planned – Carol sat down at her desk, the baby monitor at her elbow, a more cheerful person than she'd been half an hour earlier.

Bunty strolled in from the kitchen, flicked her tail a few times, then jumped up and curled herself into a ball on the newspaper Carol had discarded at the far side of her desk. Poor Bunty, thought Carol, knowing better than to pet her now-settled calico cat. She was pleased her companion of almost a decade had adapted to Albert's arrival so well, but was concerned that she still largely avoided him, preferring to spend more time than usual in the kitchen, and less and less at Carol's side when Albert was in her lap – Bunty's old haunt.

Carol felt she'd had an unproductive day, particularly annoyed she couldn't locate any records, anywhere, for a Daisy Dickens, and was wondering what she could do next. A text from Mavis told her she'd have a busy time ahead, because Bryn Jenkins had given the go-ahead for the WISE women to set up a surveillance operation at his shop.

Carol attacked her keyboard and, despite the fact it was a Sunday, within a couple of hours she'd secured the loan of enough expensive equipment to keep watch on the Crown Jewels. She relayed her news to Mavis via text, who phoned her a few moments later.

'Do you think this'll be practical?' were Mavis's first words.

Carol knew what she meant. 'It's a lot of equipment, but the advantage is it's all small, light, wireless and a doddle to put in place. Those are its selling points, and that's what the manufacturer is looking for us to test in action. They're going to send installers too, and it'll all come in well within budget. It's almost free. We just need Bryn to allow us onto his premises for one night to set it all up. While they are there doing that, I'll monitor the output here, make sure everything's in order – and then we're off.'

Carol could sense Mavis's apprehension at the other end of the line. 'It all sounds too good to be true, which, I fear—'

'Usually means it is. I know. But it's not. There's a chance the system won't live up to the sales pitch, of course, but if it doesn't work, we'll know within a couple of days and we can go back to doing it the old-fashioned way.'

Mavis still hesitated. 'Will you phone Bryn to make the arrangements?'

'I'll do it now. I'll text you. Because they're in the security business the company I'm talking to operates 24/7. I'll see if we can get it done tonight.'

'Aye, well, go on with you then. Let's give it a go. But make sure it's all in writing, and that everything is properly dealt with in terms of liabilities for damage and so forth. We don't want to end up with anyone chasing us down because something costing thousands of pounds has been knocked about on site.'

Carol tried hard to keep the chuckle out of her voice when she replied, 'I've got all the paperwork here. And I've been through it with a fine-tooth comb. You won't have to sell your lovely Mini to pay for any damages, Mavis.'

'Ach!' said Mavis, then she was gone.

Carol got on with her tasks, and was finished by the time Albert woke. It was all arranged: the installers would arrive at Crooks & Cooks at closing time that day, and she'd be ready to begin her observation when the shop opened on Monday morning.

TEN

Monday 23rd June

Alexander drove along the narrow, winding lanes of the Gower peninsular with great caution. Tall hedges blocked any useful views of the road ahead and on several occasions he was taken by surprise when a vehicle raced toward him on a tight corner.

Christine recognized he was out of his element, and wished she was behind the wheel; she'd learned to drive at an illegally tender age in the lanes of rural Ireland, and would have felt much more confident in their current circumstances than the Londoner did. After what seemed like hours, they found the turning that promised to lead them to the Llewellyn cottage; a small, rather amateurish sign – hanging onto its post by one nail – announced its location. The Aston didn't enjoy the bumpy climb up the hillside, but they finally stepped out of the car in front of a whitewashed stone building with black-painted woodwork trim. They were treated to a magnificent view down to Oxwich Bay, a wonder of nature if ever there was one, with its arcing sandy beach and a picturesque church perched on its prominent headland.

'Reminds me of parts of the coast back home, so it does,' said Christine quietly.

'Nothing like Brixton,' replied Alexander. 'Thank goodness.'

A sign pronounced the place was OPEN, so the couple went in. As they entered, a narrow staircase as steep as a ladder rose before them. To the left was a sitting room, to the right, a kitchen.

'I'm in here,' called a voice from the kitchen, so Christine stuck her head into the room. A massive fireplace kitted out with a black-ened iron hearth, boasting two oven fronts, was set up with a kettle and a fake pig on a spit above what would have been an open fire. A small, white-haired woman sat in the shadows at the back of the room. As the couple entered she raised herself off the spindle-backed wooden chair upon which she was seated and beckoned them to the rectangular scrubbed-oak table. 'There's lovely to see someone on such a pretty afternoon. Thought everyone would be down the bays on a day like this, I did. But no, see, some have the sense to come and enjoy art instead of all that sand. I'm Gwen Llewellyn. Welcome to the place where my children created artworks of such beauty they shame Nature herself. Have a sit down by here, will you?'

Christine and Alexander took the seats she indicated. The cottage was cool, and there was a hint of fresh baking in the air. Christine felt suddenly hungry. Taking charge, she made the introductions and explained why they were there. When she'd finished telling the elderly woman about the miniatures and what they'd been told in London by the expert Fliss had suggested they contact, who'd grudgingly agreed to meet with Christine the previous evening, the three of them sat quietly for a moment.

Eventually the woman said, 'Have you got them with you then? Let's have a look.'

Christine was pleased the woman wanted to get right to it, but she wasn't prepared for her almost immediate reaction when she laid the photocopies on the tabletop; Gwen Llewellyn began to cry. Tears rolled down her wrinkled cheeks; she didn't sob at all, it just looked as though someone had turned on a tap in her eyes.

Gwen pulled a tissue from a pocket somewhere in her voluminous floral skirt and mopped at her face. She turned the sheets with what Christine judged to be reverence. Other than her silent tears, there were no reactions but awe and concentration for at least five minutes.

Finally looking across the table at the couple Gwen said, 'These are lovely, aren't they?'

'Are they by Lizzie?' asked Christine, convinced the woman's reaction meant they were.

Gwen looked at the pair with teary eyes. 'I'm as sure as I can be. Yes, these are my daughter's work. Well, well. And you say these just showed up in a book at a shop in Hay?' Christine nodded. 'All I can say is the person who gave them away must have been blind – because anyone can see how beautiful they are – and stupid, because they'll be worth a good few bob, these will.'

Christine's excitement rose. 'How can you be so sure they are by your late daughter?'

Gwen's face creased into a smile. 'I understand. I'm an old woman and maybe a bit sentimental about the work of my own children, but I know it as well as I know the lines on the face I see in the mirror, I do. I wasn't one of those parents who constantly fuss over their children, but I was so proud of what they both did I made sure I saw everything I could of their work.'

Feeling she had to acknowledge the impact of what she was asking the woman to do, Christine leaned forward and said quietly, 'I'm sorry this is so upsetting for you, Mrs Llewellyn, but I'd be pleased to hear anything you can tell me about your daughter's work. There might be something that could place these somewhere in her background, so we could be more sure they were created by her.'

Gwen replied, 'Don't mind my tears. Can't stop them. Can't help them. Every day I cry. Bound to. You'd think, being here where they used to live with rooms full of their work in the gallery upstairs, I'd get used to the idea that she's gone forever, and he's in prison. That's why I did it – opened up the cottage. I thought it would help, but it seems it doesn't.' She dabbed at her eyes. 'This used to be such a happy place. A lot of people don't know that Lizzie and

Nathaniel used to get on like a house on fire. None of that came up at the trial, see. All they talked about in the court was how they hated each other. But it wasn't always like that. They shared this place in the early days, right after Lizzie came back from France. Lived and worked together they did, back then. That was the time when his stuff got bigger and hers got smaller. Funny that. But they said it meant they weren't competing with each other, see? Then Nathaniel won that big competition, and he started to get lots of money for his jobs, and poor Lizzie? Well, miniatures aren't everyone's cup of tea, but she said she wanted to use them to do something no one had done with them before – show modern life.'

'And she managed to completely change the way the public thought about the miniature form,' said Alexander gently.

Gwen sighed. 'She certainly did that, which she said was all that mattered to her. And Nathaniel did very well too. A lot better than her. Poor thing, she couldn't seem to get the commissions he did; even though the critics liked her work, it just didn't catch on like his did. She wanted to make the stuff of normal life into art that would appeal to normal people, as she put it, whereas Nathaniel wanted to make art on a grand scale, using grand themes. He was the one who got all those commissions from public bodies to make works that were on public display, and she ended up with her work selling to private buyers with fat wallets and no real social conscience. It was the ultimate irony, she said. Ate into her, it did. I could see it changing her. She'd never been a bitter girl; not an ounce of spite in her. But the way she'd talk about gallery owners, wealthy buyers, and even her brother, changed so much. Hid inside her work, she did, toward the end. I worried about her.' Gwen looked furtively at the table in front of her. 'Then . . . well, you know.'

Christine allowed the woman's fresh tears to fall for a moment or two before saying, 'How about Alexander and I pop upstairs to see what's up there?'

The grieving mother smiled. 'Yes, you do that. There's a lot of stuff by both of them upstairs. Go on with you now, I'll make a pot of tea. Be careful coming down those stairs, mind you – try coming down backwards, they're that steep, it helps.'

The stairs were, indeed, a challenge, and Christine was glad Alexander was behind her offering the promise of a soft landing should she need one. Once in the room in question, the dark-stained wide-plank floorboards, whitewashed walls and minimal furnishings allowed the works to sing aloud. Pieces of varying sizes filled the walls, all signed by the siblings.

'Oh my goodness,' said Christine. 'I prefer her work to his. And yet he was the one who was famous?'

'I see what you mean, but his appeals more to me. It's more – powerful. But both of them were good. What a waste. What a loss,' said Alexander.

They spent some time looking at more works by the brother and sister in a large, leather-bound portfolio displayed on a bed, which was just a frame with wooden slats.

Many of the pieces signed by Nathaniel were dated within the period since Lizzie's disappearance, but before his arrest. It seemed to Christine he'd treated the view of Oxwich Bay from the window of that very room in much the same way Cezanne had treated Mont Sainte Victoire – as his obsessive subject . . . drawn, sketched and painted many dozens of times.

Having taken time to enjoy the works in the second room upstairs, Christine took Gwen's advice and descended to the ground floor rump-first.

'I'm in here now,' called Gwen from the sitting room. 'Want a cuppa?' She'd done more than make tea – she'd also put out a plate full of sweet treats.

'Welsh cakes,' she said proudly. 'Made them myself, not from the shop, they aren't. Hope you like them. Tuck in.' They all did. The conversation flowed with the tea, and Christine enjoyed seeing Alexander alight with the enthusiasm he felt for the work of both the Llewellyn siblings. It became clear to Christine that, although Gwen was knowledgeable about both Nathaniel's and Lizzie's output, she wasn't a recognized expert, nor a known and respected valuer whose opinion about the miniatures would carry any weight. Indeed, as Lizzie's mother, her opinion about the attribution of any unsigned pieces would be highly suspect.

'As I mentioned, we met with an expert at a gallery in London yesterday,' said Christine. 'His name is Jeremy Edgerton. We showed him these photocopies of the miniatures and he said they might be by your daughter, but he wasn't prepared to confirm as much. Do you think you could talk to him about them?' She was hoping Gwen would agree.

'If that stuck up, high-and-mighty Mr Lah-di-dah Edgerton wants to speak to me ever again, he can climb down from his Olympus in London and come here. Not that I'm saying I'd let him set foot in the place if he was doing it for himself, but I would, I suppose, be prepared to let him come and see Lizzie's works that I have here, if it was for you, and to have these miniatures authenticated.'

'You don't like him then?' asked Alexander through crumbs of Welsh cake.

Gwen smiled. 'Highly perceptive of you, young man.'

'Dare I ask why you're so anti-Edgerton?' ventured Christine.

Gwen folded her arms over her flat chest. 'He put on an exhibition of Lizzie's work a few years back. About nine months or so before she went missing. Never invited me, did he? And I was the one who'd spent time putting all the background notes and photos and so forth about Lizzie's life together for the blessed thing. Not that I wanted more than a thank you – no money, you know – but no, not even a mention or an invitation. Rude, that's what it was. Just plain rude. I'd done all the research, all the work, and he took all the glory. I thought it was a terrible thing to do, not invite me, her mother. If it hadn't been for me, the blessed exhibition might never have happened; Edgerton was the epitome of the sort of person Lizzie had come to think of as representing the establishment she'd grown to hate, but I knew the exhibition was the only way to help her keep selling work so I talked her into it. Had a right up and down about me helping out, she and I did. Tears. Tantrums. Throwing things.' Gwen looked up. 'Her, not me, of course. But I did it anyway. And it paid off. Sold a lot of stuff for her, he did, even if she thought she was doing a deal with the Devil. I'd never missed any of her showings around here, even when she didn't want me there, I went, but that one? No invite.'

'She didn't want you at her local shows?' asked Christine.

'They'd never been her favorite thing to do. It was always hard for Lizzie to talk about her work, and what it meant to her. She'd made it clear she didn't want Nathaniel at any event where her work was on display years earlier, but she'd always let me go. Grudgingly. Then she stopped showing her work altogether. The exhibition at the Edgerton Gallery was her last ever. I heard she was there for about ten minutes, then flounced off. She . . . she found it hard to cope with people sometimes. Nathaniel was always the more outgoing one, though I have to be honest and admit neither of them developed what you could refer to as excellent social skills.'

Silence.

'It would be very useful if Edgerton were able to see what we've seen here, Mrs Llewellyn. There are some pieces upstairs by Lizzie that bear a striking resemblance to some of those in the books that have been found. That might swing it. If he could come down squarely on these miniatures being by Lizzie's hand, it could mean a great deal to the person who owns the books in which they appear.'

Gwen half-unfolded her arms. 'I dare say you'd have to be able to give him something to prove provenance too,' she said quietly. 'You say you don't know where those books came from, before they turned up at the bookshop?' Christine shook her head. 'Well, I can't help with that. I've never heard of your Daisy Dickens, but, if you need something to prove to Jeremy Edgerton the miniatures are by Lizzie, I think I can offer you something pretty convincing.'

'What exactly?' Christine felt excited.

'Well, this one—' Gwen indicated one of the miniatures – 'and this.' She leaned heavily on a stout walking stick as she crossed the room to the back wall, where she opened the double doors of a tall, built-in cupboard. Mounted in a simple clip-frame, inside was a three-foot round version of exactly the same scene of Swansea Bay on what seemed to be a simple piece of white cardboard, and the piece was signed by Lizzie.

'See, there? That's definitely by her. No one's ever seen that except Nathaniel and me. Well, I suppose the police and all those other people will have seen it too, but you know what I mean. She did it that last time she stayed here. I put it in that frame myself, and locked it up in here.'

Christine was elated. 'That'll do it. They both have to be by your daughter. Maybe the original miniature was in her mind when she created this larger piece.'

'No question,' added Alexander.

'So I suppose you'd better bring him here, then, because this one is not leaving my sight, and I'm certainly not about to haul it all the way up to his place in London,' said Gwen with resignation. 'If he'll come, that is.'

'I'll make him come, somehow,' said Christine gently. 'I'm sorry, this must be terribly difficult for you.'

Gwen smiled. 'Yes, my dear, it is.' She nibbled her lip. 'My real problem is that I'm the only person who doesn't believe Nathaniel killed his sister, see? Since they found him guilty they've stopped listening to me. Not that they ever did before; I'm his mother, so

I'm bound to not believe it of my own child, that's what they think. But they're wrong. See now, Lizzie I *could* have believed it of, but not him. When they were alone, boy oh boy, she'd let her brother have it. Nathaniel told me about their fights, and she had a terrible temper on her, even as a child. But Nathaniel? Soft as butter, he was, since he was a boy. Only time he ever said a bad word about anyone was when that lot on the telly goaded him into saying some not nice things about Lizzie. Lapped it up, she did, as though all she was interested in hearing was every little criticism of her work. It's a terrible thing, to have everyone look at you in the street, or in the shops, as though you raised a murderer. But I honestly don't believe I did. I don't know who killed my Lizzie, but I do know, in my heart, it wasn't my Nathaniel. And nothing I can do to stop them saying it.'

Christine shuffled uncomfortably and half-glanced at Alexander.

Gwen raised her head, gasping with excitement as her eyes lit up. 'Hang on a minute – now there's a thought! You're a detective, aren't you?' Christine nodded apprehensively. 'Right then. I'd like to take you on, hire you – or whatever it is people do. Could you and your colleagues find out who really killed my daughter? Because I know my son didn't. Never looked for anyone else, the police didn't. Said it was an open-and-shut case. I begged them, I did, but they didn't take any notice of me.'

Christine's sympathy for the woman led her to say something she almost immediately regretted, 'Of course I'll discuss the possibility of taking on your case with my colleagues.'

As Gwen Llewellyn wrapped her little arms around Christine in a tight hug, Alexander rolled his eyes and Christine shrugged at him.

'What else could I say?' she mouthed.

ELEVEN

With no need to make their way to the office for their usual Monday morning meeting, Mavis and Althea were enjoying the comfort of the morning room at the Dower House as they caught up with work.

'And is Carol all set up with her spyware at the shop?' asked Althea eagerly, sipping tea. Mavis nodded her reply as she petted McFli. 'I bet she's got some wonderful gadgets. The sort of thing they have at MI5 and MI6. Do you think there's an MI7 they never mention?' Althea stared hopefully at her friend and colleague. 'Probably an MI8 and 9 too, I shouldn't wonder.'

'Ach,' said Mavis indulgently. 'We're not spying on people at all, Althea. We're simply using equipment to watch people at our client's premises. It's all above board.'

'I know we don't have lots of street cameras around here, like they do in the cities and suburbs, but they have a few in Hay-on-Wye already, I hear. They *say* they're for the traffic. Do you think that's true?' Althea sounded unconvinced.

'The police might have cameras in Hay, but we have no access to them,' said Mavis, 'however, with the owner's permission, and by announcing to people that they will be filmed when they are on his premises, we can do what we are doing. But let's move on. What have you discovered during what you grandly described as your telephone research, Althea?'

Althea arranged herself more comfortably on the sofa and took a moment to acknowledge that McFli was being a good boy. 'I've had such fun! I've talked to quite a number of people I haven't spoken to for some years, and a few I thought were dead. Always nice to know they've just forgotten to send a Christmas card rather than having actually dropped off the perch.' Althea paused, staring down at McFli with a wistful expression.

'And?' prompted Mavis.

'Ah yes, I made notes,' replied Althea, tipping her handbag onto the sofa cushion and triumphantly pulling a little writing pad out of the jumbled mess. 'Most of them remembered Daisy from the old days, when she was younger – as one would expect given her seat – but most hadn't seen or heard much from her once she married. His name was George Drayton, though he's dead now, I'm told. That said, I did speak to one person who received a birthday card from Daisy a few years ago, and in it she mentioned the area she was moving to live after her husband's death. It's quite close by really. Three Cocks. Aberllynfi is the Welsh name, Three Cocks is the English name. There's been a coaching inn there for over five hundred years – the Three Cocks Inn. Hence the name. Very important junction area when the steam trains used to run that way, I believe.' Althea paused and wrinkled her nose with glee. 'Funny name for a place though, I'll admit it.'

'I think that's enough of the schoolgirl humor for today,' said Mavis sternly. 'Did you get an address, or just a general area?'

Althea's nostrils flared as she tried to stifle a giggle. 'Just the area. She said in the card she wrote that she was taking a little cottage there. However, I got it from another old chum that she'd subsequently moved to a retirement home. She probably stayed in that area, because it's swarming with old folks' homes thereabouts,' replied Althea.

'Would Daisy have been likely to be wealthy when she moved there?' asked Mavis. 'Would she have favored an up-market place, do you think?'

'My source said her husband left her pots of money – no children, you see – and she did like the good things in life, so I expect it would have been a pretty posh one,' replied Althea.

Mavis glanced around the grand room in which the two women were sitting. 'Posh is a relative term, I'd say.'

Althea nodded. 'I know what you mean, dear. Even at my age I still sometimes think I should pinch myself that I've lived the life I have, given my background.'

'As you've mentioned several times before, a mother born in Wales of Welsh and English parents, and a father born in England to a Scots and Irish couple, managed to produce you – a girl who grew up on the outskirts of London with enough spirit and drive to drag herself from suburban poverty to the stage in the West End of London where she met her duke and became a duchess. Like a fairy tale.' Mavis tried to move the conversation back to the topic in hand. 'I'll give the information to Carol and see what she can come up with. That's most helpful, Althea, dear. Anything more?'

Althea looked disappointed. 'Not really, though I thought that was quite a bit. I got it from two different people, and I know how you like to have information from more than one source.' Althea tilted her head in challenge.

'Aye, it's the proper way to investigate, right enough. It can save a lot of wasted time and energy too,' Mavis paused. 'What about where Daisy was born? Did anyone know if she was definitely still alive or, even dead? Any of that information might help Carol with her searches. She's no' having much luck.'

Althea shook her head with disappointment. 'We're all pretty sure she was from Swansea, but that doesn't mean that's where she was born. No one was certain she was dead.'

Mavis's expression softened as she smiled at her friend's hopeful face. 'I'll tell Carol in any case. Christine too. I think Christine and Alexander will manage very well together researching those miniatures.'

'They usually manage pretty well together,' replied Althea. 'Nudge, nudge, wink, wink, eh?' Her eyes glittered with mischief. 'Say no more, say no more,' she added in a comic voice and accent.

'I'm beginning to see what your son means about this Monty Python thing becoming a little annoying,' said Mavis wearily.

TWELVE

Tuesday 24th June

'You awake?' Alexander spoke quietly, hoping he wouldn't disturb Christine if she hadn't fully awoken when his phone had rung. When she grumbled into the pillow, pulling the duvet over her head, he smiled and shut himself in what could only be described as the world's smallest en suite bathroom; he had to stand in the shower stall to be able to have his conversation, or else sit on the loo. He chose the shower.

It wasn't a call he'd wanted to have; one of the chaps he had looking after his interests in London was telling him the people with whom he'd requested a sit-down to discuss the houses he wanted to buy, didn't want to play ball. He kept his voice down so Christine wouldn't hear his side of the conversation.

'You've got to get them to say yes, Jim,' he hissed. 'You mean he'll only talk to me? OK, I'll phone him. I'll get out of here so I can speak freely. If he won't consider negotiating on those properties, I don't know what I'll end up having to do.'

He disconnected, and moved as silently as possible about the bedroom, pulling on his clothes. Finally ready to leave, he bent close to Christine's beautifully tousled hair. 'I'm off out to find some coffee. There's just a couple of packets of instant in the room, and I don't hold out much hope for anything better in the little restaurant downstairs. I'll be back as soon as possible. I'm taking a key.'

A truffling sound from beneath the covers told him Christine had heard what he'd said, so he set off. The tall, terraced house was on the road that ran parallel to Swansea Bay, overlooking the sea. They'd only agreed to stay there because Gwen Llewellyn had said she'd get them 'a lovely room at her cousin's B&B'; it wasn't until they'd arrived that they'd realized the place was a bit rundown and what an estate agent would have undoubtedly described as *bijou*.

As he emerged from the building, he wondered if he should walk, or drive to find coffee. He didn't know the area at all. Taking the advice of a local who was passing by with her dog, he headed off toward a pub she'd pointed out. She assured him it might look pretty rundown but it did good breakfasts because it catered for the guards who worked shifts at Swansea prison which, ironically, also stood right on the seafront.

Her mention of 'a fancy Italian coffee machine' at the pub filled him with hope; Alexander reckoned he wasn't exactly addicted to caffeine, but he had to admit he sometimes suspected his bloodstream was about fifty percent espresso.

As he walked he made the call he knew he had to initiate; he didn't like to be seen as coming to an out-and-out crook, cap in hand. After five minutes he'd managed to talk his opponent into a face-to-face meeting. He'd have to wait a while, but he hoped it would settle the matter once and for all. He tucked away his phone, hoping for a good outcome.

When he opened the door to the pub it was as though he'd been transported back in time; he'd opened so many doors of so many pubs back in Brixton in his youth, never knowing what would be required of him, that the sight of barstools, stained carpeting and the glint of brass beer taps always took him back to his teen years. Back then he'd been a legendary and all-but-invisible transporter of packages; on this occasion he was anything but invisible, and became the immediate point of interest for a group of four burly men who were huddled at a table munching on what appeared to be bacon sandwiches, with mugs of coffee in front of them.

Leaning across the table to grab a paper napkin to catch the tomato ketchup oozing from his lips, the biggest of the bunch said, 'Mornin'. Nice to see the sun out for a change, isn't it?'

Inside Alexander's head he was sixteen-year-old Issy, illicit courier, but he forced the adult, well-bred, moneyed man he'd become to speak. 'Good morning, gentlemen. It certainly is a delightful day. One that could only be improved by a couple of cups of excellent coffee, which I've been advised I might find here. The sign outside says you serve Illy, is that correct?' He looked at the young woman who was wiping down the bar as he spoke, hoping his response would peg him as some sort of coffee snob in the eyes of the men.

'We do,' the girl replied.

'Know your coffee, do you?' asked the slimmest of the four men, his eyes twinkling.

'One has to,' replied Alexander in his most refined accent.

'Prefer Lavazza myself, but Illy will do at a pinch. Got a good machine here they have. You'll enjoy it.'

Alexander was surprised to be having such an exchange, but was glad these men who had clearly worked all night at the prison were affable and content to imagine he was an English tourist.

'I'll take two triple espressos, each with a topping of steamed milk, please,' said Alexander to the woman, who was already preparing her machine.

'Anything else?' she asked. 'The bacon butties are lovely.'

Alexander looked at the butter dripping from the thick, soft white bread on the men's plates, and couldn't resist. 'Go on then, two of those as well. All to take away, please.'

A general chuckle rippled around the group of men. 'Hard to resist the smell of bacon, isn't it?' said the big man. 'Join us while you wait? We can all budge up a bit. Where are you visiting from, then? Staying at one of the B&Bs along the front, are you?'

Alexander joined the men, who he judged were glad to have someone other than a work colleague to talk to, and recognized a chance to really help Christine. He threw himself into his full Alexander Bright routine, and nonchalantly asked about Swansea prison's most famous inmate, Nathaniel Llewellyn.

After about five minutes the girl behind the bar called, 'Ready to go now, it is. Let the poor man escape while it's all hot, you lot.'

Wry laughter was shared by the group. 'Says that all the time she does,' commented the slight man, 'thinks it's funny because we work at the prison.'

Alexander shared the men's jailhouse mirth, paid for his items, and left. The sea breeze felt good on his skin, and he felt he truly *had* escaped . . . something. Maybe the shadows of what might have been had his younger self not been as clever at slipping through the fingers of the coppers?

As he walked back to the B&B, where he was sure Christine would still be snuggled down and half-asleep, he reminded himself he still had to be clever and slippery because, sometimes, some of the things he had to resort to doing to help those who needed a hand to get out of the gutter weren't exactly the actions of a law-abiding citizen. The situation developing back on his old home turf of Brixton was a case in point.

Climbing the creaking staircase to their room he swore he'd get it all sorted when he got back to London.

THIRTEEN

Carol Hill was absolutely exhausted when she dragged herself out of bed. Albert had given her a particularly sleepless night, and she wasn't in the best of moods as she fed him and attended to the mess that had somehow accumulated in the kitchen.

Once her son was settled, she successfully accomplished most of the filing and sorting she needed to do for the day, then opened the digital recordings coming in from Bryn Jenkins's bookshop. She patiently scrolled through the files from that morning, not hoping for much, but knowing she had to focus on the images which passed before her eyes.

She slowed the recording whenever a customer, or browser, entered the frame in one of the six cameras she was monitoring, but saw nothing untoward. Finally, she saw something odd, scrolled back, and replayed the recording. The camera just inside the door of the lower level of the shop had caught the book depositor in the act toward the rear of the shop. Carol was thrilled, and immediately told the now wideawake Albert how delighted she was. Albert looked utterly unimpressed, choosing instead to attend to pulling on his toes with glee.

Carol carefully captured three excellent shots of the woman in question; she had made no effort to hide her face. Carol put her in her sixties; she had short, permed, gray hair and was quite stout. So, utterly unremarkable. Carol noted she not only deposited books, but also purchased one – *The Man in the Brown Suit* by Agatha Christie. Sadly, she could also see she'd paid with cash. Carol phoned the shop and had a terse conversation with Sam, who claimed not to recall the woman at all, despite the fact she'd dealt with her within the past hour.

Carol emailed the photographs to her team to allow them to see the woman's face, but had to admit that was all she had. Despite that sad fact, she organized a virtual meeting with her colleagues; by eleven, all the members of the agency were able to discuss the case.

Mavis called the meeting to order. 'Carol, you set?' Carol nodded into the camera on her computer in her home office. 'You, Christine?' Christine nodded into the camera on her phone, while sitting on the seafront in Swansea. 'Althea and I are here at the Dower House, so let's begin. You've all seen what Carol saw, I believe. We have photographic evidence of a person leaving books at the Crooks & Cooks Bookshop. Neither Val nor Sam at the bookshop are able to identify the individual. Questions, observations, anyone?'

Silence.

'Come along, ladies – this is a meeting. Its purpose is for us to discuss, and progress with the case. So, I'd like your input please.'

Althea thought Mavis sounded cross and decided to do something to avoid her dagger stares. 'Seems to me we've nabbed the culprit red-handed, so we give that photo to the client. We've done what he asked.'

'I agree,' said Christine, speaking clearly, 'but I do have one question. Are we sure she's the one who's done it before?'

'Good point, Christine,' said Mavis. 'Comments?'

'We could continue with the surveillance, and we might find more people doing the same thing,' said Carol as she soothed Albert by bouncing him on her shoulder, 'or we could watch for another month and see nothing more at all. I was thrilled we saw something so quickly. If our client claims he only notices more books at the end of each month, it looks as though our timing was serendipitous.'

'You mean you were just lucky?' asked Althea, winking at her distant friend.

'Ach, a piece of good fortune is never to be sneered at,' retorted Mavis.

'Call it luck, serendipity or spectacularly good planning,' continued Carol, 'the fact is we've got the person on film, and that's what the client asked for. I filed the contract he signed, Mavis, that was *all* he asked for . . . to find out who was doing it. We've done that. What he chooses to do with that information is now entirely up to him.'

'Agreed,' said Mavis slowly, 'though "finding out who's doing it" could also mean identifying the woman in the photographs, and there's still the question of whether the books belong to the woman who left them, or not.'

'I wonder why she's doing it,' said Althea quietly. 'What makes a woman wander the countryside depositing books in bookshops, willy nilly?'

Mavis tutted. 'There might be a very good reason for her actions . . .' She paused. 'Though I must admit one doesnae come to mind. And a photo's not much to go on.'

'It's a start,' said Carol, 'and I don't know how much more we can expect at this point; it's hardly likely someone will walk about with their name neatly printed on a badge on their lapel, is it? If we were TV cops, or the FBI, I'd have one of those handy-dandy face-identification programs and could run this elderly lady's photos through it. But we aren't, so we don't, and I can't. But it's not a dead end – it's a starting point.' Carol paused, then added, 'Step two in identifying this person should be for us to show the photo to other shopkeepers in Hay-on-Wye. Not just the bookshops. It might be she's known about the town. Of course we'll have to ask Bryn Jenkins if he recognizes her. Bryn wasn't at the shop when I phoned. Val said he was at Chellingworth Hall today, and I know I can't send the photo to his phone because that thing he has is too old to be able to do that. Maybe you could walk it across to him, Althea? And maybe Mavis could go into Hay and show the photo around there?'

'I could do both,' said Mavis quickly. 'Althea and I could walk up to the hall together. It wouldnae be any trouble. Then I could head off to Hay. There's almost the whole day ahead of us.'

Carol noticed Althea's wrinkled brow furrowing. 'You said earlier on you were a bit pooped, dear. Feeling revived, are we?' The tone in Althea's voice meant Carol had to hide a smirk.

'A brisk walk will do us all good,' retorted Mavis, 'and it certainly won't go amiss for McFli. I think he's been having a few too many treats since wee Gertie joined us.'

McFli lifted his head from his paws and looked at his human. 'Ssh,' hissed Althea. 'I've told you to spell that word.'

'T.R.E.A.T.?' asked Mavis. Althea nodded. Mavis smiled. 'I think McFli can spell that one, and a few other words too.' She looked down at the pink tongue and appealing eyes and couldn't resist saying, 'Aww, little sweetheart,' as she stroked McFli's ears.

Althea said, 'We like to think of them as furry people, my dear, but they're not, you know. They need their routine, and they need to be taught their boundaries. But this one? Spoiled rotten. It's all my fault, of course; he was the runt of the litter so I raised him with tiny bottles of milk all by myself. Melted my heart, did this one. I was never the same with him as with all the dozens of other dogs I've had over the years. And he knows it.' Althea stooped to rub McFli's little head.

'Right then, come away with you. Let's get up to the hall if we're going,' said Mavis.

The meeting concluded, and McFli displayed his enthusiasm for the idea of getting out and about by racing the women to the front door.

FOURTEEN

'**M**other, how wonderful! Just the person,' Henry beamed as Althea and Mavis entered his private sitting room, and showed his concern when McFli shot in behind them.

'You actually want to see me, Henry?' Althea sounded genuinely surprised. It annoyed Henry.

'Why shouldn't I wish to see you, Mother? I'm your son. You're my mother. Of course I want to spend time with you. An appropriate amount of time, spent in an appropriate manner of course, but—'

'Stop, dear,' interrupted Althea. 'You've never properly understood the concept of tact, have you? Ah well, it's too late for you to learn now, I expect. My fault. What did you want? Just get to the point, as I am here for reasons other than to spend time with you.'

Henry felt somewhat disgruntled. He didn't think he'd deserved to be snapped at, and in front of Mavis, a relative stranger. 'It's

Clemmie, of course,' he said. He recognized his tone as he spoke; he knew he sounded much as he had when he was a teenager complaining about his annoying little sister. He cleared his throat and added, 'It's not about the nurse leaving this time. It's Clemmie's desire to move back to London and take said nurse with her. They're at loggerheads about it. Clemmie says there's a contractual obligation for the woman to accompany her if she wishes to spend the last few weeks of her recuperation at the Belgravia house, whereas Nurse Thomas maintains she was retained to a post specifically here, at Chellingworth Hall. Stephanie is retrieving the original paperwork now, and we were planning to take it from there. You know, get the two of them in separate rooms and try to get them to calm down. Personally, I think Clemmie *should* go back to London, and the sooner the better. For all concerned.'

Althea took a seat near the window. 'My dear boy, you only say that because then she'll be out of your hair. She has almost an entire wing at her disposal, I have no idea why the two of you cannot avoid each other in a place this size.'

'We both need to eat, and she's started to join Stephanie and myself in the dining room in the evenings. It's not fair, Mother. We're thinking about taking dinner in our own apartment until she's gone.'

Althea tilted her head, something Henry knew she did just before telling him off about something. He steeled himself. 'She might be lonely, Henry, have you thought of that? You know she's never been a girl who's been happy with her own company. I noticed when she was not much more than an infant that she thrived only in the presence of others. As she grew up, I wondered if it was healthy, and now she's in her fifties I'm quite sure it's not; your sister has no sense of self-identity. She sees herself only as others reflect her. That's why she's seeking you out – she cannot survive alone. Despite the fact she wants to drag the poor woman to London with her, I cannot imagine Nurse Thomas pussyfoots around Clemmie. She hasn't since she arrived, which I must admit is endearing, but maybe it's finally worn your sister down. I tell you what, I'll go to the estate office, which I expect is where Stephanie has stowed the contracts, then I'll have a word with Clemmie. If she goes back to London now I can only imagine the trouble she'll get herself into by seeking out the company of some of those questionable friends of hers. She might do something that means her leg will never mend properly. Imagine if she ended up in a wheelchair for life.'

Henry took a moment to do so, and didn't like the future he could imagine for himself and his bride if his sister found herself becoming a permanent resident at Chellingworth Hall. He realized maybe it was worth putting up with her for just a little while longer, in order to ensure her eventual, and permanent, departure. 'Very well, Mother. I appreciate your help. You're right, of course.'

'Will you come with me, or will you go up to see Mr Jenkins?' asked Althea of Mavis as she set off.

'I'll head off to see Bryn, I think,' replied Mavis.

'If that's who you're after I should remain here, if I were you, Mavis. He was due to meet me here five minutes ago,' said Henry, looking at his watch. 'He promised me an update before he goes back to his shop this afternoon. You might as well wait with me. See you later, Mother.'

Right on cue, a flushed Bryn Jenkins was ushered into the room by Edward.

'Ah, Mr Jenkins,' said Henry expansively, 'I'm interested to hear how things are progressing with our books.'

'Yes, Your Grace. All coming along very nicely. The drying out hasn't done any damage as far as I can tell, it seems. I have some repairs to make to a little wear in places, but I think I can confidently project a fully successful restoration will be completed within the week.'

Henry clapped his hands in glee, and was surprised when Mavis joined in. The impromptu round of applause led to the book restorer's cheeks turning red.

'Jolly good job, Mr Jenkins,' said Henry. 'Mother will be delighted to hear your news. She's just popped to the estate office. Should be back in two flicks of a lamb's tail with my good lady wife.'

During the somewhat awkward pause that followed, Henry watched with interest as Mavis sidled toward Bryn Jenkins and pushed her telephone in front of him. 'We have a photograph of a woman seen depositing books at your shop earlier today. We wondered if you recognized her.'

Bryn pushed his spectacles up his nose and squinted at the phone's screen. 'Can't say I do,' he replied, 'though she's not a very notice-able sort of person, is she? She's the one who's been doing it though?'

'She certainly did it today, and right under your assistant's nose. Carol has a filmed record of her depositing half a dozen volumes on the shelves in the rear part of the shop.'

Henry sounded engaged. 'There's someone delivering books to your shop and you don't know who they are? Sounds a bit off to me. Wouldn't you know all the delivery personages in your sort of field?'

Bryn looked at Mavis with puzzlement. She said, 'His Grace has not been informed of the enquiries we have been making on your behalf. Her Grace, the dowager, does not share professional information with family members. It's up to our clients to decide what information they want to share, and with whom.'

Brightening, Bryn spoke directly to the duke. 'Some unknown person has been leaving books in my shop without my permission, Your Grace. It's given me a bit of a strange feeling about my business, and the WISE Enquiries Agency has been investigating on my behalf. They have used some natty equipment to spot who's been doing it, and now at least I can see the person's face.'

Henry nodded sagely. 'But you don't recognize them, eh?' Bryn agreed. Henry was desperate to see the face of the nefarious character for himself. 'Mind if I take a look. I get to see a lot of faces around these parts.'

'With pleasure, Your Grace,' replied Bryn, just as Althea and Stephanie entered the room.

Henry had to admit, with disappointment, that he didn't know the woman in the photograph. He handed the phone to his wife who peered at the photograph and delighted everyone by announcing, 'I have definitely seen this woman before.'

A chorus of 'Where?', 'When?' and 'Who is she?' followed. Stephanie swatted away all the questions, and closed her eyes. Henry thought she looked very young when she screwed up her face with the effort of recollection.

Eventually she admitted defeat. 'I'm sorry, I can't think where I've seen her, or why.' Stephanie sounded frustrated. 'I . . . I seem to think she was wearing a hat when I saw her. A rain hat? Maybe we met outdoors? Maybe in the winter? Oh dear, I'm so sorry. I do recall she had an accent that told me she was from the north of England somewhere. It was quite strong. Maybe Yorkshire? That's all I can grasp.'

'In the classes I took about how to recall information to be a better witness, they said it helped if you sat in a dark room and tried to talk your way through the memory. You have to work through things like sounds and smells. You get to the other information that way. I could do it with you if you like, Your Grace,' offered Mavis.

Henry noticed that, for some reason, Althea looked proudly at Mavis when she spoke. He wondered why.

'Thanks, Mavis, I might take you up on that,' replied Stephanie, 'but I have to deal with something else of immediate importance. Henry and I have to meet with Lady Clementine and Nurse Thomas.'

Henry felt his tummy turn. 'I'd almost forgotten about that,' he admitted.

'How surprising,' remarked his mother acidly.

'If Your Grace were to be available, maybe I could come to the hall tomorrow morning to help you with some recollection techniques,' ventured Mavis.

'That would be marvelous,' blurted out Bryn before adding with embarrassment, 'though I don't want Your Grace to go to any bother.'

'Anything I can do to help you, Bryn, and Val, of course,' replied Stephanie. 'How about meeting me at the estate office first thing, Mavis? We could find a quiet place where we can work together. How long would it take, do you think? We have a fete committee meeting at nine thirty sharp. I'd need to be able to attend that. How about eight thirty? Would that suit?' Henry beamed with delight to see his wife in action.

'Very well then, it's a date,' said Mavis, pulling her phone from her pocket and making notes on the keyboard. Stephanie did the same thing.

'The things one can achieve with technology these days is quite something, isn't it?' noted Henry.

'Aye, the world's changing, no doubt. So long as we use it, and don't allow it to run our lives, I dare say it's generally a good thing,' observed Mavis.

'Of course it is,' agreed Althea. 'All the equipment Carol stuffed into Mr Jenkins's shop, and being able to now look at the culprit, none of it would have been possible without technology.'

'I dare say one human being sitting in the shop might have achieved the same results, Mother,' said Henry. 'Don't you have someone working there while you're here, Mr Jenkins?' It seemed to Henry that would be a necessity.

Bryn nodded. 'Indeed I do, Your Grace, but it seems she's not the most observant type. Young people these days seem to be so completely unaware of their surroundings.'

'However many signs there are in a place, we don't think cameras can see as much as they do. Carol showed me the website for the company that makes the equipment she used. It was fascinating. Do you know they have tiny little cameras that look like buttons? You can hide them all over the place. I could stick one onto a cardigan, and you'd be none the wiser,' said Althea merrily.

Henry didn't like that idea at all. 'Surely it's illegal to just go about filming people in goodness knows what sort of private situation? You'd have to get their permission, wouldn't you? What if people started showing up here with gadgets all over their bodies and secretly filming our home? Good heavens, they could be working out how to rob us blind and we wouldn't even know.' Henry was unsettling himself as his mind raced through the possibilities.

'We make it quite clear that no filming is allowed on the premises, Henry,' replied Stephanie. 'Photographs are allowed, of course . . .' Henry noticed she looked suddenly concerned. 'But you're right, dear, there's very little we can do to prevent people from filming those parts of the hall for which they have paid to gain access. But let's just rest assured we have a new, and extremely thorough, security system installed that would thwart most attempts to rob us of any items of value. Unlike a year ago.'

Henry didn't feel as comforted as he suspected he should have done, and wondered if his worries had shown on his face.

FIFTEEN

Mavis MacDonald was wearing her comfy walking shoes, and was on the job. It had been agreed – in other words she'd informed the team – she was going to spend the rest of the day making the rounds of businesses in Hay-on-Wye with the photographs of the woman who'd deposited books at Bryn's shop. She'd promised herself a spot of tea at The Swan as a reward, and planned on suggesting to Bryn he might like to join her, if he could get away.

Mavis reckoned it was best to work on a door-to-door basis, and she began as she meant to go on – entering the premises in question, waiting until the person in charge was available for a quiet word, then introducing herself and asking those working there if they recognized the person in the photographs. As was always the case in such circumstances, she knew she might need a good reason for asking, as a suspiciously hesitant response wasn't unusual. Since she didn't want to give the real reason for her enquiries – thereby ensuring her clients' privacy – she had decided to resort to a backstory that usually worked: a friend of the unknown person's family had lost contact and was trying to get in touch with urgent news, so they'd asked Mavis to undertake some professional enquiring. Since Mavis was the designated 'public face' of the agency, she didn't have to worry about retaining an undercover profile. Indeed, she made sure she carried a bundle of business cards to hand out if there was the merest hint of interest in the services the agency offered. She'd picked up quite a few contacts that way, many people not knowing a discreet enquiries agency existed in their neck of the woods.

A couple of upmarket women's clothing shops yielded no information, a bookshop specializing in maps and atlases was no more helpful. Mavis hesitated on the doorstep of an outlet offering children's clothing, handmade toys, yarn and other knitting and crocheting paraphernalia, but went in believing it was best to be thorough. Nothing.

After forty-five minutes, and about ten more shops, the retired nurse was beginning to flag. The whole process was so repetitive, and dispiriting. Two pubs, a coffee place and a shop specializing in children's books later, and knew she needed to pause for a rest. Just a wee one. The feet that had carried her thousands of miles along hospital corridors were letting her down. She hated it when Annie Parker used the term 'gumshoeing,' but she was beginning to wonder if a pair of something squishy and 'gum-like' on her feet might have helped.

A couple of worn wooden chairs on the pavement outside a thrift shop looked inviting. She picked up one of the little leaflets, that told her all about how the money raised by the shop would benefit cancer research, as she rested her rear on one of the rickety seats.

'You thinking of buying those chairs?' asked a sharp voice. 'They're for selling.'

Mavis looked up into a mass of just-colored-and-set dark, tight curls and a pair of tired eyes. 'Sorry,' she said, smiling, 'I was just reading your pamphlet. You're supporting a good cause.'

The woman eyed her suspiciously. 'Yes. We are.' She hesitated. 'If you want to come in we've got comfier seats inside, and I could get you a glass of water.'

Mavis hoped it was the chair creaking when she rose. 'Very kind of you. Don't mind if I do.'

With Mavis enjoying a glass of cool water and the two women who staffed the shop peering at the photographs following her explanation of her task, Mavis felt much better.

'I know her,' said the manager.

Mavis's spirits rose even further. 'That's good news. Do you happen to know her name, by any chance?' She pulled a notepad from her handbag.

The woman looked suspicious. 'I thought you said you knew her, or at least that you were acting for people who knew her. You're sure this is all above-board, are you? How come you don't know her name?'

Mavis nodded. 'I do,' she lied, 'I just need to make sure you do.' She could tell the woman was sizing her up.

The women shrugged at each other. The older one spoke. 'Sarah Cruickshank. Runs a posh old folks' home in Three Cocks. It's called Oakdene, or Oakview, or Oakdale . . . something like that. I'm pretty sure it's Oak-something, anyway. She's only brought in a few little pieces now and again. Nothing to write home about. The odd vase or two, a few boxes and bits of general bric-a-brac.'

'Would you happen to know where she gets the items she brings in?' asked Mavis.

The women exchanged a significant glance, then the older of the two lowered her voice, as she said, 'None of our business.'

Mavis decided it was best to not say more than: 'No matter. I'm sure I'll be able to find her with the help you've given me. The friends and family trying to get in touch with her will be pleased, I'm sure. I understand from them she's a caring sort, so an old folks' home doesn't come of much of a surprise. Is she married, do you happen to know?'

The more junior of the two women – in age and station – replied, looking coyly at her superior, 'Oh yes. He sometimes meets her outside here. I expect they come into Hay together and go their own ways. A lot of couples do that. To be honest with you, it's why we have the chairs outside. Husband Chairs we call them – lots of places have them. Somewhere for him to perch while she browses.' She looked furtive as she lowered her voice and leaned toward Mavis. 'He's a bit of an old goat, truth be told. Filthy laugh on him. Talks like something out of a *Carry On* film, he does. Puts me in mind of Sid James, even though he looks nothing like him. Wears one of those hats, he does. She'd have to be a patient sort to put up with him, or maybe he's not like that with her all the time, who knows. I couldn't cope, myself. It's all well and good to see it on the telly, but to have that sort of banter at all hours? Drive me *twp* it would. But there, she's giving us odds and ends we can sell, so I shouldn't speak ill of them.'

'Got anything here at the moment she's brought in?' asked Mavis hopefully.

The two women cast their eyes about the shop. The younger one pointed to a wooden box on top of a chest of drawers. 'She brought that in a while ago, didn't she?' They both agreed she had.

'Mind if I take a look?' asked Mavis. She got up and strolled to the item in question. The worn, light-oak wooden box that had clearly once held a cutlery service in its velvet-lined interior was empty. 'The cutlery wasn't in it?' she asked.

Both women shook their heads. 'We were thinking maybe someone would be able to get all the innards out and just use it for odds and ends,' said the younger of the pair.

'How much do you want for it?' asked Mavis.

Sensing a sale, the more senior woman took the box and gave it a good going over. 'Fiver?' she said.

Mavis glared. It was contrary to her nature to not haggle on such an occasion, but she reasoned the money would go to a worthy cause, and she could pass on the cost as an expense – or find a use for the box herself. Either way, she felt she had to accept the price quoted.

A few moments later, invigorated by what she hoped was useful information – and in possession of a box she wasn't sure she really wanted – Mavis paused on the pavement and sent off a few texts, then headed toward Bryn's shop to invite him to join her for a pot of tea. She planned to return to her task of entering every establish-ment in Hay and asking about the woman in the photographs after she'd properly refreshed herself. Having information from one source was handy, but having it verified or augmented by a second, and even a third if possible, was Mavis's preference. However, she believed she'd earned a break, so set off with a spring in her step.

SIXTEEN

'And you're sure it'll be alright for me to join everyone for dinner up at Chellingworth Hall tonight?' asked Alexander of Christine as the sleek Aston Martin purred along through Ystradgynlais.

'Yes, I checked with Althea. We're all to be her guests, she said. Something about wanting Clemmie to have a proper dinner party to enjoy. So you'll be expected to be your most charming self.'

'I'll do my best. Want to stop for a spot of late lunch on the way? Those bacon butties we grabbed for breakfast won't keep us going until eight o'clock tonight.'

Christine gave the matter some thought. 'We'll be passing Craig Y Nos Castle soon. It's a fascinating place; built by a sea captain in the 1840s, all his family died out in Shakespearean style and a chap named Morgan Morgan bought it, lived in it, and then his son did too. He was also named Morgan Morgan. No wonder they all give each other nicknames around here.' She grinned at Alexander who smiled, but didn't take his eyes off the narrow, winding road. 'So then along comes Dame Adelina Patti, the world-famous operatic soprano, who falls for the place, buys it and pours money into it. She built a theatre there that seats a hundred and fifty. Anyway, the great and the good all visited; she even had her own private railway station and traveled the world from her Welsh home until she died. The place became a hospital, and now it's a hotel. With a bar. We could go there. I've always fancied seeing the place.'

'Thought you knew it inside and out, the way you were talking,' said Alexander grinning. 'How d'you know so much about the place?'

Christine shrugged. 'Places like that call to me, somehow. Growing up in our draughty old Georgian pile in Ireland meant I knew what it was to live in a big house but with no money available to make it more than shabbily comfortable. I've always wondered what it would be like to do a place up just as you want it. It would be marvelous, don't you think?'

'You've seen where, and how, I live. I don't care for a lot of stuff about the place.'

Christine knew he was right, and it bothered her a little because she preferred the idea that more was good, and layering was even better. Some called it clutter, she liked to think of her preferred style as 'Victorian' . . . but in a good way. 'Well, it's not far now, so what do you think? We could try.'

'Agreed.'

Ten minutes later they were back in the car and heading off again. 'Shame about that. I should have guessed it would be the time of year when they'd be busy with weddings, but not on a Monday. What an odd day to get married. I mean, it's a lovely day for it, to be sure – and can you imagine those photographs? The place is stunning. Maybe we can come back some time?'

'I'll phone them up and see when they can fit us in. Booking for two hundred people, OK?'

As the last syllable left his lips, both Alexander and Christine clamped their mouths shut and looked out of their respective windows. Christine could feel her heart pounding in her chest. She knew Alexander had *not* just proposed marriage, but she also knew what they were both thinking at that precise moment. She forced herself to breath. Silence reigned until they'd wound their way up to the Crai Reservoir and stopped to take in the view.

Standing in a little lay-by, the patchwork-green of the rolling Brecon Beacons around them and the view across the vast body of water before them, Christine felt she had to break the tension somehow, but wasn't sure where to begin.

'It's grand here,' she dared.

'Are you aware you revert to full-on Irish when you're off in your own little world?'

Christine wanted to say so much, but satisfied herself with: 'We're neither of us quite what the world thinks we are, are we?'

Alexander's eyes narrowed as he replied, 'It's good we have each other then – someone we can be our whole self with.'

Suddenly nervous he was going to utter words he would never be able to un-say, Christine was relieved when she was, quite literally, saved by the bell; her phone rang.

She pulled it out of her pocket, looking puzzled. 'I can't believe I can get a signal up here.'

She listened to her call, and shouted above the gusting wind which, if the shape of the few stunted trees that could be seen was anything to go by, blew constantly, and in one direction. Finally she hung up. 'OK, new plan. There's a place out past Brecon and Talgarth called Three Cocks. It's on our way back to Chellingworth from here. Mavis has asked us if we can find an old folks' home in the area called Oak-something, run by a couple named Cruickshank. She believes the wife's the one who's been dumping books in the shop. I said we'd do it. Apparently there's a decent old coaching inn there too, with a good reputation for its food. So let's press on, eh?'

'Happy to be your chauffeur to anywhere your heart desires, Miss,' mugged Alexander, and they were off, pausing intermittently to avoid the sheep strolling across the road as they foraged the ancient mountainsides, just as they had done for possibly thousands of years.

As Christine settled back into her seat, she felt the tension between Alexander and herself had been defused. She was also pleased to be able to help with another part of the case for the Jenkinses.

It took about forty-five minutes to reach their goal. As far as Christine could see, Three Cocks was quite a going concern, and much more built-up than she'd imagined it would be. Signs of light industry, an activity center for those she thought of as yomping-types, a high school, a garden center set up at what used to be a railway station, then finally, on the way out of the village in the direction they were heading, she spotted the Three Cocks Inn.

'Here we are. I suggest lunch and enquiries.' Christine unclipped her seatbelt.

'So, just the usual then,' quipped Alexander, hurrying out of the car to open the door for her – something Christine allowed him to do on the basis that he wanted to, and she liked it.

A sunny afternoon in June meant the delightful beer garden was busy. Inside, though the fire in the large fireplace wasn't lit, the pub was warm – despite all the doors and windows set into the lovely old stone walls being open. The pewter mug-bedecked bar was bustling, but the pair managed to find two barstools, and the depar-ture of a couple of men ferrying drinks to the smoking area outside allowed them a little elbow room, though they were still squashed together.

'It might be difficult to attract anyone's attention to get served, let alone beg information,' noted Christine. 'Doesn't anyone around here have a job to go to at this time of day?'

'Looks like we've hit a busy patch. Maybe it'll quieten down soon. Do you think people around here start work early, and finish early because of it?' said Alexander, checking his watch.

They chatted, took in their surroundings and were soon served their halves of foaming Felinfoel ale. Christine ordered an oak-smoked salmon sandwich, made with fish caught in the local Usk River, while Alexander opted for a beet and goat cheese salad, the cheese having been supplied by a goat farmer who, according to the menu, raised the animals in question just up the road. They agreed they were surprisingly peckish, and Christine kept a beady eye open so she didn't miss the chance to talk to the landlord as soon as he was able to spare a moment.

A couple of brief, and several-times-interrupted, exchanges later she'd established the old folks' home in question was probably Mountain Ash House, run by a couple named Fred and Sarah, though the landlord didn't know their surname. He looked at the photograph on Christine's phone and confirmed it was the Sarah he knew. Just as their food arrived, a table beside the open door to the garden became available, so they grabbed their plates and scurried off, glad to feel the breeze and enjoy some sustenance. The babbling in the bar meant their conversation was pleasant, but not deep, something for which Christine was grateful and, within forty minutes, they were off again, following the directions they'd been given at the pub.

SEVENTEEN

Mavis MacDonald was happy to be finally sitting on the edge of the seat of her Mini in the car park at Hay-on-Wye. The windows and doors were all wide open to allow it to cool down from oven-temperature, and she rubbed her feet with gusto. Not since she'd been running the Battersea Barracks Hospital had she felt this bad. She reckoned she was getting soft in her old age . . . then reminded herself she wasn't old at all. Your mid-sixties was a time when activities like working, traveling, and even hiking and hill-walking were still real possibilities, and when there were still enough years ahead of a person for them to make plans. It was when the results of a healthy lifestyle would pay off – of that she had no doubt.

She was pleased with her day, even if she wasn't delirious about her feet. Not only had she found out about Sarah Cruickshank at the charity shop, she'd had her information confirmed by the manager of another such establishment that specialized in clothing and clothing accessories. Mission accomplished!

She'd also enjoyed a very pleasant break with Bryn Jenkins. Luckily for her he'd recommended a little place in a back-street where, he assured her, the tea was just as good as it was at The Swan, but at half the price.

Impressed with her achievements, Bryn had agreed he'd like to know more about the circumstances of the woman in the photo, this Sarah Cruickshank, so Mavis was glad she'd already phoned Christine, knowing she'd be on her way back from Swansea with Alexander. Mavis thought at the time her colleague had sounded a bit strange on the phone, but suspected that would be something to do with the enigmatic Mr Alexander Bright – so none of her business.

Squeezing her swollen foot back into her sandal, Mavis was grateful for the Velcro on the straps that allowed her a little extra wiggle-room. She made the call she knew she had to, to let Althea know she wouldn't be taking their usual late-afternoon stroll on the estate, then pulled out of the car park to head back to the Dower House where she planned on putting her feet up for an hour and having a cool shower before she dressed for dinner at Chellingworth Hall.

Just as Mavis revved her engine, her phone rang. It was Stephanie Twyst.

'I'm glad I caught you, Mavis,' said the duchess, sounding rushed. 'I sat and did what you said – I shut my eyes in a quiet place and tried to think about all the feelings I had when I talked to that woman, and I got it. Her name's Cruickshank, and she runs an old folks' home somewhere in the Three Cocks area. It's not much to go on, and I'm afraid I can't find any paperwork relating to her visit. I know she talked to me about gaining access to Chellingworth Hall without those in wheelchairs or using walkers getting wet, which was when I put two and two together. But I can't remember the name of the home. Does that help at all?'

'It most certainly does, Your Grace. It helps me be more certain we're on the right track, since your information confirms what I have gleaned from other sources. I appreciate you taking the time to think it all through. Thank you, Your Grace.'

'You're most welcome, Mavis. I really like Val Jenkins and I'd like to help her out if I can. She was always most generous with her cooking tips. I'll let you get on now. See you later for dinner, I understand.'

'Aye, indeed. I'm looking forward to it, Your Grace.'

As Mavis drove along the busy roads, she felt satisfied with a good afternoon's work. She replayed her conversation with Bryn, and realized, to her consternation, he'd quoted the Bible at least half a dozen times during their tea break. To Mavis's mind, that seemed like a lot. Indeed, she wasn't used to spending time with anyone who quoted the Bible at all. She wondered if he was given to doing it all the time. Maybe it was because he was restoring biblical texts at the moment? Or maybe it spoke to the nature of the man more deeply.

EIGHTEEN

Christine wanted to be able to turn up at dinner that evening with concrete news about the Cruickshanks and the old folks' home, so she felt excited as Alexander's car nosed gently along the uneven track that led from the road to the substantial Victorian structure the signpost had announced as simply MOUNTAIN ASH HOUSE. The place was an inviting, large, solid-looking building, with well-maintained landscaping and several of the trees for which it had been named arcing above garden seating. A few white-haired women were sitting in the shade offered by the trees, a couple of walking frames beside them. The front door of the house was open, inviting them inside.

'I'll talk, you follow my lead,' said Christine before they left the car. Alexander grunted his agreement.

Christine chose to not enter the grand old building, but instead made her way toward the three probable residents who were enjoying cups of tea set on a sturdy wooden table.

'Hello there,' she began, bringing her best Irish brogue to bear, 'I was wonderin' if any of you lovely ladies would be livin' here by any chance? I'm helpin' out a wonderful friend of me dear old grannie to find a place to settle down and meet some good folk like yourselves.'

Christine noted the three woman were all wearing outfits that suggested the warmth of the sun wasn't quite enough for their elderly bodies to feel comfortable in anything less than a lightweight twin-set. Three pairs of eyes looked Christine up and down, then all settled upon Alexander as he strode to her side. Christine worked out what was going on.

'This is me friend, who's got a fancy car he just loves to drive about in the countryside, so I said he could bring me here to visit. I'm Christine and this is Alexander.'

Playing his part to the hilt, Alexander beamed at the three ladies, for whom he was now the center of attention, then reached forward to take the extended hand of the woman who was the most upright and spry-looking of the trio. Once he'd bowed his head to *almost* touch her knuckles with his lips, each of the other two offered up their hands, relinquishing their teacups in a trice.

'Join us,' said the woman who'd been kissed first. She waved to some vacant wooden chairs. Christine took the one Alexander gallantly held for her, then he himself sat.

Addressing Alexander the woman said, 'I'm Maisie, this is Mabel and that's Megs. The Three M's we're called, for obvious reasons.'

'A pleasure to meet you all, ladies,' replied Alexander. Christine noticed he'd polished up his accent a bit, just as she knew he would at dinner that night; he'd managed to eliminate almost every trace of South London from it by taking elocution lessons many years earlier, he'd told her. The efforts he'd made were paying off, as they did on many an occasion.

'Your grannie's friend will need a few bob if they want to live here,' said Mabel.

'But it's worth it,' replied Megs.

'It's not about the money, it's about the lifestyle,' added Maisie. 'They do a good job here; not too overbearing, good food to suit all tastes and enough activities to keep our minds alive, if we want to participate. Quite a few of our fellow residents are attending a local lawn-bowls tournament in the minibus they have. As you can see, we prefer our own company.'

'They keep the place lookin' good out here,' said Christine surveying the freshly-mown, emerald grass and well-weeded borders. 'Are the rooms nice? Do you have just a room, or are they more like apartments with a kitchen and so forth? Me grannie's friend's a great cook, so she is. It would be just grand if she could keep on bakin'.'

'She could bake in the main kitchen, couldn't she, Megs? There was that woman from Scotland who did that, and we got to eat what she baked. Very good shortbread, I recall,' said Mabel brightly. 'Dead now, of course,' she added on a more somber note.

Maisie sat even more upright, 'Many of us are glad to leave behind the necessity to plan meals, go shopping, cook and clean. It's why we're here. But those who wish to, do, I know. Is the lady Irish, like you?'

'She is that,' said Christine, wondering what the response would be.

'Good, we have no Irish here at the moment. It would make watching the international rugby more fun,' said Megs. 'We have a bit of a flutter on it, and it's nice when all the countries have someone to support them.'

'Do you have a lounge where you all mix, then? Do the owners encourage that?' asked Christine, desperately trying to find a path to the place she wanted to be.

'I wouldn't say they need to encourage it,' replied Megs. 'Some prefer company, some don't. You don't have to leave your room if you don't want to. We've all got our own tellies and little fridges, and we can make a cuppa too. But they arrange cards- and games-nights, that sort of thing.'

Christine took her chance. 'The folks who run the place, are they good sorts?'

The three women all nodded.

'Fred and Sarah Cruickshank. Nice enough. He's the jolly one who drives us to various places in the minibus, she's the one who does all the work. She'll be in there now, checking the cleaners have done a good job, that the cook is on budget and has the timing right for dinner later on, and she's making all the arrangements for our concert,' offered Megs.

'You have entertainment coming in?' asked Alexander.

Megs beamed. 'A nice young man comes to play the piano a couple of times a week. Local boy, still in school – only about seventeen – but he's good and he makes an effort to play tunes we all know. The good, old ones. We enjoy it. Beyond that, this Friday we're giving a concert ourselves, for the public.' She leaned across toward Alexander, her eyes glinting. 'I bet you can't guess what we three will be doing.' Her mouth pursed wickedly.

Christine saw Alexander was going to play along. 'Now, let me think,' he began, stroking his very attractive chin, 'there are three of you, and you're all too young to remember the Andrews Sisters, so not them.' Coy head-tilting and giggling ensued. 'And you're all quite refined, too. Maybe something by Gilbert and Sullivan?'

Megs and Mabel squealed. Even Maisie grinned when she replied, 'Very clever. Yes, we're doing "Three Little Maids," with all the necessary costumes, of course. Megs is on that, aren't you, Megs?' Megs nodded. 'It should be fun. You could come. And bring your grannie's friend with you, she could meet us all and see if she likes the place. They have a couple of rooms here for folks who want to give the place a bit of a test-run before they commit. She could do that. See if she likes us, and the Cruickshanks. Though I don't see why anyone wouldn't. Most people become quite fond of them. See over there?'

Christine followed Maisie's nod and spotted a threesome walking across the lawns; she reckoned the house was set in a few acres of land, and could see most of it was grassed, with paths that allowed for the use of walking aides. She and Alexander acknowledged they saw the people Maisie had indicated.

Maisie continued, 'They turn out to be distant relatives of a lady who passed a couple of months ago. Finally showed their faces. Never bothered when she was alive. Lived here four years without a single visitor, she did. Anyway, they turned up today to collect what she'd left them – a couple of old brooches by the sound of what they said over lunch. Not best pleased they'd motored from Birmingham for just that. Not that Birmingham is that far away, but they seem the type to never want to stray. The daughter drove them, she's the tall one. Kicked up a bit of a fuss.'

'And why would they be doin' that?' asked Christine, truly eager to know.

'Expected a lot more, I suppose,' replied Megs conspiratorially.

'The people who come for the personal belongings – if anyone does – usually do.'

Christine couldn't help but wonder how many times these three women, all of whom she put in their eighties, had seen the same situation play out . . . and how it made them feel about their own mortality. 'You mean the person who's passed hasn't left much for them to collect?'

'Left it all to the Cruickshanks. A lot of them do, because, as I said, people grow fond of them.' Christine was beginning to get an uncomfortable idea about the Cruickshanks, but didn't know how to dig much deeper without either causing concern, or irritation.

As she gave the matter some thought, a voice behind Christine made her jump. A short, round woman in her thirties wearing a lurid green nylon tabard had appeared, presumably from the house, and was hovering at the tableside. 'Hello, I'm Amy. I help out. I see you've rustled yourselves up some guests, ladies. Are they staying for tea?'

Alexander's eyes asked Christine what she wanted to do. She looked at her watch. They really needed to get away if they were going to be ready for pre-dinner drinks at Chellingworth Hall. 'I'm so sorry, we can't. We just dropped by on the off-chance. But we'll be back,' she said, rising from her seat. Alexander sprung up and held it for her. The Three M's looked suitably impressed.

At the moment she was about to leave, Christine decided to go out on a limb and said, 'Grannie's friend heard about this place from another friend of a friend, a Daisy Drayton. I believe she lived here for a while. Did any of you ladies know her, by any chance?'

Three suitably sad expressions looked up at her.

'There was a Daisy here. Was she a Drayton? I'd have thought I'd have remembered that, because it's a bit unusual. Too many of the Davies, Rees, Roberts and Morris around these parts to keep track of them all, but Drayton?' She shook her head. 'We don't use last names a lot here, you know. She died, anyway,' said Megs.

'Before my time,' added Mabel.

'If it was the same Daisy, she'd been going downhill for a little while, and there was talk of her having to go to a proper nursing home – the sort where they can cope with the ones who need real medical attention all the time, not like here. But then she was taken ill one night, before they could move her, and she was rushed off to hospital. Never came back. It was very quick.'

'Best way to go,' said Megs.

'All round really. Never know what to say, do you?' added Mabel.

'Lovely woman, full of life. Bent almost double, though, lots of broken bones over the years. She rode,' said Maisie.

'Grannie's friend rode too, so it might be her,' replied Christine. 'I gather she was very good in her day.'

'Maybe she was. Certainly had one heck of a time sitting and standing, I can tell you that much. She always said she should have had her hips and knees done donkey's years ago, but she'd left it too late and didn't want to risk it. Some don't, you know – they'd rather suffer than go under the knife. Not that she was a woman afraid to take a risk on a horse, I gather, but she didn't like hospitals.'

'She often mentioned that,' said Megs.

'A lot don't, you know. Afraid they'll never come out,' added Mabel.

'Died a while after Christmas, I think it was. A great pity. Wicked sense of humor,' said Maisie.

'That's a shame. If it was the same Daisy, it might have been someone to help Grannie's friend feel at home here. Did she have a family to leave everything to? Did they come to collect her stuff? I might be able to put Grannie's friend in touch with them, if so.'

'No one,' said Megs.

'She left the lot to this place. The MAH Trust, they call it. That's where they put all the money they're given, then spend it doing the place up and keeping it nice,' added Maisie.

Mabel chuckled, 'As if what we pay isn't enough.'

Amy chimed in with: 'Got new curtains and one of those really thin tellies for the wall in the lounge after that Daisy went, we did. Very nice it is, isn't it, ladies?' Christine noticed she shouted, unnecessarily she thought, but maybe the young woman was so used to doing it she didn't notice anymore.

'You're right, Amy,' said Maisie. Looking at Christine she added, 'Some of us get together to watch *Strictly Come Dancing* and we raised a glass of sherry to her after they'd installed it, didn't we?' Her pals agreed they had.

Christine knew she had what she wanted, however much she didn't like it. 'Thanks ladies, I'll tell Grannie's friend all about it. Come on, Alexander, I think we'd best be off.'

Alexander kissed all three women's outstretched hands, and that of the surprised Amy, before they left.

'I'll be sure to speak very highly of the people who live here to Grannie's friend,' said Christine as they began to move back toward the car.

'And come for the concert if you can. Friday, six o'clock, with tea beforehand,' called Maisie.

'Maybe we will,' replied Christine, and she started to hum the Gilbert and Sullivan standard as they crunched along the drive, heading for the road.

NINETEEN

Carol had phoned to say she was running late for dinner at the hall, so Ian Cottesloe had been sent in the Gilbern to collect Annie from her cottage in Anwen-by-Wye, then he picked up Althea and Mavis on the way. It was a cozy journey during which Annie shared the tale of how she'd managed to get photographs of two rather dim thieves at the Swansea sweet factory making off with cases of product, all the while hoping no one would notice. Tudor had sent his apologies, and Annie emphasized to Althea how very keen he'd been to join them for dinner, but that he had no cover at the pub that night. What she didn't mention was that Tudor had been spitting nails to think he'd missed his chance to get one up on Marjorie Flaming Pritchard – as he usually referred to the woman.

Alighting from the car at seven o'clock on the dot, they entered Chellingworth Hall to find Bryn and Val Jenkins had also just arrived. Edward ushered everyone into the drawing room, where drinks were being served.

Annie hadn't seen Lady Clementine for some time, which she suspected was a good thing; she didn't like the woman but, of course, had to act as though she did. She suspected Lady Clementine didn't like her either, but was stuck with the same dilemma. They greeted each other with politeness and Annie was surprised to see the woman had blue and purple hair. She'd never seen it dyed two colors before, it was usually just one, hideous shade, all over.

As Annie cast her eyes about the collection of people in the room it suddenly struck her that polite society was really very odd; no one ever said what they truly thought – or, if they did, they were treated as though they'd grown a second head.

Christine and Alexander already had drinks. Annie sighed with just a hint of jealousy as she admired the way the peach chiffon Christine was wearing glowed against her lightly-tanned skin, and made her look almost ethereal. She also noted that Alexander looked as sharp and dashing as ever in his navy suit and crisp white shirt. She thought Stephanie looked a bit out of sorts; maybe she'd been rushing about, which was why she looked a bit pink in the face. She was pounding down fizzy water with a lot of ice in it so was maybe trying to cool off, though she was wearing a sleeveless shift-dress, so she couldn't have worn much less. Henry, on the other hand, was bedecked in a somber-looking charcoal three-piece suit, sloshing his drink about as he told some tale or other.

Annie's lightweight, silky black trousers and vivid red blouse were just right for the temperature in the room, though she knew that, at some point, the unwelcome whoosh of heat would hit the back of her neck and envelop her entire body for a few moments; she hated the feeling, but steeled herself for its arrival, and decided an extra couple of cubes of ice in her G&T would help.

The chatter was muted, but pleasant. Annie would have found such a gathering horribly uncomfortable just six months earlier; now she was able to take in her surroundings and feel pretty much at ease within them because she knew the people in the room. The portraits were the things she always wondered at; it was so alien for a girl from the East End of London to imagine living with paintings of predecessors, some of the canvasses twenty feet tall, peering down with dead eyes. It made her shiver a bit.

'Feeling the cold?' asked Alexander solicitously.

'Nah, I'm fine,' replied Annie quickly. She looked around to make sure no one could hear her. 'I know I don't know much about you, but I know you're a Londoner, like me, and not from a family with pots of money like this lot. It's the paintings. I feel like they're watchin' me. 'Orrible, it is. How do you feel about 'em?'

Alexander allowed his native accent to emerge as he lowered his voice. 'Best this type 'as someone to keep an eye on 'em. Never know what they might get up to otherwise. Need someone to keep 'em in line, they do.'

Annie laughed aloud, though the tone of Alexander's voice had given her another chill. She just couldn't make up her mind about him at all. Handsome, definitely; dangerous, probably; criminal? She wondered.

'What are you two nattering about?' asked Christine, joining them.

'Them paintings,' answered Annie honestly.

'Annie doesn't care for them,' added Alexander, his accent re-polished.

'Don't get me wrong,' said Annie feeling she had to explain herself, 'I can see they're good. But . . . do you have stuff like this at your place in Ireland?'

Christine nodded. 'Yes, but fewer of them, and they are smaller. Most of the ones that were worth something were long gone before I came along, my wastrel of a grandfather saw to that being a necessity. Ironically, so my father tells me, it was a rather fine portrait of said grandfather, by a well-known and sought-after Irish portraitist, that he was able to sell to pay my school fees. So some good came from the family art, I suppose. By the way – since you're not mentioning it, dare I ask how your case in Swansea went?'

Annie grinned. 'Of course, you don't know . . .' And she proceeded to tell the couple about her recent triumph. It kept them entertained until dinner was announced.

Nurse Thomas joined the group to dine, otherwise they'd have been eleven at the table because Tudor hadn't been able to arrange for a stand-in at the pub. Annie didn't think the world would have ended if eleven people had eaten instead of twelve, but she didn't say anything. Henry sat at the head of the table, which Annie had to admit looked magnificent with its gleaming silverware, glinting crystal and tasteful porcelain.

Finally settled next to the just-arrived Carol, Annie accepted wine and sorted out her napkin. She noticed Carol checking her watch. 'Oi, you only got here five minutes ago, and Bertie's with Dave – so, come on, relax.'

Carol glared at her friend. 'It's true that *Al*bert is with his father Dav*id*, but, other than popping across the village green for something from the shop, this is the first time I've left the two of them alone. It's a worry.'

Annie patted her chum on the leg. 'Did David push you out and tell you to have a nice time?' Carol nodded. 'Well since you're here, try to do exactly that then. They'll be fine. *They* need time to bond an' all.' Annie hoped she was saying all the right things, though she wasn't really sure she was.

Carol sighed, but didn't look convinced. The dinner conversation was muted, but jolly enough. Annie noticed Lady Clementine knocking back a couple of glasses of wine under the withering gaze of her nurse, and she seemed to be having a rare old time telling stories about her friends back in London. Alexander and Christine were absorbing most of her excited chatter, which Annie reckoned was to be expected. Val Jenkins and Althea seemed to be hitting it off like a house on fire, while Bryn and Mavis – who were seated next to each other – seemed to be having quite an intimate *tête-à-tête*. Annie wasn't sure she liked that so much. Nurse Thomas was at the far end of the table and kept herself pretty much to herself, even when Annie tried to draw her into the conversation.

Eventually the subject of the imminently-successful restoration of the religious volumes from the lower library came up, and celebratory toasts of thanks to Bryn were made with raised glasses, then the topics of the bothersome books, the mysterious miniatures and the curious Cruickshanks were broached.

Henry and Stephanie were brought up to date with the progress that had been made across the board, while Clemmie sipped her wine and looked more bemused than anything else. Everyone was pleased to hear about Christine's foray into the world of the Mountain Ash House old folks' home.

'I'd still like to know why Sarah Cruickshank is doing it,' said Bryn when all the information had been shared around the table. 'It's very nice of her to donate the bric-a-brac and clothing the departed residents leave behind to such good causes, but she should realize my shop doesn't work the same way. I buy and sell books – I'm not a dumping ground for unwanted dross.'

'Maybe she thinks she's doing you a good turn, Dad,' said Val, 'giving you something you can sell on and make some money from. Some of the books have been in good condition – just not the type you, or I, sell.'

'Well, why not hand them to me then? Either I, or someone else, is always there. Why sneak them onto the tables and shelves? It's suspicious, if you ask me. I've thought so from the outset.'

'But you wouldn't accept them, would you, Dad?' said Val a little sharply. She explained to her tablemates: 'The bookshop owners in Hay are all experts in their fields, in a way, and they can be pretty particular about what they will, and won't, accept for sale.'

'Which is the way it should be,' replied Bryn. 'I owe it to my customers to only offer a carefully curated selection of specialized works. It's what they expect.'

'Bryn has a point,' said Mavis, tipping her head coyly in his direction. 'It's no' the way I'd go about handling books that have been left to me. I'd be looking to sell them, or even give them, to someone, openly.'

Christine piped up with: 'I have to admit the idea that elderly people with no one left in the world are leaving their belongings, and maybe all they have, to the Cruickshanks did make me worry a little. Your Daisy Dickens, or Drayton, leaving her worldly goods to them must have amounted to a good deal of money, Althea. Rather more than what would have been needed for some new drapery and a television – however thin it might be.'

'Do you think they're running some sort of murderous scheme?' asked Althea, horrified. 'Knocking off octogenarians to feather their own nest?'

'Mother, that's a dreadful thing to suspect,' responded Henry, looking mortified. 'Of course, one finds it difficult to understand why one would leave all one's money to such a place, or such people, but if one is alone in the world – at the end – it has to go somewhere. Where would it go otherwise? It's not something I, nor anyone in my family, has had to consider.'

'Taxman,' said Althea heavily. 'Death and taxes? Tax you to death, they do.'

Annie thought Henry looked almost apoplectic. 'Mother!'

'Oh shush, Henry. It's not as though the Inland Revenue has a secret agent up the chimney. I can say what I want about them. Blood-suckers. Over the decades they've done their best to remove this estate from this family's control. Your father was always worried about taxes. The state gets enough. Why shouldn't a woman leave her fortune to a couple she's come to know and like, and to a home where she's been happy? I tell you, it's that or the taxman gets it . . . and if it's not the taxman it'll be someone who works along the corridor from him.'

Annie'd never seen Althea cross. Indeed, she'd only ever thought of her as a fluffy old bird with a love of Monty Python and a deep affection for most things with four legs. She was beginning to see where the woman's reputation as a human Jack Russell had come from – she had a bark, and Annie suspected her bite might be quite nasty.

At a tilt of the head from Mavis, Althea took a sip of wine and composed herself. But Annie – and probably everyone else at the table – could tell she wasn't finished.

Althea, calmed, continued, 'All that being said, I don't like the idea that Daisy, or anyone else for that matter, might have been coerced into changing whatever they might have had planned for the distribution of their estate by a couple with an eye for a killing – if you'll pardon the pun.' She paused, then added, 'You don't think they really *are* doing that, do you?'

'Doing what, Mother?' asked Clemmie loudly. Everyone turned to look at her, which made her giggle. 'Do you think that in the middle of Wales there's a couple who are getting little old ladies to sign away everything to them, then bumping them off? Here? That sort of thing? Rubbish.'

Clemmie emptied her glass and looked hopefully at Edward, who retreated, bottle in hand, at a warning glance from Nurse Thomas.

'It seems a little far-fetched, Mother,' said Henry. Annie reckoned he didn't enjoy agreeing with his sister. 'Let's not forget this all began over a few books. One shouldn't get carried away.'

Althea grunted and indicated she'd like a little more wine. Edward complied, then passed Henry's request for the table to be cleared to the rest of the serving staff.

As plans were being made for after-dinner activities, during which Annie had to plumb the depths to come up with as many reasons as possible for not wishing to learn to play bridge, she overheard Althea asking Christine for details about the guest accommodation available at the old folks' home and she knew immediately where Althea was headed.

'I thought I was our undercover specialist,' she whispered to Althea, chuckling. 'Sometimes I think it's all I'm good for – so don't go nickin' it from me.'

Althea looked as innocent as a pup when she replied, 'Undercover work? Me? The idea had never entered my head.' She smiled sweetly, but there was no lightness in her tone when she added, 'Though I am concerned that this issue has raised some rather worrying questions. What if people are being taken advantage of at the Mountain Ash place? What if poor Daisy was duped? I know there's a lengthy process that usually ends up with everything owned by someone who dies intestate going to the state, but what if she'd had some previous plans to allow some specific charities to benefit after she'd gone, and those greedy people talked her into leaving them the whole shooting match?'

Annie could feel the level of tension increasing around their circle, a shift in the dynamic that seemed to draw Carol to them so they were, all five, together at last.

Althea rallied and added, 'Now we're all present and correct, *I'd* like to retain the WISE Women to investigate the goings-on at this old folks' home. Post haste.'

All eyes turned to Mavis. Clearing her throat she began, 'Aye, well the first thing to say, Althea dear, is that there's no indication the Cruickshanks have done anything questionable at all. To be fair to them, there's nothing to suggest they are anything but a solicitous couple running a delightful retirement home. With happy residents, if what Christine tells us is true, which I believe it to be. And as for you becoming our client – *again* – I suppose it falls to me to point out we're not really your private band of investigators to be put to work on any pet project you might have.' Annie noticed Mavis had moderated her sometime-harsh tone to be sympathetic.

Althea looked puzzled. 'I can become a client like anyone else, can't I? Isn't my money as good as the next person's?' The four women nodded their heads, reluctantly. 'And I know for a fact you don't have any other cases pending for next week.' Shoulders shrugged. 'So why not work for me for a few days? I realize I'd lost touch with Daisy, but this is a bigger issue. None of you is as old as me, but, as the years pass, you'll begin to realize how very little our society cares for its elders. Out of sight is out of mind in so many cases. It shouldn't be so. I would at least like to know that this one little residential home, almost in my own back garden, is at least respecting the real wishes of its residents, even when they have no one to speak on their behalf. I'm fortunate that I am able to afford your – our – agency to look into this. And I propose we do so. You can draw up a proper contract and everything, Carol.'

Once again eyes rolled until they finally all came to rest upon Mavis. Annie could tell by her expression she was on the verge of capitulating.

'And what would your desired outcome – as a client – be for this case, Althea?' she asked.

Althea gave the matter some thought. 'To be certain that no undue pressure is being brought to bear upon the residents of Mountain Ash House to give their all, after they die, to the proprietors of said old folks' home,' said Althea, looking satisfied.

'The Case of the Over-generous OAPs? Or what about the Swindled Seniors? The Ripped-off Retirees? The Gypped Geriatrics?' risked Annie, with a wink.

'Not even slightly appropriate,' chided Mavis.

'Have you got a thesaurus in your head?' asked Carol with a twinkle in her eye.

Althea smiled. 'You have a way with those case-file titles, Annie. I like it. Though I don't like the implication, I'd go for The Swindled Seniors. Which I hope is *not* the case. But I'd like to be sure. I'd like a proposal, please, and a quote. Just like you do for other clients.'

'With no idea of going undercover yourself,' said Mavis firmly. 'You're far too well-known in the area in any case. I'm guessing your photograph has appeared in the local newspaper hundreds of times over the decades, so you'd be spotted in an instant. No, this one has to be approached in a different way.'

'Excuse me, ladies – might I have a word?' Val Jenkins towered over all the women except Annie, with whom she drew level.

'Certainly,' replied Mavis. 'Is it about your father's books?'

Annie wondered why Val looked so coy. It was strange for her to be able to look another woman in the eye – not many were as tall as she was – and it gave her a new perspective on the woman.

Val shifted her weight awkwardly. 'Thanks for all the updates. You're all doing so well. We really are keen to know if whoever left those books in our shop had the legal right to do so. To know if they really owned them, and chose to give them to us freely. If they did, then the books are ours. And if they are ours – and the miniatures can be authenticated so the books might be worth a fair bit – I'd like to liquidate them. It would mean I could get myself a place of my own again and move out of Dad's house. I'm a bit old to be living in the land of "not under my roof."'

Annie knew what Val meant; when she'd moved to Anwen-by-Wye her mother had stayed with her for several weeks and, while she hadn't had the ultimate veto of owning the house, Annie had felt the weight of her displeasure as though she were a teen. She couldn't imagine what it must be like for Val to be living in her father's house without a bolthole of her own.

'I just want you to clearly understand that Dad and I do want you to press on with looking into the Cruickshanks. Sometimes he babbles a bit, and gives people the wrong impression,' added Val.

'You mean you're telling us to continue working to discover the ownership status of the books at the time they were left at your shop, as well as whether the miniatures were created by Lizzie Llewellyn?' asked Mavis.

'Yes, that's correct.'

Annie nodded her agreement, along with all her colleagues, and Mavis smiled at Val. 'We're happy to continue on that basis, though I'd like Carol to revise our contract with your father to contain your name. I'm sorry we didnae do that in the first place, but your father gave us to understand it was a personal undertaking on his part.'

'He always speaks of the bookshop as his,' said Val quietly. 'I don't really mind.'

Mavis drew everyone's attention back to the topic in hand. 'Very well, Val, we'll progress as we have discussed. This means there's no need for you to become a client at all, Althea. Now, I think an early night is called for.' She placed her arm gently on Althea's shoulders. 'It's been a long day. I'll ask Edward to call Ian to bring the car. Annie – Ian can return to collect you when he's delivered us back to the Dower House.' Annie was aware this wasn't a request.

'Okey dokey, I've been wantin' to learn all about bridge in any case,' she lied.

'Don't worry, Mavis,' said Carol. 'If Annie's happy to leave now, I'll give her a lift back to Anwen. I've had a lovely time, Althea, but I'm not going to be able to settle any longer. I'd like to get back to David and Albert, if that's alright with everyone.'

With a general consensus reached, leave-takings began.

TWENTY

Tuesday 24th June

When Henry opened his eyes and turned over, Stephanie wasn't there. He panicked. He was surprised her absence made him feel so anxious; she'd been getting up exceptionally early in recent weeks and seemed to be spending an inordinate amount of time in the bathroom. He checked. She wasn't there either. Where could she have got to? It was only . . . he looked at the casement clock beside the wardrobe. Good heavens! It was nine thirty. He wondered why no one had wakened him. Edward knew he preferred a little time to move about the hall freely before the public arrived.

It took Henry half an hour to get out of his apartment and down to the breakfast room. It was deserted. He rang for Edward who appeared a few moments later.

'What the blazes is going on, Edward? You didn't wake me, my wife has disappeared and there's not a soul to be found about the place.'

Edward assured Henry all was well with Her Grace – who was already taking a meeting with Elizabeth Fernley in the estate office – and that it was she who had asked Edward to allow the duke to sleep in. Indeed, Edward went so far as to enquire after Henry's health, which led Henry to suspect his wife had told his butler he'd been unwell the night before. Maybe that last, rather large, brandy had been somewhat ill-advised, after all.

Miserably sipping strong coffee and crunching thickly-buttered toast, Henry only found the balance he'd been seeking when his wife joined him at just gone ten thirty. They hugged, and everything was marvelous again; his tummy had settled, as had his emotions. His spirits revived, Henry left the breakfast room and made his way across the great hall, planning to hide away before the hordes descended, and was more than a little discombobulated to see an elderly woman, with one of those walking frame things, merrily pottering about taking photographs of the colonnade beneath the staircase. There was no question the colonnade deserved such attention, but the woman had somehow managed to gain entry to the hall fifteen minutes before the doors were opened to the public. Immediately irritated, Henry had half a mind to turn on his heel and use the back corridors to avoid an interaction. Then he stopped himself. *Why may I not walk through my own home as I wish until the appointed time?* he asked himself, and strode toward his goal – the door to the lower library.

'Young man – do you work here? Are you a volunteer or something?' The old woman's accent was thickly Welsh. 'What can you tell me about these big columns here, then? Special, are they?'

Henry took a deep breath and looked down at the woman, forcing a smile. 'I'm afraid I don't work here, but I can tell you that the marble came from Carrara in Italy, and they were crafted here, *in situ,* during the last two decades of the seventeenth century by a band of specially commissioned Italian artisan sculptors. They have an overall harmony, but each one differs just a little from all the others. Each is unique, in the true sense of the word.' He felt he'd done his duty, nodded and moved as fast as he dared to the open door of the library, which he closed behind himself. *Blessed tourists!* He'd have a word with Glyn, who was supposed to oversee public access to the estate; Henry knew he had to put up with the people crawling all over his home for hours every day, but to have them almost catch him in his pajamas? An appalling state of affairs.

He rushed through the library and worked his way through connecting rooms to the safety of the working part of Chellingworth Hall. In the offices, workshops and converted out-buildings, he was able to seek sanctuary among those who worked at the estate, and he hoped to find Stephanie too, but she was in yet another meeting it seemed – something to do with the honey they harvested on the estate to be sold in the little shop, which he knew was important, because a good deal of income was made by the retail end of things.

He sat at Stephanie's desk, which was covered with examples of greetings cards, bookmarks, printed window decals and strings of decorative bunting. It looked a bit of a mess to him, but he didn't dare fiddle too much. The bunting was jolly enough, but the greetings cards puzzled him; they were Christmas cards.

'Ah, there you are darling,' said Stephanie rushing in and delighting him. 'I thought you were off to see Bryn. Isn't that what you said?'

Henry thought Stephanie looked a little pale, and said so. She admitted she hadn't enjoyed her last meeting as she gathered up the bunting and the greetings cards.

'Are we going to be selling those cards at the shop?' asked Henry.

'I'm considering it,' replied Stephanie, pulling open cupboards and packing away the detritus from her desk.

'Isn't it a bit early for Christmas cards?' asked Henry.

Stephanie paused in her task and looked indulgently at her husband. 'Not at all, dear. Decisions must be made, and orders must be placed in good time to have them on the shelves for the last visitors of the year. These are all made from used Christmas cards, so they have an artisanal quality. Just what we're aiming for here. They're made by a co-operative in Tenby employing women who have escaped abusive relationships. All the money raised from their sales goes to providing safe housing for the women and their families. It's a good cause and they are well made.'

Henry stood and held his wife close. 'How awful they need such help. You're a wonderful woman, and I'm lucky to have found you,' he said. 'Not all men are dreadful, you know, my dear. I'm not.'

His wife looked up at him, smiling. 'Of course you're not dreadful, you're delightful. But not everyone is like you, Henry. That being said, and however much I love you and am enjoying this hug, I am terribly busy and I must press on. So, what will you do today? The doors are open now, where will you hide?'

'Actually, I'm going to get hold of Glyn and ask him how an elderly lady I just encountered managed to gain access to the hall at least fifteen minutes before the gates were supposed to be opened to the public. You didn't have anyone coming here for a meeting about the fete, or these cards, or something else today, did you?'

'No, not today. You say someone managed to get past Glyn and his guards? That's worrying, Henry. Did you get a name?' Henry shook his head. 'What did she look like?'

Henry paused, gave the matter some thought and replied, 'Old, with a walking frame, bowed back and a sadly obvious wig; it was dark brown and looked as though it was made of nylon.'

'Tall? Short? Glasses? Clothes?'

Henry returned to head shaking then said quite firmly, 'She was short. Definitely short.'

Stephanie looked as perplexed as Henry felt. 'That's not terribly helpful, but it's better than nothing, I suppose.' Her face softened. 'Maybe the poor thing was wearing a wig because she'd lost all her hair? Maybe cancer? It's hard to know, of course. Yes, I believe you should put some effort into investigating how that might have happened. Not the wig-wearing, of course, I mean how she got into the hall. Then pop along and have a bit of a chat with Clemmie, will you dear? She mentioned to me at least three times at dinner last night that she believes you're avoiding her. Now we both know that's exactly what you're doing, but she's spotted it, so you must make an effort. We're all lunching together at one o'clock in the upstairs dining room, but maybe you could drop into her apartment before that and bring her to lunch yourself? She'll need help on the stairs, of course, but if you do it, it would give her a break from Nurse Thomas, and vice versa.'

'Yes, dear,' muttered Henry as Stephanie rushed out of the office. He managed to fill an hour locating, then talking to Glyn on the telephone. The man claimed the gates hadn't opened a moment before they were due to, and he had no idea who the woman in question could be. Henry was more concerned than ever, so instructed Edward to check if any member of staff had invited the woman onto the premises. As he finally trudged toward Clemmie's rooms he told himself off for not asking the rogue tourist her name, but felt quite proud that at least he'd been on the ball when it came to the wig. As he reached Clemmie's apartment he also recalled the woman had been wearing spectacles – shaped like cats' eyes. *Why hadn't he remembered that earlier?*

He showed Clemmie the common courtesy of knocking before he entered her rooms, and Nurse Thomas opened the door. 'What a pleasant surprise, Your Grace,' she said with what Henry judged to be a genuine look of pleasure on her face. 'Lady Clementine will be pleased to see you. Two visitors on one day, there's a turn-up for the books. Do come in.'

She stood back and Henry entered. 'Two visitors, you say?' he asked.

He looked across the spacious sitting room and there was his sister sitting on the sofa with the interloping visitor.

The elderly woman rose to her feet and walked toward Henry with her hand outstretched saying, 'There's lovely. We meet again. I had no idea you lived here. You should have said. So you're the horrible duke who's been victimizing this poor girl over here then, are you?'

Henry was at sea. His sister was a quivering wreck on the sofa – was she sobbing into a handkerchief? Nurse Thomas's face was a picture of torment, then she dropped her head, shaking it slowly. The old woman added, 'You don't look the type to let her fade away, ignored and lacking in any sort of familial support. But, there, they do say you can't judge a book by its cover – and I suppose you can't judge a man by his title, can you?'

Henry could feel himself getting hot, and he wished his wife had been there with him. She'd have known what to say – what to do. Not being sure of either, he said and did nothing. Then the old woman started to laugh at him. Right in his face!

'Oh Henry, your face is a picture,' said the old woman, with a voice he recognized.

'Mother?'

The woman pulled the wig from her head to reveal his mother's neatly-trimmed almost-white hair. She took off the spectacles and he saw her twinkling eyes. The brownish lipstick made her look washed out, and the purple floral dress was – well, it made him feel quite bilious.

'Ta-daa!' said his mother with a flourish. 'You truly had no idea it was me, did you dear?'

Henry was cross. 'I've had half the staff running about trying to find out who you were, and how you'd managed to get in. I'll never hear the end of it. Really, Mother. What on earth were you thinking? And you can take your face out of that handkerchief now, Clemmie, thank you very much. Hysterics at your brother's expense – your favorite blood sport, eh?' He said nothing to Nurse Thomas, who he felt was at least making a real effort to not be amused.

'What are you playing at, Mother? Is this another one of your so-called "jokes," because you know I don't usually find them at all funny.'

Althea rejoined her daughter on the couch, and beckoned her son to sit at her other side. Nurse Thomas left the room.

With a hand on a knee of each child, Althea kissed them on the cheek in turn. 'I'm sorry, Henry dear, I had to find out something for my own satisfaction. And I can tell you now it wasn't just you who didn't recognize me. Come along, Clemmie, be honest, you had no idea it was me either, did you?'

It was unusual for Henry to be sitting beside his mother, and sister – and even more unusual was the fact Clemmie had a genuine smile on her face . . . the smile he recalled her having as a child. 'I confess,' she said, 'I had no idea it was Mother. Indeed, if Nurse Thomas hadn't arrived when she did, I think I'd have talked to the unknown woman for another ten minutes before the penny would have dropped. Didn't she do well, Henry?'

It was agreed Althea had done a splendid job, and a germ of an idea wriggled in Henry's brain. 'I say, Mother, how d'you feel about getting all done up again and joining us for lunch? Let's see if you can fool Stephanie and Edward. That would be great fun, don't you think?'

The mother and her children spent the next half an hour making sure her disguise was back to being perfect, then taking the trip, via back staircases, to the private dining room which enjoyed a view to the west; Althea and her late husband had named it the supper room, because they'd enjoyed watching the sunset there, but the name hadn't stuck, it only having had a few decades to do so in the face of hundreds of years of the room being known as the small dining room.

As the threesome slowly mounted the stairs, Henry helped Clemmie along and could feel the excitement build inside him. It was absolutely thrilling to be playing a joke with his sister and mother, and not have them playing one on him, which was the norm. He had no doubt Stephanie would be a good sport about it all, and was delighted by the look on her face as the three of them entered the room where she was already seated.

Henry could tell she was surprised to see an extra guest – *how wonderful* – and she rose to greet the woman. Henry noticed a curious look on his wife's face as she approached.

'Look, I found my "mystery woman,"' said Henry with a flourish. 'Mrs Gladys Pugh.'

'Pleased to meet you, Mrs Pugh,' said Stephanie, extending her hand. 'Henry mentioned meeting you earlier. If only I'd known you were joining us I could have asked someone to help you up the stairs. Henry, you've had your hands full with both Mrs Pugh and Lady Clementine. Here, let me lend you an arm, Mrs Pugh.' She helped Althea to a seat while Henry steered Clemmie, who was doing rather well with her cane.

Once they were all seated – his mother had selected the seat that meant she had her back to the window – he noticed his wife peering at his mother with a puzzled look on her face. 'Have we met before, Mrs Pugh?'

'Don't think so, Ma'am . . . er . . . Madam. Never been in a posh place like this before, I haven't.' Althea feigned shock when she saw Edward entering the room with a silver tray. 'Oh my giddy aunt – is he a *real* butler? I thought they were just on the telly.'

Edward took note of the additional guest, placed the tray on a sideboard and magically set an additional place at the table. 'Ta very much,' said Althea, touching Edward's sleeve.

Henry watched as the butler managed to restrain himself from looking shocked, then smiled when the man made direct eye contact with his mother and replied, 'You're welcome, Your Grace.'

'Drat!' said Henry, slapping his thigh. 'He's spotted you, Mother. Well done, Edward. No flies on you, eh? Eh?'

'Indeed, Your Grace,' said the man, leaving the room.

Stephanie sat open-mouthed, staring at Althea. 'You rotters,' she began – then the foursome enjoyed an extremely jolly lunch.

TWENTY-ONE

Mavis waited as patiently as possible while Annie organized coffees and teas for the unusual afternoon meeting, Carol tidied her desk and checked for messages from David about Albert, and Christine finished sending a couple of emails.

'It's unusual for there to be just four adult humans here. So let's make the most of it,' announced Mavis, calling the meeting to order. 'Carol will begin.'

Carol had soon caught the women up on invoices sent and paid, money in the bank and levels of pay to be expected on the 1st of July.

Annie stuck up her hand.

'You know there's no need to do that,' said Mavis with a sigh.

'I like to play it safe,' said Annie. 'I wondered if you had anything more for me this week?'

'Now that Carol's updated our contract with Val and Bryn Jenkins, we'll discuss how we'll progress with our enquiries into the legal ownership of the books containing the miniatures when they were deposited at Crooks & Cooks by the Cruickshanks,' replied Mavis.

'Love the alliteration,' mugged Annie, drawing a warning glare from Mavis.

'Alliteration aside,' said Christine, smirking, 'the whole thing seems a bit odd to me. Why would Mrs Cruickshank be dropping off the books people have bequeathed her at bookshops all over Hay-on-Wye?'

'Exactly,' agreed Mavis, 'and that's where Althea's idea that residents are being conned falls down.' She spoke with assurance. 'If the Cruickshanks were trying to get their hands on the stuff so they could cash in, that's exactly what they'd do – they'd be selling it, not just giving it away.'

'We only *know* they've given away stuff that's not worth much; some books and a few bits and pieces, plus some items of clothing. It doesn't amount to a great deal, does it?' said Carol thoughtfully. She turned to her keyboard and started tapping the keys. Everyone knew she was off on some sort of digital trail, so let her get on with it.

'Car's right,' said Annie, 'if we're to understand if this truly is some sort of big con or not, we'd need evidence of them selling high-priced items and pocketing the loot to even begin to make a real case.'

Mavis began pacing. Everyone watched her as she argued aloud with herself. 'If there is wrongdoing at that place, we should inform the police. But we don't have anything concrete about which to inform them. I cannae see that a few books and some old clothes can underpin some sort of murderous scam-artists' business. But it could be the tip of the iceberg. However, that sort of thing? In the depths of Powys? Run by a middle-aged couple? It seems preposterous.'

'Is it as preposterous as the Cruickshanks giving a ringing endorsement of a certain Tristan Thomas and his antiques business A Taste of Time?' said Carol, lifting her head from her keyboard.

'Tristan Thomas?' said Annie. 'That 'orrible man with all them teeth who used to run that antiques shop on the green in Anwen-by-Wye?'

Carol nodded. 'His website is still up, even though the shop is closed. The Cruickshanks gave a glowing testimonial to the quality and range of the items he offered. Which I think is interesting.'

Annie did a quick calculation in her head. 'His antiques shop closed around about the time those books started showing up at Bryn's place. I bet you that slimy little toerag was the bloke who bought all the stuff they wanted to shift before he was forced to shut up shop. He'd be the type. They've had to change their entire modus operandi because he's out of the picture.'

'Nice use of terminology,' said Christine with a grin, 'but I think that's a bit of a leap, Annie. To be fair, I understand why you'd believe it of him, but we know nothing about the Cruickshanks. The truth is, of course, even if they *were* selling items to him they would have had every right to do so if residents had left them the pieces in question in their last will and testament.'

Carol had continued her tapping. 'The Cruickshanks seem keen to lend their online praise to several companies it seems,' she added. 'There's a florist in Builth Wells they think has the most wonderful floral displays at the best possible prices; they cannot say enough good things about a firm of solicitors in Brecon; they've apparently received wonderful service from a company specializing in moving precious items from homes around the United Kingdom to their premises and have had excellent interactions with a company in Cardiff that provides well-trained catering and cleaning staff for their business.'

'You found this all online?' asked Mavis. 'Just now? How is that possible, dear?'

Carol blushed. 'Once it occurred to me to search, it wasn't difficult. I use the same principles as Google or Yahoo, but I have a little program I've written that searches out names or terms a much more general search engine might miss . . . or would have appearing on page seven thousand of its discovered entries.'

'And what you're doing is quite legal?' asked Mavis, arching an eyebrow.

Annie noticed Carol looked much more confident when she replied, 'Quite. The Cruickshanks have agreed – I assume – to allow their names to be associated with these businesses. Once that information is out there on a website, it's in the public domain. I'm not accessing anything private here, just using a bit of code to find what's there for anyone to see.'

Mavis retook her seat at her desk. Annie thought she could see her mind working behind her darting eyes. Her face was a bit twitchy, too.

'If the Cruickshanks are up to something, they'd need a solicitor to make sure everything was aboveboard,' mused Mavis, almost to herself. 'The florist, the moving company, the staff-providers – they're all to be expected. But the solicitors? Hmm. What's the name of the firm, Carol?'

'Phillips, Bennett, Wilson & Jones. Like I said, they're in Brecon. Have you heard of them, Mavis? I know you're the one who's been pounding the pavement bringing our services to the attention of this type of business.'

Mavis nodded. 'I know Phillips the younger. I met her back in – oh, it must have been April, I'd say.' Mavis pulled open a drawer in her desk and started riffling through files. She pulled out a large brochure and held it up. 'I picked this up from them. It talks about their services, and the people who work there. However, before we even consider doing anything like questioning the Cruickshanks of Mountain Ash House, there are other avenues we can pursue to discover all we can about them and their establishment,' said Mavis.

'Such as?' asked Annie.

'I could do some more *legal* digging about on the Internet,' offered Carol. 'I don't know what I'll find, but I could do all the usual stuff – financials and so forth might be available, depending on exactly what type of entity it is they operate – and I could let you all know what I find. We could take it from there.'

'Doctors,' said Annie. 'You should find out what doctors they use when residents are taken ill, and what hospital they'd use, too.' She glowed with pride when Mavis nodded in her direction.

'We could phone around a variety of local antiques shops and ask if they buy from them,' suggested Christine. 'Some story about an erroneous sale on behalf of a resident?'

The group all nodded as Carol tapped keys, making a list. 'I'll also source a list of places which deal in estate jewelry. Local art galleries and dealers too,' she added.

'There are a lot of antique markets held on various days in the towns hereabouts,' said Mavis slowly, 'the people who have stalls there might be difficult to get hold of on the phone but we could visit the markets when they are set up and ask around. That would need a car, so I would do that.'

Annie added, 'We might all pitch in on a bit of everything. How about you make up some lists, Car, then divvie them up? If you've finished with investigating those miniatures, Chrissy, you could help us out. The Case of the Imperiled Pensioners,' said Annie triumphantly.

Mavis tutted. 'Aye, we'll investigate the Cruickshanks because we certainly need to understand if they legally owned those books when they deposited them at Crooks & Cooks, as well as gaining an insight into what they might be up to at Mountain Ash House, in more general terms. But no' all of us. Christine, you should follow through with getting a definitive attribution for those miniatures, if you can.'

'About that,' began Christine, 'there's actually something else I need to talk to you all about.' She spent the next fifteen minutes telling her colleagues about Gwen Llewellyn's desire to have her son's innocence proven, which led to a hush falling over the entire group.

'The entire legal system has come down against him,' noted Mavis. 'What can we four do, even if his mother believes in her heart he didnae do it?'

'Find out who did it if he didn't,' suggested Annie quietly.

A sharp intake of breath from Carol signaled her disquiet. 'Annie, trust me, I've read pretty much all the coverage of the court case. There's no other explanation. Nathaniel killed Lizzie.'

'Gwen truly believes her son didn't do it,' insisted Christine, 'and I suspect you read all the coverage from the point of view of someone trying to find out about Lizzie the artist – because that was our original angle – rather than as someone quizzing the evidence from a different perspective . . . that of someone trying to spot holes in the Crown's case.'

'As a mother, I understand why Gwen Llewellyn would feel as she does about her son,' mused Mavis. 'But that's no reason for us to agree to help her. Even if we could, which I'm not sure is a possibility.'

'Did the cops have anyone else in the frame?' asked Annie.

Carol shook her head. 'Christine's right, I did read everything with my brain seeking information and patterns relevant to the case we were on at the time. I dare say another reading wouldn't hurt. I'd probably focus on different aspects of the facts if we were to take on the mother's case. However, as I recall, the police viewed it as pretty much an open-and-shut case.'

'There then, the cops even look for anyone else, did they? A quick collar was all they were after.' Annie sounded triumphant. 'You're brilliant you are, Car, I bet you could ferret out some tasty bits of stuff here and there in all that legal banter if you was to look at it again.'

'The way you speak, Annie,' said Mavis tartly. 'Come along now, seriously, what on earth does this woman want? Does she really expect us to prove her son didn't do it and someone else did?'

Christine shrugged. 'To be honest, I think she just wants someone to hear what she's saying. It seems no one has listened to her at all.'

Carol added, 'Now that's an opinion I'd back; even on my first reading of the news coverage, I recall the mother tried to speak out in defense of her son throughout the trial, but didn't get much press coverage.'

'If you don't want in, I could do it myself. Take time off. Not take wages for a bit. I've already done a bit of digging around, actually,' said Christine blushing faintly. 'I was intrigued, you see, and I realized I recognized the name of the barrister who represented Nathaniel Llewellyn. It turns out he was at school with my brother, so I reckon it should be easy enough to get him to agree to talk me through the whole thing. I might get a less biased view from him than from the mother.'

Annie rose. 'Course you know some posh barrister-type. Good for you, doll. Let's use all them contacts to our advantage. I'll walk me feet to stumps going around market stalls looking for bits of fenced old tat, while you have a snifter with a bloke who wears a wig and frock for a living.'

'Annie,' warned Mavis.

Annie pouted. 'Not going to want to visit the artist bloke himself in clink, Chrissy?'

Christine also rose. 'I plan on doing exactly that.'

'Ever visited someone in prison before?' asked Mavis.

Christine shook her head. 'It'll be a first for me. But I believe it's what I must do if I'm to try to decide for myself if Nathaniel killed his sister. Surely there can't be anything better than looking a person in the eyes when you ask them if they murdered someone?'

'Depends how good an actor he is, I'd have said,' replied Annie.

'Well, I'll see about that,' said Christine sticking out her chin and picking up her handbag. 'Alexander heard from some of the guards at Swansea prison that Nathaniel was a very quiet, unassuming man, and that they actually feared for his safety while he was there. He didn't strike them as the sort of person who'd fare well within the system that necessarily operates in that environment.'

'You mean he's getting hit about and taken advantage of?' asked Mavis.

'Sounded as though he was having a pretty difficult time.' Christine's tone was bleak. 'And I admit I felt sorry for Gwen.'

'Aye, his poor mother believing he didn't even do it, and knowing he's there,' said Mavis.

'While the jury believed he did it,' said Annie.

'As you said earlier, Annie, the question is, if Nathaniel didn't kill Lizzie – who did?' said Carol quietly.

'I don't feel comfortable charging a woman a fee for an investigation that's no' likely to lead to the end she desires,' said Mavis, 'though the work we have to do will be the same either way.'

'I don't think there's any great hope for us coming up with the outcome she desires, either,' agreed Carol.

'I read the stuff Carol sent us, and even I have to say I reckon he was the one what did it, Chrissy. I think you have to go into it understandin' that,' said Annie.

'All Gwen wants is a little hope,' said Christine. 'I want to follow through.'

'We're all able to tackle cases independently, and, if we're no' in agreement, you'd be tackling this on your own,' said Mavis. 'I'd prefer it to be something the agency takes on professionally, as a team, but with no payment being asked for up front. We could put in a clause about negotiating after the outcome of our enquiries. If he's innocent, maybe there'd be some sort of compensation. How say you all?'

All the women agreed.

'Very good then. Carol, draw up a contract, please. You be careful with this case,' said Mavis, nodding at Christine. 'Will Alexander be accompanying you during your enquiries?'

'Why do you ask,' snapped Christine, 'don't you think I'm up to it on my own?'

Annie and Carol exchanged a quick eye-roll as Mavis replied, 'Ach, of course you are, you're a perceptive and intelligent woman. What I mean is that Alexander has a certain . . . presence about him.'

'You're not kidding,' remarked Annie with a cheeky grin.

'You mean he looks like my minder?' said Christine, mock-strangling Annie.

'Aye, you could say that,' replied Mavis.

'Maybe he will, or maybe he'll be too involved with his own business,' said Christine as she started to climb the circular staircase to her apartment above the barn. 'Either way, I'll be fine.'

TWENTY-TWO

By the time Mavis arrived back at the Dower House she had a thumping headache. She didn't suffer from headaches. She *wouldn't* suffer from headaches. She also wouldn't give in to taking medication that might help her aching head, but dull her senses. Althea had announced she thought the rain would keep the visitors largely inside the hall, so she was taking McFli for an early walk before attending an emergency meeting of the sub-committee responsible for organizing the marquees for the summer fete up at the hall that afternoon. She hadn't returned, so Mavis took tea alone watching the heavy rain beat against the windows. Maybe thunder was on the way; that would explain a great deal.

When McFli burst into the sitting room, stood beside Mavis and shook himself with great delight, she ended up with extremely wet legs. 'Could you no' have done that in the hallway, you wee scamp?' she asked the dripping creature, whose expression seemed to indicate he'd given the matter a good deal of consideration.

Althea's entrance was less damp, but equally discombobulating. 'I say, Mavis,' she opened, making her way toward the teapot, 'I bumped into Christine out toward the office and she told me she was going up to London this evening. *Again.* What's all that about?'

Mavis wondered how much to say. 'I think she and Alexander have had a wee skirmish. He was away back to London last night, after dinner, I gather. She's been sulking since then. She just sent me a text saying she'd managed to get another appointment with that gallery chappie tomorrow – but I think she jumped at the chance to get to London to try to see Alexander.'

Althea sat on the sofa and petted McFli at her feet – in spite of his wet fur. 'I worry about her. I shouldn't, I suppose; I have my worrying all pre-arranged by my son and my blessed daughter, it seems. But Christine? She's so desperately independent. Do you think her parents are fully apprised of the situation between her and Alexander?'

Mavis smiled warmly at her friend. 'Aye, I think she's trying to be open with them. I know she's arranged a few dinners and weekend visits for the four of them together. However, I cannae help but imagine they must share our concerns; Alexander isn't an easy man to get to know, or read. He's highly adept at showing people only that which he chooses to share. I'm sure Christine knows a good deal more about his background than we ever will, but as for what he gets up to in his own business dealings? He strikes me as the sort of man who might end up doing bad things for what he judges to be good reasons.'

'You mean like Robin Hood? But without the tights? Though I suspect Alexander would look rather good in tights.'

Mavis shook her head. 'I wasnae thinking of Robin Hood exactly, dear.'

'Dennis Moore then?'

'I don't think I know him at all.'

'Lupins. Your life, or your lupins. Lupins in a basket with sautéed lupins. You know?'

Mavis twigged. 'Ah, Monty Python. Got it. No, I don't mean Alexander is like anybody who stole from the rich to give to the poor, I just mean I think he might have a peculiar idea about right and wrong.'

Althea sat up and wiped her damp hands on her backside. 'They're complex concepts. Highly subjective.'

'Not where the law is concerned.'

'"The law is a ass," that's what Dickens said, and he might have had a point.'

Mavis walked across the room to sit beside Althea. 'Monty Python *and* Dickens, before tea-time? Something bothering you?'

Althea looked Mavis squarely in the face and replied, 'Yes. You. You know Bryn Jenkins is making overtures toward you, and you seemed to be enjoying his company immensely at dinner last night. But you haven't said anything about him to me. About how you feel about him. I thought we were best friends.'

Mavis was genuinely shocked. 'But there's nothing to tell. He's a pleasant enough man, I'll grant you, but more than that? Nothing. He's happy with his lot; pleased his daughter lives with him; he's a good head for business – canny when it comes to a deal; bit of a bible basher. That's it. And I can tell you he's made no "overtures" toward me, as you put it. He's no' even tuned to middle C, as far as I can tell.'

'But you two had your heads together all through dinner. I saw you. You even had the odd giggle. I thought you were enjoying yourself.'

'I was, dear. It's not as though I'm averse to the company of men.' Mavis sighed. 'Mine has been a life of quiet duty; raising my sons, nursing in the forces, running the barracks for retired soldiers. Nowadays I make sure this agency works well. I am, like Bryn, happy with my lot. My marriage was a solid one. I am not a seeker after frivolity.'

'But you could do with a bit of fun, Mavis. You're young yet.'

Mavis wondered why Althea was pursing this line of thought. 'Is there something you're not telling me, dear? Any health issues?'

Althea rose. 'I'm as fit as a fiddle. It's just that I have a Big Milestone coming up, and it's making me think; would I have done anything differently when Chelly died if I'd known then I'd have all these years ahead of me? I hit my late sixties and thought it was all behind me – marriage, life, discovering new places, new people. Then you four arrived here, and poof! It all changed for me. You helped me realize there were new horizons even at my age. I hope your settling down here with me doesn't make you miss out on opportunities you wish, in a decade or so, you'd taken.'

Mavis watched as the dowager poured herself a cup of tea. 'That'll be stewed and cold. Let me ring for Lindsey to get Cook to make a fresh pot.'

'It'll be fine. I'm not as particular about my tea as you. You're deflecting.'

'Have you been reading books on psychology?'

'One or two. I'm enjoying learning new things. You might enjoy getting to know new people. Seeing new places. You and Bryn could travel.'

'Ach, I've traveled.'

'I don't mean as a nurse with the army, I mean as a tourist – seeing nice things, not horrible wounds.'

'I didnae see so many of those, I'm pleased to say.'

'That's not my point. You're deflecting again.'

'Ach, this is a pointless conversation. I am happy, Althea. I do not need a man in my life to feel complete. Should I feel I require more than my own company I have good friends – yourself most of all – and the knowledge that my being will continue in the genetic code I have passed to my grandchildren. That is more than enough for anyone. I do wish, however, to do something useful with my time. Solving cases that bother folks – even if they are not "important enough" to be given attention by the police – is something I feel good about doing. Look at this case, for example: we have the chance to allow a woman, Val, to strike out and get herself a home and feel a freedom in her life she gave up to help out her father. That's a good thing to do, and not something the police would have the slightest interest in helping with.' She noticed that Althea looked deflated, so moderated her tone. 'I don't mean to snap, but I have a headache, dear.'

'I miss my Chelly, Mavis. It's times like this I miss him the most.'

'Times like what?'

Althea slumped. 'I agreed with Henry and Stephanie to celebrate my eightieth birthday at the Chellingworth Summer Fete. I do so hate to be the center of attention – though it's something I have learned to deal with over the past fifty-odd years.'

'It'll be a lovely celebration, my dear. You'll glow with it, I know you will.'

'That's not the problem. The problem is I know they're only going to be cheering because I'm still on my perch. They're celebrating the fact I'm not dead yet, not the fact I've achieved something while I'm alive. That's what birthday celebrations are – a big party to congratulate a person on not being dead.'

Mavis could tell her friend was holding something back. She waited quietly.

After a moment Althea sighed heavily and said, 'And that's another thing. This place. The Dower House. Look around – it's quite beautiful. Everything a woman needs for her final years, when her husband has shuffled off his mortal coil and left her without a real role to fill, her son having taken the title. It's nothing more than a gilded cage. Think about all the old women living out their useless, fussy lives here before me. Our discussions about that old folks' home have made me see this place in a new light. That's what this is, really, isn't it? Dower Houses are no more than the original form of somewhere for the younger generation to stow away the old biddy and forget about her.'

Mavis thought for a moment about how best to respond. 'It's no' a bad grannie annex,' she said, trying to get Althea to look up and acknowledge the sparkle in her eyes. She'd honed her skills in dealing with the infirm, then the elderly, throughout her nursing career but didn't usually need to call upon them at all with Althea. Her friend's pink eyes told her maybe this was a day when she should.

Organizing fresh tea and a towel to rub-down McFli, and having managed to negotiate an early dinner, Mavis settled with Althea to try to buff the approaching evening to a rosy hue.

TWENTY-THREE

Wednesday 25th June

Jeremy Edgerton looked annoyed, and Christine was none too happy. She, Alexander and the gallery owner were standing in front of a massive piece of what she could only describe as 'junk' – because that was what exactly it was, all squished into the shape of a cube – displayed as the centerpiece of a much-vaunted exhibition at Edgerton's premises off Bond Street.

'But it's not convenient,' the ruddy-faced man was whining, 'not today. I must be here for the opening at 7pm. It's critical. The press, the artist, key buyers – it's all arranged. The caterers will be here within the hour. You must see it's impossible for me to accompany you to the Welsh coast this afternoon.'

Alexander whispered something into the man's ear. Edgerton's expression changed from annoyance to terror, then compliance. 'Just a matter of a few hours?' he squeaked. Alexander nodded. 'Back by five?' Again, Alexander nodded. Christine was puzzled; she hadn't the faintest idea how it was possible for the three of them to drive to and from Gower, and allow for a useful amount of time while there, in so short a time.

Edgerton straightened his bow tie and said, 'I expect my assistant can cope with the caterers, but I need ten minutes to brief people properly. I'll be with you momentarily. Wait here.' He scurried toward a hidden office.

'How on earth are we going to manage that?' asked Christine. 'He'll never be back in time.'

'I have a plan,' said Alexander quietly.

'And does that plan involve a helicopter and a couple of fast cars?' quipped Christine.

Alexander smiled. 'As a matter of fact, it does.'

'What?'

'We leave from the heliport in Battersea and land at Swansea Airport. I have a car booked at that end to take us to the Llewellyn cottage. Depending on the weather – which looks not too bad at the moment – the flight should only take about an hour, and we're in Gower when we land. If we give him an hour with the Llewellyn artworks, we'll be back here before you know it.'

Christine admitted to herself she felt a mixture of pride and misgiving. 'You've got it all worked out, haven't you? How could you be so sure he'd say yes?'

Alexander winked.

'What did you whisper to him? Did you threaten him?' She felt her tummy tighten.

'With what could I possibly threaten the owner of one of London's pre-eminent art galleries? Dear old Jeremy lives a blameless life, with a stain-free history. Just like you and me.'

Christine allowed the meaning of his words to sink in. 'So you've got something bad on him, and threatened to go to the tabloids with it?'

Her companion's entrancingly light eyes narrowed. 'Not much chance of getting anything past you, is there?'

Christine didn't enjoy her range of emotions. 'How on earth did you manage to pull all this together so quickly? I didn't even mention this meeting until we were having breakfast this morning.'

'I'm good at making fast decisions.'

It was a slightly cowed Jeremy Edgerton who joined them at the door and urged fleetness of foot. 'If we're going to do this, then let's get going,' he snapped.

Alexander silenced him with one glance, then held open the door for Christine to exit. 'Our car will be here presently,' he said.

Christine didn't enjoy the trip; she wished she could have, but she didn't. She wasn't annoyed because Alexander had taken over – she knew he was better equipped financially to be able to make the whole thing happen – that wasn't it; she just felt a bit inadequate. The views of London as they flew over it were spectacular, and she didn't take her eyes off the magnificence of the landscape changing beneath her for one moment. She'd never seen it that way before. Despite the dreadfully noisy, and frankly less-than-comfortable, environment, the most marvelous thing was that they flew so low – relative to an aeroplane.

The bumpy landing at Swansea Airport and the hurried journey in the chauffeured car Alexander had booked behind them, Christine, Alexander and Gwen Llewellyn were all finally standing around Jeremy Edgerton as he peered at Lizzie's signed and framed work on the wall of the cottage in Gower, sucking his thumb.

The excruciating silence was pierced by the whistle of Gwen's kettle. She scurried off to make tea, the tension clearly too much for her. By the time Edgerton turned from the painting, the tea was ready. Three pairs of eyes stared at him, the atmosphere vibrating with anticipation.

'Congratulations,' he said, 'you have yourselves a collection of almost thirty miniatures made by the impressive, and I dare say, desperately under-appreciated, artist Lizzie Llewellyn. There are a couple of other people I'd like to bring to see this particular piece, as well as the portfolio you have upstairs, Mrs Llewellyn, and the original miniatures, of course, but – and I hope this doesn't sound as though I'm blowing my own trumpet too loudly – it's my word and opinion that will hold most water. Despite the fact I've not had the pleasure of seeing more than photocopies, I can say I am more than likely going to be able to confirm your miniatures are by the hand of Lizzie Llewellyn, Miss Wilson-Smythe. I am sure your client will be delighted. May I also say I would be happy to present them to the market, if that's what your client chooses to do with them?'

Christine suppressed a cynical chuckle; of course the man would like to get his foot in the door to make a potential profit.

'I'll pass the news, and your kind offer, to my client. However, whatever my client might choose to do, they will require an official attribution. When might they expect that to happen?'

The gallery owner looked at his watch impatiently. 'If we could just get back to London so I'm on the spot for tonight's opening, I can get in touch with my esteemed colleagues – one of whom I will see at this evening's event – and we can make arrangements to return here, together, at a more convenient time. The originals will, of course, have to be inspected.'

'Why don't you just take photos of this one here on the wall, then you won't have to come back and bother me again. It's not like I'm getting anything out of this – not for all my inconvenience.' Gwen sounded irritated and glared at Edgerton as she spoke.

Christine gave the matter some thought. 'Hang on for two minutes while I make a quick phone call?' She didn't wait for an answer, but dashed out of the cottage and phoned Stephanie Twyst. She returned a few moments later.

'On Saturday July 5th, the annual summer fete is being held at Chellingworth Hall, the ducal seat of the Twyst family in Powys. I have an invitation from the duchess herself for all of us to meet at the hall that day. I'll bring the original miniatures along with my client – should they choose to attend – and we'll make sure you have adequate transportation for yourself and this framed piece, Mrs Llewellyn. The duchess has offered to send the family's Bentley for you, which should suffice.' Gwen glowed. 'I'm sure you can manage to convey yourself and your colleagues to Powys, Jeremy. Why not bring your team to the hall, meet the duke and duchess – and maybe enjoy a private tour of their wonderful artworks? Maybe you and Mrs Llewellyn could even discuss an exhibit of Lizzie's works, and possibly a book about her. I understand she has furnished you with valuable background information pertaining to her daughter before now.'

Jeremy's eyes gleamed with the light of a possible commission. 'I'd be thrilled to get behind such an undertaking. After all, I would think everything would be up for discussion with your client. Surely all he's really interested in doing is bumping up the value of the books containing the miniatures?'

Christine couldn't resist. 'Did I say my client was a man, Jeremy?' She was unreasonably delighted when Jeremy blushed.

'Well, no, I suppose you didn't. Why? Is it a woman?' He sounded horrified.

'If my client chooses to meet with you at Chellingworth Hall, you'll have the chance to find out,' was all Christine was prepared to say.

'Best we get back to London now, don't you think?' said Alexander, looking at his watch.

'I'll join you in the car in just a moment,' said Christine. 'Before I leave I need a private word with Mrs Llewellyn, if you don't mind. You go ahead. I'll join you as soon as I can.'

TWENTY-FOUR

Thursday 26th June

Christine had been inside several jails, by way of curiosity and research; the places where people were housed on a temporary, or at least short-term basis in police stations, weren't, to her mind, too awful. But she'd only seen the inside of a prison on television, so wasn't at all prepared for the two things that most affected her as she made her way through the various layers of security at HM Prison Swansea – the smell, and the sounds. Her nose wrinkled as she reckoned disinfectant could only be expected to do so much when it came to disguising the engrained stench of thousands of men inhabiting a confined space with little by way of ventilation, throughout a period of pretty much 150 years. She told herself she'd get used to that in a little while, so tried to put it to the back of her mind. But the echoing of heavy gates and doors clanging closed and being locked? That was something she'd keep with her forever. She knew she was merely visiting, so wondered why the sounds hit her in the pit of her stomach and made her feel more desolate, more truly alone and abandoned than she had ever felt before. Even before she met Nathaniel Llewellyn he had her sympathy, which she told herself was unprofessional.

As Christine sat in the interview room awaiting the arrival of the convicted man, she peered longingly at the few inches of barred window set into the upper part of one wall of the room. The cries of seagulls she could picture swooping on the ocean breeze beyond the twenty-foot-high walls taunted even her. She found it hard to imagine how the sound of those gulls made the inmates feel. 'Hopeless' was the word that came into her mind, swiftly followed by 'trapped.'

As the heavy door swung open, the man who entered seemed to embody the words she'd just conjured; the robust, swaggering Nathaniel Llewellyn she'd seen enthusing about the new age of grand public art he was spearheading in Britain when the BBC cameras had been rolling was gone – she saw only a rake-thin, bow-backed man with a shaved head and patches of red, flaky skin on his face that gave him the air of a vagrant. Christine was shocked, and tried to hide her emotions as he took his place across the table from her.

'How's Mam?' were his first words. His expression was that of a small, lonely boy.

Christine gathered herself. 'She's fine. I saw her yesterday. She sends her love.'

'Send mine back,' he said, his voice lacking any emotion.

'I will.'

'She knows I didn't do it. It must be killing her, this. Are you sure she's alright?'

Knowing she couldn't reach out to touch or comfort the trembling man, Christine said, 'We haven't got long, Nathaniel. Only an hour. Your mother tells me you couldn't have murdered your sister' – the words sounded as harsh as the act they described – 'and the agency I work with has agreed to investigate her claims. I met with your barrister yesterday evening in London, and he's given me access to the papers he used at your trial. I spent hours poring over them last night, but I still have a long way to go. I've come here today so you have the chance to tell me anything – *anything* – that might help our investigations. Face to face. Just you and me. The jury found you guilty. There's no need to hold anything back now. We need something new – something that wasn't presented in court. Some little fact you might have recalled, or insight you might have remembered. Maybe something you thought wasn't relevant at the time. Nathaniel, can you help us?'

Nathaniel sighed. Christine noticed the deep, dark hollows beneath his eyes, the sagging skin and dry lips. The sleek, well-paid and respected artist she'd seen on TV had shrunk and aged to this thing in front of her. The shock of ginger hair was now a fuzz of graying stubble, Nathaniel's trademark vivid, patterned clothing replaced by the shapeless garb the prison service saw as appropriate for a man who was going nowhere any time soon.

'How can *I* help *you*?' The man's voice rasped helplessly. 'I thought *you* were here to help *me*. That's what Mam said – she'd found someone who was coming here to help me. Now you want me to help you? How can I do that?'

Christine replied calmly, 'You and I both know how the jury viewed the evidence and the testimony against you. At your trial you said you couldn't imagine why the witness to your actions the morning your sister disappeared was lying. Your barrister told me that didn't endear you to the people in the court. Now you've had time to think, and assuming the woman didn't lie, can you come up with any ideas as to why she said what she did? Why did Mrs Wynne Thomas say she'd seen you loading something that looked like a body into your hatchback? Any ideas at all?'

'No. It wasn't me. It couldn't have been me. I really was asleep until I woke up.' He shook his head slowly. 'You know what I mean.'

Christine dug deep. 'So you maintain you were not the red-headed man she saw stuff something into your car, and drive off with it?'

'Correct.'

'If, as you claim, your sister just walked out of your cottage of her own volition, where did she go? Why hasn't she come forward to say she's just grand after all, knowing you've been convicted of her killing? And where on earth did all that blood come from?' Christine tried to keep her voice as calm as possible, but she knew her frustration was showing itself in the bits of Irish peeping through.

'I don't know, I don't know and I don't know,' squealed Nathaniel, dropping his head into his hands.

Looking at the man's juddering back, Christine could quite understand how Nathaniel had managed to come across as such an unlikeable character in court. She felt sympathy for him, but no warmth. His manner was just a bit . . . off. It was like interacting with a boy who'd never grown out of the truculence of his teen years.

Finally Nathaniel raised his head; his eyes were red.

'Nothing? You have no ideas at all?'

He shook his head, tears dropping onto the tabletop. Christine checked with the guard that she was allowed to hand Nathaniel a paper tissue. He wiped his eyes and nose.

'The blood,' he said sobbing. 'I can't stand the sight of blood. I threw up when I saw it all and I think I passed out too. I couldn't have done anything to a person that would have made all that blood fly about the place. I'd have been unconscious on the floor in five seconds flat,' he croaked plaintively. 'There's that. I told my solicitor, and my barrister, that. And Mam knows that too. I've always been like that with blood.'

Christine had seen those notes. 'It's not much to go on.'

'Sorry. It's all I've got.'

'What do you think happened at your cottage that morning, Nathaniel?'

'I. Don't. Know. She must be dead, mustn't she? All that blood. Never getting in touch with anyone ever again. Who would do that to her? I know we didn't always get on, but who would do that? She was alright, really. Why would anyone kill Lizzie?'

Christine pushed on. 'What was she really like, Nathaniel? You were her brother. Explain your relationship with her to me, as best you can.'

Nathaniel heaved a sigh. 'She was my sister. Have you got a brother?' Christine nodded. 'Well, then – you know. Brothers and sisters can be a bit . . . off with each other sometimes. But they're still brother and sister.'

'My brother was quite cruel to me when I was small. Were you and Lizzie cruel to each other?'

Nathaniel's face softened. 'I thought she was a pain, but she was the cruel one if you can call it that. She was my big sister, see? Everything I did, I did it because I wanted to be like her. Mam thought she was wonderful, that everything Lizzie did was fantastic, so I copied her – so Mam would be proud of me too. I even used to dress up in high heels and necklaces like she did, 'till Mam told me I couldn't do that anymore.' He looked wistful. 'Made fun of my hair, did Lizzie. She had lovely brown hair, chestnut highlights, always shiny – like yours. I had red hair, like my granddad. And freckles, as you can see. She thought they were hilarious. Drew all over me with a felt-tipped pen joining up the freckles once when we were little, she did. Mam had to scrub and scrub to get it all off. But I didn't mind, 'cos Lizzie said it was fun doing it, so I let her. I wanted her to like me, see? I wanted to be like her.'

This was a dynamic Christine hadn't expected. It wasn't something that had come out at the trial at all. She wondered if the jury's lack of sympathy for Nathaniel might have been dented if only he'd shown this part of his character on the stand.

'So you loved your sister?'

'Of course.'

'Did she love you?'

'Maybe once, when we were little, and even for quite a long time when we were grown up. But maybe not toward the end.'

'Could you be more specific?'

Nathaniel chewed the corner of his lip. 'She changed. Over the years, I mean, not all at once. When she came back from France and we shared the cottage in Gower, things were great.' For the first time during their interview Christine noticed a spark of life in the young man's eyes. 'You've no idea how empowering it can be to be creating in the same space as someone who had as much passion for art as Lizzie. I learned so much from her. Her technique was magnificent, and, although I thought she wanted her art to do too much, socially speaking, she also made me think of the way the man in the street interacts with art on a daily basis. If it hadn't been for her, I'd never have found the courage to enter the first competition I won for a piece to be put on display in a square in Liverpool. That was what got me going. After that, I was in great demand when it came to imposing pieces for public spaces. It . . . it seems horrible to say it, but I believe she became jealous of my success. She seemed to think I was doing well just to spite her, which was stupid, because she was the one with more talent than me, and I always told her that. But she didn't want to listen. That last couple of years, before she disappeared, she just got more and more angry, and less and less communicative. She shut everyone out. Eventually, I don't think she loved anyone or anything except herself and her art.'

'Didn't she have any friends, or people in her life she loved or cared about at all?' Christine knew the only people testifying about Lizzie at the trial had been business acquaintances and people who knew her from the art world.

'No, she didn't have anyone. And she was always going on about Mam. She took to phoning me at all hours. Said horrible things about Mam, she did. I didn't get it. Mam had always been lovely to both of us. Without Mam we'd never have been able to go to art school or anything. Worked her fingers to the bone so we could do what we did, did Mam. Dad died when we were little, so she did it all herself, see? And, eventually, Lizzie didn't have a good word to say about her. I felt so sorry for Mam. She'd always done all she could for Lizzie, and me, of course.'

Christine didn't know what to say. She drew upon her basic understanding of psychology and offered: 'Did Lizzie feel she wasn't loved? Wasn't appreciated?'

Nathaniel peered across the table at Christine, then he screwed up his eyes in anger – like a small child. 'Not appreciated? That's what *she* always said. Always whining on about no one understanding her artistic journey, she was. Like I said to her on more than one occasion, if you're going to paint things so small that no one can see them, how on earth do you expect anyone to understand what you're trying to say? But she wouldn't listen. Let it get to her, she did. Hit rock bottom a few times.'

'Did she ever try to harm herself?'

'What, did she do that "cry for help" thing? Yeah, she did that alright. Stuffed herself full of pills, then phoned Mam. Twice she did that. Terrified poor Mam she did. Not fair. Totally selfish.'

Christine made notes. This was the first time anyone had mentioned Lizzie being suicidal, and she wondered if it might have a bearing on the case.

'Did she ever make an attempt on her own life but not call for help?'

Nathaniel shook his head. 'Not her style.'

Christine decided it was time for a couple of Big Questions. 'So, Nathaniel, you're telling me you didn't kill your sister?'

He lifted his chin. 'I didn't.'

'And you didn't find her dead, by her own hand, and take her body away somewhere to hide it?'

Nathaniel looked shocked, then puzzled. 'Why would I do that? Even if I'd thought something that stupid was a good idea at the time – which I wouldn't have done, because I'm not an idiot – I certainly wouldn't have let it come to this. I'd have told them where I'd put her body. If there was a body, there'd be some way to prove I didn't do it.'

Christine tried a different approach. 'At your trial, you said you couldn't think of anyone who would want to harm your sister. Have you changed your mind about that since then?'

Nathaniel's eyes grew round. 'I wish I could think of someone, but there wasn't anyone.'

'No boyfriends? No artistic enemies?'

'She had a boyfriend for a while when she went back to live in London. The tattoo artist guy. I told the police about him.' Christine couldn't recall any mention of a tattoo artist in any of the case notes she'd seen, and Nathaniel's barrister certainly hadn't mentioned one.

'Tell me about him,' she pressed.

Nathaniel looked surprised. 'He was some bloke she was living with for about two minutes in London, about a year before she . . . disappeared. She called him Baz. That's all. Got a shop in Soho. That's all I ever knew.'

'Nothing more?'

Nathaniel shrugged. 'He did her tattoos, that's all I know.'

'So Lizzie had tattoos?'

'Yeah. On her arms, her back – all over the place. Nowhere you could see them unless she chose to show them off, though. But this isn't news. I told everyone about them. Tattoos of her own work. Weird thing to do, that.'

Christine made some notes.

Nathaniel began to look impatient. 'Look, where's all this going, exactly? Do you believe I didn't kill her, or what? Why have you even bothered to come? Are you just ripping off my poor old Mam? I bet that's what this is.'

'First of all, we're not charging your mother for this work, so there's that. The reason I'm here at all is because your mother believes you didn't kill your sister and I've promised your mother I'll do what I can to give her, and you, hope. So help me out, will you? Ollie – *Oliver* – your barrister, warned me you weren't a person who was over-anxious to endear yourself to people, not even when you took the stand in your own defense. Since I'm here on behalf of your mother I feel able to tell you your attitude isn't helping me at all. Have you even considered I'm on your side?'

Nathaniel's face reddened, his fists clenched and he whispered, 'Don't you tell me I'm not helping myself. I'm doing everything I can to hold onto my sanity. I woke up one day to find my sister gone, my cottage covered in blood, and everyone thinking I'd killed her. I *know* I didn't. But I cannot explain what happened. It's like a nightmare. And I'm not waking up.' Tears rolled down his face again.

Christine stood, moved to the guard on duty, showed him what was in the folder she'd brought with her and retook her seat.

'I know this must be difficult, but I'd like you to look at some photocopies of some drawings. I'm trying to establish if they were created by your sister. It would help me to know if you've ever seen them before.'

Nathaniel wiped his face with the back of his hand. 'Go on then. I'll look.' He stared at the enlarged versions, then the smaller ones. 'Yes, they're by Lizzie.'

'How can you tell?'

Nathaniel laughed. The sound echoed in the bare room. 'Ha! You ask me to critique the work of the woman I've been found guilty of killing, then question me about my artistic opinions? That's rich, that is. Look, here, and here – see where she just hints at shapes she thinks aren't important to the composition instead of finishing them off properly? Always did that. Really annoying. It was as though she couldn't grasp the meaning of her subjects, just their form.'

Christine was taken aback, and realized her surprise must have shown on her face.

'I'm not going to lie,' said Nathaniel. 'Call me a perfectionist – many people have. Indeed, a lot of people have called me a lot worse than that. What I say is, if you're going to try to be realistic, you should be totally realistic. See that one of the Great Hall at Swansea University's Bay Campus? Now that's good. All the angles right, the detail of the building is perfect. She could do it when she tried – when she put her mind to it and followed through – she just didn't always bother. I don't like lazy artists.'

'Thanks,' said Christine, pushing the copies back into their folder. 'I'll tell Jeremy Edgerton you agree these are your sister's work.'

'Edgerton?' Christine nodded. 'Creep.'

'Your mother agrees with you on that matter too,' said Christine, offering a smile.

'Poor Mam,' said Nathaniel, with feeling. 'Sorry I snapped, but it's hard in here. Have I helped at all?'

'I've got a tattoo artist in Soho to track down for a start,' said Christine. 'Anything else from you?'

Nathaniel shook his head.

TWENTY-FIVE

Mavis MacDonald was livid. Staring at Ian Cottesloe, the dowager's factotum, and Lindsey Newbury, the dowager's aide, in the entry hall of the Dower House she felt herself boil inside.

'You have colluded with the dowager to pull the wool over my eyes,' she began, using the soft, determined tone that had been known to terrify junior nurses. 'How could you? I realize she pays your wages, but you have allowed her to put herself, quite possibly, in harm's way, and that is unforgiveable. Loyalty is one thing, poor decision-making quite a different matter.'

Lindsey spoke first, her lip trembling. 'I'm so sorry, Mavis, she made us promise. On our honor, she said. It's not that she pays us, it's that we love her. It's more than working for her, you see? She had a plan and we helped her. I spoke to her last night and she was just fine. She's not far away, and there's no way she could get into any trouble.'

Mavis could think of a thousand ways Althea could manage to get herself into trouble. 'What time did you drop her off, Ian?' she almost whispered.

'Around two, yesterday afternoon.' The young man, strapping though he was, looked like a small boy who'd been caught scrumping apples.

'So Cook outright lied to me when she told me the dowager was having supper in her room last night? She's in on it as well?' Two heads nodded. 'Ach, it's unbelievable. She's no business going off on her own like this. How did you come to speak to her, Lindsey?'

The young woman shook her head. 'As her ladies' aide, I would prefer not to say. But, out of respect for you, I can tell you she phoned me from her mobile phone.'

'But she hasnae got a mobile phone,' snapped Mavis.

'She has now,' replied Lindsey.

'Tell me the number.' Lindsey and Ian exchanged a worried look. 'Stop that. You both know I'm right. She has no business going undercover at that old folks' home with no one to watch over her.'

Lindsey's eyes rolled at Ian, and he frowned, shaking his head.

'Out with it,' snapped Mavis.

Althea's handyman sighed. 'I'll tell you,' said Ian. Lindsey poked him in the ribs with her elbow, but he continued, 'Her Grace said if you found out, and told us we had to tell you what was going on, that we weren't to, but that we should tell you to speak to Carol.'

Mavis was puzzled. 'Carol? You mean Carol Hill?' They nodded. 'Why? What does Carol know that I don't?' They shrugged. 'Very well. You may go about your business.' They turned on their heels, looking relieved. 'This is not over,' called Mavis at their retreating figures.

She speed-dialed Carol's mobile phone.

'Hello, Mavis, what's up?'

'It's Althea – *she's* up to something, and I think you know what.'

'You mean doing her bit for the agency up at Mountain Ash House?'

'Aye.'

'She's doing really well. Her feed's been coming through just fine at this end. I'm running through her input a few hours behind time, but it turns out she's a real pro. Good job with the briefing, Mavis.'

'Briefing about what?'

'Pardon?'

'I know nothing of this, Carol. She's taken herself off all alone, with no one's knowledge.'

'Now, hang on a minute, Mavis. She told me you two had come up with this plan together. She said you'd agreed she could go to the old folks' home for a couple of days so long as she filmed everything. I sat down with her for hours yesterday going through how she was to use her new phone and all the apps I loaded onto it. She told me that was what you said you wanted. Are you telling me she's . . . what, made the whole thing up?'

Mavis's tummy unclenched. 'Aye, the wee . . . you know what . . . has lied to us all. Now, tell me again, you *know* she's alright?'

'Like I said, I'm a bit behind with watching her filmed feed, but . . . hang on, let me check the time-code. There – as of 9.26 a.m. she was lovely. Having breakfast with a very nice woman named Maisie, who's already roped Althea in to giving some sort of performance at the concert party tomorrow night.'

Mavis was at a loss what to say or do next. Her initial misgivings had been alleviated, but she was still cross with Althea.

'Do you think she didn't tell you about her plans because she knew you'd try to stop her?' asked Carol gently.

'Aye, I've no doubt that crossed her mind,' replied Mavis now feeling more in control of her emotions. 'And she'd have been quite correct in that assumption. She's been hatching this plan for a while, it seems.'

'I'm sure she'll be fine, Mavis, and she's gathering some useful insights, really she is.'

'So how's she doing that then?'

'She's using a smart phone I gave her for the purpose.'

'So you're in this up to your neck too?'

'Honestly, I thought this was an agreed plan, on behalf of the agency. That's what she said.'

'You didnae think to consult with me about it?'

'Well, with respect, Mavis, you don't run the agency – we're all partners, and I . . . well, I took Althea at her word.' Carol paused. 'You're right, I should have spoken to you about it. I spoke to Annie about it and she thought it was a great idea.'

'So I'm the only one who didnae know?'

'No, I haven't discussed it with Christine. There wasn't any point.'

Mavis sighed. 'Aye, well, I'm going to run over to the place and fetch her back right now.'

'But why? She's already managed to get conversations going that have pointed me in the direction of which doctor to check out in the area – the one they use there – and she's also had a very interesting chat with an extremely elderly lady named Bronwyn who's going through the process of deciding whether to leave all she owns to a cat sanctuary in Chester, or to the Cruickshanks. It's all good stuff.'

Mavis felt the wind go out of her sails. 'And this is all legal? All this recording?'

'Yes, don't panic. She discussed her use of recording equipment with the owners when she got there, and it turns out they positively encourage it. They often have people visiting and wanting to film the place, it seems, and all the residents have signed the appropriate waivers. Althea's only recording when she's in public places. The residents' rooms are off limits, she knows that, but those areas where she, a paying guest, is allowed to be, we're good there.'

Mavis gave the matter some thought. 'Ach, well if the owners said it was all well and good to film, I cannae think they have anything to hide. And Althea tells everyone she's recording what they say?'

'She does. She's an elderly lady trying to decide if she wants to spend the rest of her good years there. She's explained she has some memory issues, and that's why she's recording everything. It's all above-board. Don't panic. We have the owners' permission, she gets the residents' permissions.'

'Aye . . . well . . .'

'If you're worried about her, and you insist upon seeing her to put your mind to rest, at least don't blow her cover.'

Mavis walked into the sitting room and sat on the sofa. 'Aye, mebbe you're right.'

'I know I am. You could always pretend to be checking the place over on behalf of a relative. If you're going to go there at least let me know so I can prepare her to see your face, and play along.'

'I'll think about it. Would you at least catch up with her feed and let me know she's alright now?'

'Of course.'

'Bye then.'

'Bye, Mavis.'

Mavis pushed her telephone into her pocket and stared out of the window. She didn't see the flowers in the border nodding in the breeze, she didn't notice Cook picking herbs, she didn't even spot the birds in the clear blue sky. All she saw was the reflection of a woman in her sixties with a worried face.

TWENTY-SIX

Carol ended her conversation with Mavis just as David brought Albert downstairs after his nap.

'What's up? You don't look too happy,' he said.

'What a very perceptive husband I have,' said Carol, taking her baby son into her arms. 'How's my boy? Oh, look, he's still all pink with sleep.'

'Edible cheeks,' said David then looked concerned, 'does that sound weird? I mean, maybe it's a bit over the top, but you know what I mean.'

'I know exactly what you mean,' said the new mother, kissing her infant son's chubby cheek with great tenderness. 'Now, can you take him while I give my attention to this bit of work?'

'Yep. Got nothing on until Monday – well, our Sunday, because the client is in Japan. I'm going to have to work through the night, so I'll be around for him if he needs anyone and you can sleep.'

'Won't they mind you breaking off work to see to your son?'

'The CEO has a nine-month-old, and she'll be fine with me taking responsibility for Albert.'

'A female Japanese CEO?' Carol was genuinely surprised.

'No, she's American. Her company is working in partnership with a Japanese outfit. Though your tone suggests you'd understand they aren't finding the relationship an easy one. Very complex view of the role of women in society the Japanese have.'

Carol sighed. 'Every country and culture has a complex view of how women should, and do, fit into society. And it's never the same across all strata of society. Trust me, I know what I'm talking about.'

David took Albert, kissed his wife, and Carol turned her attention to the feed coming from Althea's camera. Unlike the output she'd watched from the bookshop where the camera had been static and the data had rolled in on a continuous basis, Althea was turning her camera on and off, and it was sometimes lying on its side on a table while in use. Carol knew she'd shown the dowager how to set the camera upright, but it looked as though she'd forgotten that part of her equipment training. At least she was turning it on and off correctly, which was encouraging.

The other big difference was that this camera was recording sound as well as vision, and the content of the conversations was what mattered, so Carol had to listen as well as watch. She was pleased she could plug in her earphones and listen intently, rather than being concerned about every little noise Albert was making – his grunts, squeals and bubble-blowing were a complex pattern of communication cues she was learning, but they needed more attention than she could give them while listening to a constantly changing parade of elderly ladies all chatting merrily to a woman they thought was Gladys Pugh from Tenby, who was looking for somewhere to spend her final active years.

As conversations repeated themselves – Where are you from? Do you know so-and-so? Have you ever been to wherever? What did your husband do? Any children? – Carol tried her best to not glaze over. It became increasingly clear Mountain Ash House was filled with widows whose children were either non-existent (rare), living too far away to visit often (more likely), or happy to ignore them (too frequent). There was one man living there among eleven women, which meant he was kept busy when it came to being courteous and doing 'manly' things like being a dance partner.

After an hour Carol had to pause the recording, because she felt an overwhelming wave of sadness, and panic, creep up on her. Statistics told her men died younger than women, and she and David were the same age. What would she do with maybe ten, or fifteen years at the end of her life without him? Would Albert grow up to be a son who emigrated to Australia, or would he live at home with his poor, widowed old mam until she popped her clogs?

She needed tea, and felt better after she'd pootled about in the kitchen brewing a pot, seeing her son and husband young, vibrant and noisily happy. Returning to the land of virtual octogenarians, she felt happier knowing she had more than forty years to get used to the idea of spending her days the way these elderly people seemed to be doing – reading, talking, watching TV and taking gentle, walkers-assisted strolls in the summer sunshine.

As the procession of elderly women passed before her eyes she thought how odd it was they all seemed to have become almost de-gendered; open-collared shirts, short or close-cropped gray hair, the odd whisker or two and not a scrap of make-up to be seen. She was interested to see Maisie, Megs and Mable – about whom Christine had spoken. She also met a Betty, a June and a Shirley. Coincidentally, the male resident's name was Bert, and she tried hard to imagine her bouncing Albert in eighty years' time, but couldn't manage it.

Bert was a jolly chap, who was happy to talk to Althea/Gladys about the way the place was run. Carol got the impression he felt he could have done a much better job of maintaining the Victorian property, and he spoke at length about the value of properly rubbing down paintwork on wooden sash-windows before repainting them. One thing she did glean from his insights was that the fabric of the house was in need of attention; the roof was losing slates, the damp was making inroads at the rear of the property and he felt the Cruickshanks were about to find themselves needing to make some serious upgrades in terms of the heating system, which apparently hadn't performed well during the past winter.

'So, they need some cash, and quite a bit of it,' said Carol – aloud, as it turned out.

David stuck his head through the door. 'Need me?'

Carol smiled and pulled out her earplugs. 'No, just talking to myself. But now you're here – any idea what it would cost to put a new slate roof on this place?'

Her husband looked bemused. 'What – because I'm a bloke I know that sort of thing? No idea, but I could do a bit of online research, if you like. Why, do we need one?'

'You're right – silly of me to think you'd know. And don't bother, I can look it up too – besides, we don't need one, but I think the old folks' home we're investigating might. I'm just trying to get an idea of how much it would cost to keep a place like that up to snuff. With what the residents are telling Althea, it's not cheap to live there, and their expectations of standards and comfort levels are understandably high.'

'OK.' David left, calling, 'Enjoy that, then.'

A conversation with a woman who'd been pals with the woman named Daisy who'd lived there was next up. Althea and she had lunched together, so Carol took a moment to text Mavis to assure her the dowager was in perfect health and spirits just a couple of hours earlier. This example of octogenarian enthusiasm was named Iris, and it seemed she and Daisy had initially gravitated toward each other because of the floral motif in their names. It seemed Iris had known Daisy quite well, so Carol listened intently. She smiled as she realized Althea had also cottoned on that this might be her most important conversation to date and attempted to ask questions that might elicit revelations about possible coercion.

Not being able to see Althea, Carol had to mentally refer to the image she had of the dowager in her disguise; she'd shown off her reflection in a mirror in the hallway of the old folks' home and it had surprised Carol – Althea looked older, shorter and more wizened, wearing a blonde wig, beige clothing and vivid fuschia pink lipstick. Althea was also affecting a thick Welsh accent as Gladys, which Carol admired; truth be told, Althea sounded very much like Carol's own mother.

'So what was Daisy like when you knew her?' asked Althea/ Gladys of Iris. 'If it's the same one, I lost touch with her back in the 1970s. Did she age well?'

'Lot of aches and pains, like all of us, but nothing out of the ordinary,' replied Iris, who Carol guessed – by her accent – came from somewhere in north Wales, rather than from the south; the nasal way she pronounced her words gave it away. 'Pretty fit for a woman who'd broken her neck.'

'She'd broken her neck?' Althea sounded genuinely surprised. 'I never knew about that. Came off a horse, I suppose?' Carol saw Iris nod. 'Lucky she could walk at all then.' Iris shrugged. 'No horses round this way. She'd have missed her horses. Did she leave everything to some horse sanctuary when she died?'

'Left it to this lot. "Us," as they like to say.' Carol inferred a non-verbal cue from Althea which encouraged Iris to say more. 'See, when we goes – us lot, the ones with no one . . . and it would be the same for you, I suppose, you being on your own now like you said earlier – well they give us a chance to talk it all through with a solicitor. Nice chap, he is. William Williams. Young chap – well, they all are nowadays, aren't they? Anyway, he's got these lovely printed booklets that go through all your options. It's worth doing. If you don't leave a proper will, with everything done right, it all goes to the state, see?'

'So I understand,' said Althea. Carol picked up a whiff of the annoyance she'd seen Althea display at the dinner at the hall, but could tell the dowager was playing her part to the hilt. 'Of course I've thought about it, and there are some people – you know, the ones who've meant something over the years – that I'd like to leave a little bit to, but, other than that, it's so difficult to know what to do. See, I'd have thought of horses for Daisy, because she was never as happy as when she was riding. But maybe that faded over the years. I've always had dogs, myself. I was thinking of the RSPCA.'

Iris nodded. 'A lot of them do leave money to places like that. If we leave it to this place it's nice to think of people coming after us here. It's a lovely spot, and there's always one person here who's paid for by the trust fund. Someone who'd be in a horrible council place otherwise.'

Carol was delighted that Althea pounced on that lead. 'Who's here like that now then?'

Iris leaned in. 'Well, no one will admit to it, of course, but I think it's Maisie. Husband died about twenty years ago and he used to work down the pits. Can't have had a lot back then, and even less nowadays, I'd have thought. Talks about her son in Australia all the time. He's also only a miner of sorts, though.'

'If her husband died of pneumoconiosis she might have got a lump-sum payout,' said Gladys. 'Terrible thing, black lung, and it gets so many men who've spent their lives underground.'

'It does,' said Iris sadly. 'I'm from the north originally, Rhyl, but I lived in Merthyr for decades – moved there when I was young, we did – and I knew too many men gone long before their time that way. A lot of my school friends grew up without dads because of it, then married men who worked down the same pits that killed their fathers. But there, it wasn't as though they had much choice. Different for you though, being from Tenby.'

'We were very lucky. Mam and Dad had a shop. Nice clean living.'

Carol waited while a silence passed. 'So they use the money the residents leave them to help others, do they?' asked Gladys; Carol was impressed by her ability to not lose focus.

'That's what the solicitor said, and he's got to tell the truth, hasn't he? Funnily enough, he's coming this afternoon to have a meeting with old Bronwyn – her who's talking about giving it all to the cats. You might want to get one of his brochures. That would tell you all about it. Oh look, there's our afters coming around now. Spotted Dick today, it is. Fancy a bit?'

At that point Althea had stopped recording and Carol could tell that was all there was to watch. She wondered if she would get a feed coming in from the meeting with the very helpful, if young,

William Williams, and decided to do some enquiring into the man's
background while she waited.

TWENTY-SEVEN

Annie was pleased to hear from Mavis, and agreed she'd get
herself ready to be able to accompany her colleague on a
visit to the antiques market in Brecon to try to establish if
the Cruickshanks were selling off items of value they'd been left
by their late-residents. She felt she was, at last, getting involved in
the case the rest of her colleagues were working on. She was also
relieved she wouldn't have to pretend to be someone else for a
while; she enjoyed undercover work, but didn't mind the idea of
being herself for a while. She rang Tudor's mobile phone to see if
he'd be able to look after Gertie for the rest of the day.

A couple of minutes later, Tudor knocked at her tiny front door.
'I thought I'd pick Gertie up here,' said the more-florid-than-usual
publican. 'I'll walk her over to my place, grab Rosie and we can go
once around the green for ablutive purposes. Got time to join us?'

Annie checked her watch. 'Yeah. Mave's not due for half an
hour. You got here quick.' She bent down and dragged Gertie out.
Once the puppy smelled Tudor, she became highly excited; Annie
was well aware that, in Gertie's little dog brain, Tudor's smell
meant she'd be seeing her litter-mate Rosie shortly thereafter. She
was also pretty sure it told Gertie she was about to get more treats
than usual, too – though Tudor always vehemently denied spoiling
the pups.

They arrived at the pub, collected Rosie, allowed the yellow
Lab to greet the black one, and all four of them continued on their
way, both dogs' noses following trails of who-knew-what smells in
all directions as they crossed the green. Gertie and Rosie's leads
were both fully extended on their little spools, and Annie and Tudor
allowed them to play as they wanted, within reason. 'No throwing
balls, no time,' Tudor had said, and Annie had agreed.

'I'm off to Brecon with Mavis to an antiques market. On the
lookout for anything for the pub, are you?'

'No, I've got enough decorative items for now, thanks. Have you found out anything else – about anything else? I'm a bit at a loss as to what you're working on at the moment. Not still these books, is it? Looking at Gertie there with her nose down, that's how I think of you and your detecting, you know – always sniffing out a lead. You love it, don't you?'

'I do,' said Annie glowing, and took the chance to bring him up to speed. 'So if we can make that final connection between this Daisy woman, and the people who run the old folks' home, we should be done and dusted, and the Jenkins family will be quids-in.'

'Alright for some,' said Tudor sounding less than happy. 'A bit like winning the lottery for them, if those books turn out to really be theirs.'

'Wish it was you?'

'You kidding? Of course I do.'

'What would you do if you won it? The lottery.'

Tudor smiled. 'Buy a bigger pub and have more staff to run it. I like having a pub, but I could do with working in it a bit less. You?'

'Take Eustelle and Dad to St Lucia for a nice long holiday so we could see the extended family and spend some proper time with them, then I'd come back here and learn to drive – or I suppose I could afford a car and a chauffeur like Althea's got. Have my own Ian Cottesloe.'

Tudor gave Annie an odd look. 'Just to drive you about? Nothing else?'

'Nah – that would do me,' said Annie, handing Gertie's lead to Tudor and entering her own front door. 'I'll pick her up later. Hopefully about five. Maybe I'll have a bite at your place.'

'I'll eat with you,' said Tudor, taking his leave.

As he walked away, Gertie and Rosie gamboling in front of him, Mavis pulled up in her Mini. 'Hang on a mo, Mave – got to use the you-know-what, then I'll be with you,' called Annie, running inside the cottage.

The drive to Brecon took longer than the two women had expected, or hoped. The traffic was heavy, the roads clogged with all sorts of vehicles. At least it gave Annie the chance to listen to Mavis as she sorted through her thoughts about the case.

'Maybe Althea has a point,' began Mavis, 'maybe the elderly are being bamboozled into doing something against their true wishes by a con-artist acting on behalf of the Cruickshanks. Carol's found nothing in the searches she's been able to conduct in the way of legal actions being taken against either Mountain Ash House as a corporate entity, nor the Cruickshanks personally, by any disgruntled family members of the deceased. Chancery's something of a mine-field, Carol's made that much clear. However, the fact there are no publicly available records of any such actions doesn't mean such legal cases don't exist, just that they are invisible to simple searches. To do more would require a significant investment of time, effort, and the likely requirement to spend money out-of-pocket to gain access to court records.'

'And that's a no-no for now, I'm guessing?' asked Annie when Mavis drew breath.

'Aye, for now.'

Annie listened while Mavis rattled on, informing her it was true the layers of approvals for care homes and nursing homes in the UK provided many checks and balances for such places. However, as Carol had pointed out, explained Mavis, those dwellings offering merely sheltered or communal living, where residents were perfectly capable of looking after themselves in all respects, but chose to live a more companionable lifestyle, were not subject to the same levels of oversight.

Mavis was also well aware that a last will and testament properly drawn up to respect the wishes of a person possessed of mental clarity as defined and agreed by a medical practitioner was difficult to overcome, so a quick meeting with a solicitor might well put a family member off taking any action. She told Annie she'd been impressed by Carol's thoroughness in contacting all the Citizens Advice Bureaus in the region to ask if they'd been approached by anyone wishing to make an informal, or formal, complaint about Mountain Ash House. There had been none.

Mavis then went on to explain how she knew only too well how hospitals, clinics and even barracks thrived on whispers, rumors and gossip. There was no reason to doubt an old folks' home would be any different – and Althea would have access to all that while in her disguise. '*Gladys Pugh*,' concluded Mavis. 'Althea really has thrown herself into her role.'

At this point Annie dared a quick, 'I bet she's lovin' every minute of it,' much to Mavis's consternation.

Mavis then moved to the matter of Daisy Drayton's death, much though she said she didn't want to contemplate it as suspicious at all. Despite Althea's insights having possibly established that Daisy Drayton had died at a local hospital rather than at the home, Carol hadn't, sadly, been able to make any further progress, there not being any death records for a D. Drayton anywhere in Powys at any point during the past ten years. That *was* a puzzle. And annoying too. As Mavis said, the woman was dead, that much was clear, but where or when exactly she'd died was a mystery, as were any intentions she'd put into her will. If only they could somehow find that, they'd know if she'd bequeathed the books with the valuable miniatures to the Cruickshanks. Mavis hoped the dowager's continuing enquiries, however bizarrely carried out, would yield some results on that front.

When they finally arrived in Brecon they found it difficult to park, so ended up walking more than a mile to get to the antiques market itself, by which time several of the stallholders were packing up. Deciding it was best to split up, Mavis and Annie applied themselves to their task, and met up again half an hour later to compare notes.

'This one—' Annie gave Mavis a business card – 'he's been buying china from Fred Cruickshank. The dealer's specialty is Gaudy Welsh Pottery. Hideous, if you ask me, but it seems to be all the rage. And he does crystal too, but they haven't had much of that. This stuff, though it looks 'orrible, can be worth quite a bit, he said. And this woman—' she passed another card to Mavis – 'also deals only with Mr Cruickshank and he's been bringing her silver. Bits and pieces, all sorts, for about nine months. None of them here had seen Sarah Cruickshank at all, and nothing of Fred much before that timeframe either. Everyone said they knew him, but not her. Didn't have anything bad to say about him, though I got the impression Fred's seen as a firm negotiator.'

'Good job, Annie. It sounds as though he'd come with a variety of pieces to sell each time. If you're telling me he's sold specialist pottery and silver, you can add furniture through this chap—' she showed Annie a business card – 'and decorative items like mirrors, figurines, that sort of thing, through these two people.'

'So only the husband's been shifting valuables.'

'Exactly,' agreed Mavis. 'The wife's been giving away little bits of bric-a-brac, here and there, clothes and books included, while he's been selling what sounds to be a fair amount, and certainly for a good bit of money. And that side of it started when that Tristan

Thomas went out of business. So maybe the idea Fred Cruickshank was selling Thomas a whole range of items before that holds water.'

'So – back to Anwen?' asked Annie, hoping the answer was yes.

'Aye, let's get you back to your Tudor Evans,' replied Mavis with a smile.

'I keep tellin' you, he's not *my* Tudor Evans.'

Mavis marched off in the direction of the car park. Annie caught up with her and linked arms with her friend and colleague, an inexplicable lightness in her step.

TWENTY-EIGHT

C hristine was pleased to be back in her car and heading away from Swansea prison. She'd felt more depressed in the past couple of hours than ever before in her life. The sound of the outer door shutting behind her had been the last straw, and she'd allowed herself to have a good cry before getting ready for the drive back.

Heading out toward the M4 she realized she was passing a site Lizzie Llewellyn had portrayed in one of the miniatures, Swansea University's new Bay Campus. On not much more than a whim she turned off the main road and decided to stop to take a look at the Great Hall and compare it with Lizzie's interpretation of it. She marveled that the woman had managed to pack so much detail into such a tiny piece of art, and realized, as she compared that specific miniature to some of the others that, to be fair, Nathaniel had made a valid point – some of Lizzie's pieces were, by comparison, a little less rigorous. The campus ran all the way down to meet the beach, and Christine gave herself permission to go for a stroll beyond the imposing buildings onto the wooden walkway that meandered among the dunes. The wind buffeted her, blowing away the stench of the prison, and she realized how grateful she was to be able to be mistress of her own fate – to be able to do as she pleased. To be free.

Turning her back to the sea she looked up at the edifice constructed on what she knew had once been an industrial site – plaques had greeted her describing how the land had been reclaimed and gifted to the university. As she stood there reading about exactly how the project had been undertaken, something niggled at the back of her brain. She returned to her car and pulled out the artwork created by Lizzie Llewellyn, then she looked at the building itself. Again she was struck by the perfection of the rendition, but she was tingling with another realization: the building hadn't been completed until a year after Lizzie's presumed death. How, then, had the artist managed to do what she'd done, if she was dead at the time?

TWENTY-NINE

When Carol sat down to watch Althea's filmed output again, she could see she was only about five minutes behind the live feed.

At first, all Carol got was white noise and a black screen. Knocking sounds and bizarre images led her to believe Althea had the phone in her pocket. Carol wondered if the dowager had pressed the 'broadcast' button by mistake, but a moment later it became clear that was not the case.

Carol worked out that Althea was holding the phone in her hands, probably in her lap, but certainly beneath a table. When Althea didn't fiddle with it, Carol could hear quite clearly, even if all she could see were fingers and a lump of wood. The conversation seemed to make no sense at first.

A man's voice said loudly, 'If you're having problems I can come there.'

Was Althea in trouble?

Gladys replied very loudly, 'Just speak up more.'

Althea's not deaf.

'Maybe I can fix it,' offered the man, speaking slowly.

'I've killed it completely this time,' said Althea.

Killed what?

'Is there some other way I can help?' Carol thought he sounded cross.

'I tell you what, I'll plug in my headphone things and you can talk into this – that usually does it.' Carol gathered Althea was pushing headphones into her phone, then she stuck it right in front of the man's face. Carol recognized him; it was the William Williams she'd been able to find listed as an office manager at the partnership in Brecon for whom the Cruickshanks had furnished a testimonial. He looked slightly less polished than in his online photograph.

'So what do I do now?' he shouted into the camera.

'No need to shout,' said Gladys in her normal tone, 'this amplifies it for me and I'm recording you, so I can listen to everything again later on. I can hear you properly now. Just talk normally.'

'Looks like it's a camera too,' said William, peering into the tiny lens.

'It is, do you mind?'

'Not really.'

'Good. I'm only using it to listen. I can see you very well. Just hold it in front of your mouth and speak. Now, what did you say about elephants?'

Carol could only see the man's lips, so had no idea what the rest of his face was doing, but even his mouth looked puzzled. 'Elephants? I don't think I mentioned elephants at all Mrs Pugh.'

'You said elephants were going on a date. Made no sense to me, that's why I remember it.'

The man's mouth pursed, then smiled. 'Oh – I think you must have misheard me saying your inheritance would go to the state. That's what I said; if you don't have a proper will, the state will take all your belongings, and all your money too, so it's worth spending a little bit now on getting your papers in order.'

'And if I move in here, does that advice come free with my rent?' Carol liked the way Althea was playing dumb.

William shook his head. 'No, but I can draw up the papers for a small fee. After you've given some thought as to what arrangements you'd like, of course. None of us is getting any younger, you know.'

'I don't think you could,' said Althea.

'Pardon?'

'You're very young. Young to be a solicitor. I thought you had to go to university for donkeys' years for that. How old are you then?'

The man smiled. 'Older than I look,' he said. 'I've always had a baby face, my mam says. I've been at the solicitors' office five years now.' Carol noted the fact he didn't say he *was* a solicitor, just that he worked at a solicitors' office. She didn't like the fact he was so careful about exactly what he said. It made Carol feel as though he knew he was skating on thin ice.

'I see,' said Althea. Carol wondered if she'd picked up on that little nugget too, and suspected she had; she'd admired Althea's sharpness since they'd first met, and loved the way it mingled happily with moments of utter vagueness.

Carol heard pages turning, and worked out Althea was looking through a brochure. 'It's very nicely printed. Big type. I like that.'

'We do our best.' *Smarmy*, thought Carol.

'Are the people in these photos of Mountain Ash House real residents here, or did you rent them for the day? I haven't seen any of these people. Do they live here in the basement or something?'

'The photographs were taken some years ago now. I believe they've all . . . left.'

'You mean they're all dead.'

Carol saw the man's Adam's apple slide up and down as he swallowed, hard. 'Some have moved to facilities where nursing care is available. Others have passed.'

'Passed?' Althea snapped. 'Stupid word to use. Passed what? Passed an exam? Passed out? Passed on – to where? When you're dead, you're dead. Use the *right* word. Trust me, when you've been a widow as long as I've been one you know exactly what "dead" means. It means gone.'

The camera jiggled as the man shifted in his seat. 'Some prefer the use of the word "passed" and I find I have to be very careful when I speak of death; it's a delicate matter.'

'It's how you make your money though, isn't it? Wills, bequests, plans for what should happen at a funeral. I bet you milk us for all we're worth.'

Careful, Althea, thought Carol.

'I'd hate to have it perceived that way. We provide essential services at a fair price. That's how I'd put it.'

'Ah well, there you are then. And if I come to live here, and if you help me with my will, what would you say if I told you I've already decided everything's going to the RSPCA?'

The man smiled. Carol didn't like this smile. 'It's a very wise choice, Mrs Pugh. It's a well-respected charity doing marvelous things for animals all around the country. Of course, being Welsh, you might want to consider giving your money to something that's just Welsh – you know, benefitting Wales alone, as opposed to

Scotland, or *England*.' Carol noted he uttered the word as though he was mentioning Hades. 'That's where they spend most of their cash, you see.'

'Is it?'

'Oh yes.'

'I had no idea.'

Neither did Carol, so she allowed her fingers to do some keyboard-digging into the matter. She immediately discovered the RSPCA had no standing in Scotland, there being a Scottish SPCA to do the job there. *So he's prepared to tell actual lies*, she thought. *Interesting.*

'I'm sure I could find something closer to home that would be ideal,' he said, smiling. 'Now let me guess – you'd be a cat person, am I right?'

'Dogs. Can't stand cats. Allergic. They have their place, but that's living outside catching mice and rats. No place for cats, a house.'

Carol looked across her sitting room at her beloved Bunty, fast asleep on a magazine that lay open on the floor. She knew Althea was play-acting, but whispered how much she loved Bunty, just in case she'd heard, despite Carol's headphones.

'Dogs then, very good. I could have a check around. There – see? I'm already offering good advice.'

'I suppose you are. It could be handy having you so close, if I come to live here.'

'Indeed. I could also talk to you about how you might want your inheritance to benefit humans, as well as dogs. They have an excellent trust fund set up here, for example, to allow for those less fortunate to enjoy the comforts of Mountain Ash House.'

So it's a real scheme? I wonder who controls the funds within it? Carol began to search for details of the fund, and the trustees.

'That sounds like a very good idea,' said Althea brightly. 'I mean, I love dogs, but people are nice too. I'm very lucky I've got so much, see. Even if I'm here twenty years, there'll still be a lot left.'

With the camera so close to the man's mouth, Carol was treated to the sight of William Williams licking his lips. He did it discreetly, but on her monitor it looked disgusting. She pulled back from the screen and let out an 'Eww!'

'Is that fund thing in this brochure?' asked Althea.

Things got fuzzy as Carol inferred William was turning pages for Althea. 'There you are – that bit mentions it.'

'So is it some sort of charity? This place can't be a charity, surely? They must make money at it, or why would they do it? So there's another "bit" is there?'

Carol spotted an insincere smile. 'It's all rather complicated – trust funds, escrow accounts, trustees, legatees, beneficiaries . . . and I could go on. That's what I do, you see, I streamline everything. All you do is tell me what you want, I write it up in plain English – or Welsh, if you prefer, our services are bilingual – and then you just sign it, get it witnessed and you're all sorted. Simple. You don't want these decisions hanging over your head. Best to do it, then forget about it, wouldn't you say?'

'Maybe. I'll think about it. Can I keep this?'

'But of course. You don't happen to have any other legal or financial advisors you'd like another copy for, do you?'

Clever way to find out if a person has other advisors he has to work around, thought Carol.

'There's no one. All my money's in a bank, safe, not floating about all airy fairy on the stock exchange, thank you very much. It's real money, in a real bank. And there it will stay.'

'Ah yes, the power of cash. You're right, it's a challenge to find safe places to invest one's money so it can grow safely. Mind you, if we meet again, there are a few people I could put you in touch with who specialize in just that sort of thing; investments that are as safe as houses, with an excellent, guaranteed rate of return – and it wouldn't hurt to know you'd be leaving even more behind, while not risking your present-day comfort.'

'All over my head.'

'Ah well, that's the beauty of it, see, I would only refer you to people who, like me, talk straight and don't make it all too complicated.'

'That would be helpful.'

'I know many of the residents here over the years have found it to be so.'

'Did you advise a previous resident by the name of Daisy? I believe she left all her worldly goods to this place.'

Carol wished she could see more than the man's mouth, which smiled rather too brightly. 'Maybe, maybe not. It's difficult for me to recall all the lovely ladies I've worked with here over the years. But time is pressing on, Mrs Pugh, so I'll say cheerio now then. I don't want to keep you, and I think you mentioned you were due to have a cup of tea with some ladies under the trees outside any minute now.'

'Ta for talking into my thingy. It made it much easier on me. You're very kind.'

'Kindness doesn't cost anything, Mrs Pugh. I hope to see you here next time I call, when maybe you'll be their newest resident.'

'We'll see. It's very nice here. Everyone's very friendly.'

'So are you, Mrs Pugh. 'Till next time then.'

After he'd left, Carol heard Althea say aloud, 'I feel I need a bath. That odious little man is an out and out crook. Investments that are safe with guaranteed returns, my eye! When you hear this, Carol, please phone me at your earliest convenience. It's not urgent, but I would like a little chat, please. Telephone the house itself, not this mobile phone. I want them to know I've had a caller. Say you're a friend of a friend. Use the name Carol.' She tittered. 'Oh, you know what I mean. All this cloak-and-dagger stuff quite gets under one's skin. Thanks.' The recording stopped.

Carol walked through to see David and Albert; they were both fast asleep on the sofa, David curled around Albert, protecting him from falling off the edge. She pulled her phone from her pocket and snapped a few photos. Such precious moments, and now they were captured forever. She wouldn't disturb them – Albert would wake when he needed something.

THIRTY

Carol cursed inwardly when her phone rang in her pocket, and she scuttled away so as not to disturb her sleeping son and husband. Shutting the door behind her she hissed, 'Yes?'

'It's me, Christine.'

'Hiya, how's it going? How was the prison? Have you been yet?'

'Yes, I've been. But that's not why I'm phoning. I need your help. Can you give me a hand, please?'

Even though she knew her friend couldn't see her, Carol smiled. 'Of course I'll do what I can. What's up?'

Several moments later Carol's fingers were doing what they were best at – flying across the keyboard, hunting out the answers to questions that would, hopefully, fuel her colleagues' investigations.

Finding a tattoo artist in London's Soho named Baz wasn't quite as easy as she'd hoped, but, by burrowing about in a few online forums where 'ink' was what it was all about, she finally achieved her goal. She was able to text a name and address to Christine, knowing her colleague would be following through as soon as she reached London, which was where she was heading. Carol took enormous comfort, and pride, in the fact Christine had had such confidence in her ability that she'd simply told Carol she'd pick up the address from her phone when she stopped at the Heston services just before hitting the last part of her trip.

Then Carol turned her attention to the construction timeline of the Swansea University Bay Campus, and especially the Great Hall, as Christine had asked. She gathered together all the artists' impressions of the building prior to its construction that had been commissioned by the architects and project-management company, as well as photographs of the finished building, and Lizzie's drawing of the place. She was elated to discover Christine had been correct – unless Lizzie Llewellyn had seen the completed building, her representation of it wouldn't have been what it was: slight differences existed between what had been envisaged and what had been built. Carol sent her confirmation to Christine, then took a few moments to think about what it all meant.

If Lizzie Llewellyn had really created the miniature portraying the building, she had to have been alive when it was finished – long after the date when she was presumed to have been killed. Carol allowed herself to imagine how she and her colleagues would be lauded for rescuing a man from a prison cell where he languished, convicted of a murder that hadn't been committed . . . at least, it hadn't been committed when it was supposed to have happened. Then she realized that fact raised some troubling questions in itself. If Lizzie Llewellyn hadn't been killed when everyone believed she had been – where was she? And why hadn't she come forward when her brother was convicted of her murder?

Had Lizzie, as her brother had always claimed, simply walked out of his cottage that fateful day, and maybe left the country by some means where her passport hadn't been recorded as being used – Carol's reading had told her the authorities had checked that at the time. Even so, because of Nathaniel's high public profile, the story had made headlines around the world. Could Lizzie be hiding out in such a remote place she'd failed to hear about her brother's fate? Or could it be some sort of dreadful plan she'd hatched to ruin her brother's life? Carol couldn't imagine that being the case. Such a level of vindictiveness was beyond reason. The impact such actions would have on her mother alone, let alone her brother, would mean Lizzie would have to be more than heartless to do such a thing.

And what about all that blood? Carol picked up the phone and spoke to Mavis. She wanted the opinions and insights of an experienced nurse on matters pertaining to how much blood a person could lose without becoming debilitated, or dying. When she hung up she sat clicking the end of her pen for some time – something that always helped her think.

THIRTY-ONE

'I'm so pleased we're sitting together for dinner, Gladys, I thought you were avoiding me. They say such horrible things about me here – but there, I should expect nothing less of this lot. All a load of ill-bred know-it-alls. Common as muck, some of them. Now tell me, my dear, where do your people come from? I heard they were in trade – but there's trade, and *trade*. I'm sure you know what I mean.'

Althea, Dowager Duchess of Chellingworth, stared across the dining table at Sylvia Trumbell and carefully weighed her response. It was true she'd been warned off the woman she was about to dine with – by pretty much everyone – but she had admitted to herself that, in a place like Mountain Ash House, gossip could run amok and reputations become sullied for no real reason, so she'd joined her with an open mind. However, having spent only three minutes alone with Sylvia so far, she had to admit the woman had already marked herself as a snob of the worst type, and the possessor of an acid tongue.

'My parents owned an ironmongers shop in Tenby,' replied Gladys, sticking to her cover story. She couldn't help but add, 'I'm not sure how you'd categorize that sort of trade.'

Sylvia pursed her mouth as she considered her response; the deep wrinkles around her lips suggested it was something she did a good deal, and had done for many years. Althea thought her mouth looked mean, and wondered what Carol would be making of it back in Anwen-by-Wye on her computer screen.

'Not the sort of thing there's much call for these days, with all these giant American-style warehouses selling all sorts, I'd have thought. And your husband? Dead, I assume. What did he do? Made a good living, did he?'

Althea noted the fingernails filed to rounded points, and the pastel pink nail varnish carefully applied. Sylvia was the only woman at the home who wore make-up, had her hair colored and styled and attended to her hands. *All the better to show off her collection of stone-encrusted rings, earrings and bracelets.*

'He was a farmer, of sorts,' said Althea – not altogether untruthfully – thinking of the six-thousand-acre Chellingworth estate. 'And we rented out a few properties on our land.' That allowed for the entire village of Anwen-by-Wye.

Sylvia shook her head. 'That must have been a hard life for you,' she said. 'Don't make any money at all, do they? Farmers, I mean. And to earn a living as a landlord? Well, you've got to be hard as nails and keep your costs down. Like the Cruickshanks do here. Good business heads, they've got, I'll give them that. How did you find this place?'

Althea steeled herself. 'Through an old friend, Daisy Drayton. Did you know her?'

Sylvia's eyes narrowed. 'Knew a Daisy Davies.'

Althea wondered if Daisy Davies and Daisy Drayton might be one and the same. Perhaps her old acquaintance had remarried. It would certainly go a long way to explaining why Carol hadn't been able to find any recorded death of a Daisy Drayton.

'A right old fusspot, she was,' continued Sylvia with a look on her face that suggested she'd been sucking a lemon. 'Always going on about horses. That's all in the past, I told her. She carried on as though she'd won the Olympics or something.'

Almost certain they were speaking about the Daisy she was interested in, Althea said, 'The Daisy I knew always rode well. I'd lost touch with her in recent years. I don't suppose you recall how things were for her . . . at the end? One of your fellow residents seemed to think the Daisy who lived here was called Drayton.' Althea made her face look sad when she spoke. She hoped it would work.

'You mean Iris? Dumb as a bag of hair, that one. Daisy was Davies, not Drayton, in the end. And how did she die? You're a bit gruesome, aren't you? I don't know the details, so I can't tell you. All I know is an ambulance took her away from here, and she never came back. They usually don't. Even if they're chucked out of the hospital – which they seem to do two minutes after you can manage to get along without all the machines they attach to you these days – they get packed off to a proper nursing home. When you asked if you could record this, is it because you've got dementia? They won't take you here with that, you know. You'd be a danger to yourself and others. It's best if you let them lock you up if you've got that.'

Althea struggled to hold onto her temper. 'I'm perfectly well, thank you,' she replied coolly. 'I don't have a good head for lots of details, and I knew I'd be trying to take in such a huge amount of new information over just a few days I wanted the chance to look back on it in the weeks to come when I'm making a decision.'

'Not a bad idea,' conceded Sylvia. Althea suspected this was a great compliment, coming from the hyper-critical woman. 'You could do worse than this place, I suppose. They don't stint on the food and the jaunts are pretty good. Fred's a card, right enough; always helps jolly us along. We're all off to the Chellingworth Summer Fete next weekend. Will you still be here then? You could come with us.'

Althea didn't panic, she simply replied, 'I'll have left before then, but I might see you there in any case. Have you been before? Is it fun?'

Again Sylvia pursed her mean little mouth. 'I suppose it's better than being stuck here all day with this lot,' she began, casting her eyes about the dining room disdainfully. 'Though I think the fete is just an excuse for the toffs at the hall to lord it over us peasants,' she added.

'Toffs?' dared Althea.

Sylvia leaned in. 'The dowager, and her son, the duke. They say she was a dancer when she managed to get the old duke to marry her.' She leaned in further. 'What sort of dancer, nobody knows.' She pursed her lips and raised her eyebrows to convey exactly what sort of dancer she imagined the dowager to have been. 'Common as muck, in any case, I heard. And the son was off swanning around the world pretending to be an artist when his father died.

Chellingworth Hall itself is falling to pieces, they say. All her fault, I should think. Not born to it, see. Not up to the job.'

Althea gritted her teeth and ventured, 'Really? Do you know her well?'

Sylvia gave the matter some thought. 'Not well but, you know, to say hello to. I hear the new duchess is the daughter of some sort of used car dealer, so it sounds like the duke's new wife is like his mother: a gold-digger.'

Althea tried her best to sound vague when she replied, 'I heard the duchess's father was a lumber merchant, but, maybe those two things are much the same.'

'Cars. Wood. What does it matter? Probably a spiv of some sort. I wonder if she'll shunt the older one out of the picture now? I hear she's about ninety.'

Althea couldn't resist. 'I thought you said you knew the dowager. Does she look ninety?'

Sylvia had the good grace to blush as she replied, 'Hard to tell with women once they reach a certain age, isn't it? She should be pretty well-kept really. Probably not done much her whole life, you know, being waited on hand and foot.'

Althea wanted to get up and leave, but dug deep and pushed on. 'Daisy didn't wear well, I understand. Someone told me she'd broken her neck, poor thing. Lucky she could walk at all, I suppose.'

'Well, if a person will go riding around on horses, what can they expect? She managed well enough. Always moaning, though. Some do. Some of us just put up with it. If she'd only had my headaches to contend with – now that's something I never mention, my headaches.'

Althea didn't bite. 'She died in hospital, you say. Do you recall when that was by any chance?'

Sylvia's eyebrows lifted. 'Want to crow about outliving her? That's a common enough pastime hereabouts.'

'I wasn't thinking of that,' replied Althea smoothly. 'I wondered if I could find out where she was laid to rest so I could pay my respects, if I'm able.'

'No idea where she ended up. Died on January 13th this year. I remember because it was my late husband's birthday.'

Althea was delighted to get some concrete information. 'Well maybe I can look it up somewhere then. If I at least know Daisy

Davies died on January 13th at a hospital in Powys, I should be able to track her down.'

'Well, you won't find her as Daisy, will you?' Sylvia looked even more smug than she had before. Althea was surprised, because she hadn't thought it possible. 'I thought you said you knew her. Can't have known her very well if you didn't even know her proper name.'

Althea was puzzled. 'How d'you mean?'

'Daisy wasn't her *real* name. Not even one of her middle names. Honoria she was. Now let me think about the whole thing for a minute – a lot of names she had.' Althea watched with as much patience as she could summon. Finally Sylvia looked triumphant. 'Honoria Estella Sophronia Dickens was her full birth name. We talked about it – seems her father was nuts about Charles Dickens, which I suppose is understandable. I've never understood what everyone saw in his books, myself. They're all so depressing. Full of the most horrible, unwashed people with wretched lives. All her real first names were from his characters. Daisy was what she was nick-named as a baby, and it stuck, she said.' Sylvia looked triumphant.

Althea smiled. 'It could have been worse; they might have named her Fagin or Fezziwig, I suppose.' Sylvia's face suggested it wouldn't have been much worse. 'I had no idea about Daisy's given names. How interesting. Thank you. That should help with my enquiries.'

'Enquiries? You sound like someone who's plodding through a detective novel,' said Sylvia, pushing away the bowl which had contained a satisfying beef stew.

Althea laughed off the jibe, and quickly turned the conversation to the topic of food, which she felt would be a useful diversion; if she tipped her hand to Sylvia, she might not get much more out of the woman. Indeed, she noticed Sylvia was already giving her some odd looks, but quickly worked out it was because her wig was slipping down her forehead, so she pulled it back into place as surreptitiously as possible.

As she listened to the odious woman opposite her moan on about a litany of sleights she felt she'd been dealt by various other residents, Althea wondered how she might be able to squeeze any more information out of Sylvia. She tried to not glaze over as Sylvia took the chance of a break between courses to show off photos of her grandchildren in a thick little wallet full of pictures she produced from her handbag. Eventually Althea realized the woman was so self-absorbed she'd be unlikely to notice a direct query, so she simply asked, 'The woman you speak of, I'd like to be sure she was *my* Daisy. Do you happen to have a photograph of her?'

'I think I might have one of her and me together.' Sylvia flicked little plastic pages. 'Here we are. I think we'd been taking tea together.'

Althea looked at the photograph of a wizened creature she found it hard to recognize as the youthful, vibrant Daisy Dickens, but spotted something about the eyes that meant she knew it was the same person. And Althea fairly fizzed with joy when she saw what was on the bookshelves behind the woman's head – an entire row of large picture books about Swansea through the ages. 'Was this taken in your room?' she asked innocently.

'Oh no, I never entertain. That would have been at Daisy's.'

Althea's heart skipped a beat with excitement. 'Would you mind if I took a photo of this with my telephone's camera? I'd be ever so grateful,' said Althea in her sweetest voice. 'Something to remember her by – and you, of course – when I leave.'

'But of course,' said Sylvia, clearly flattered.

With dinner finally finished, Sylvia stood and took her leave. Althea thought it was high time to go back to her own room for a bit of peace and quiet. She admitted to herself she was missing McFli terribly, and realized she hadn't seen any pets about the place. If she needed any reason for never returning to Mountain Ash House after her undercover operation was concluded, that would be it – no pets allowed, and her not able to leave her beloved McFli. She remained at the empty table long enough to send the photo she'd just taken and Daisy's full name to Carol, then she pulled herself to her feet and waved her farewells to the folks still enjoying after-dinner chats in the dining room.

As she made her way toward the staircase that would take her to the privacy of her room, Fred Cruickshank appeared at Althea's left elbow, 'Ah, there you are, Mrs Pugh. I understand you've been having a good old chat with several of our residents, and you even managed to spend a little time with one of our advisors, Mr Williams, this afternoon. He told me you were asking after one of our previous residents, a lady by the name of Daisy. Now would that be Daisy Davies, I wonder?'

Althea smiled, despite an odd feeling of apprehension. 'Yes, it would be, though I must admit I only just discovered she'd remarried toward the end of her life. For the third time, would you believe it, Mr Cruickshank.'

'Always was a lively one, was our Daisy,' said the man with a cold grin. 'I wonder if you'd like to join me in the office for a little bit of a catch-up.'

Althea didn't fancy the idea at all, but it was clear to her she had no choice in the matter.

THIRTY-TWO

Christine's Range Rover darted through the rush hour traffic crawling around Hyde Park Corner as fast as she dared push it. She leaned on her horn as some idiot in a Smart car crawled along at about two miles an hour in front of her, to no effect. As she avoided tourists scampering across the road in the most dangerous of spots, she couldn't help but wonder what she'd find in Soho.

She used the underground car park in Chinatown she knew was the best spot for accessing the West End, and headed toward the address on Greek Street Carol had sent her. The shop-front didn't look particularly salubrious, but she walked in, her head held high and ready to face whatever might be thrown her way.

She was surprised to discover a very pleasant set-up with no horrible sounds or smells, and not so much as a hint of large, bare-chested – or worse – bikers, which was what she'd feared. Instead, a petite Indonesian woman greeted Christine with a bow.

A little flummoxed by this greeting, Christine explained she was hoping to see Baz.

'He is with client. Will be for next hour. I do not interrupt his work. He is true artist. You like tea while you wait? Or you prefer come back later?' replied the woman.

Not wanting to miss her chance to talk to Lizzie's ex, Christine agreed to tea and sat quietly.

When she pulled out her mobile phone the young woman said, 'No signal. Baz jams signal. Is not good for aura, he says.'

Christine wondered how long it would take her to drink her scalding tea so she could get to the street outside and do some work, but, since she felt she had to at least make a show of accepting the woman's hospitality she sipped it and said 'Mmm' a few times.

Ten minutes later, she was itching to know if Carol had any more news for her, and was keen to carry out a few of her own online searches. She impressed upon the woman how important it was that she spoke with Baz, and ascertained he had another four appointments that evening, so wouldn't be leaving any time soon. She realized tattoo artists didn't keep regular office, or even shop, hours and felt more comfortable in her decision to pop to the pub across the road, from where she'd be able to keep an eye on the front door of the establishment.

She ducked into the pub and ordered a bottle of fizzy water, then stood at the narrow shelf along the window, where she elbowed her way in and pulled out her phone, delighted to find she had access to Wi-Fi, though with a weak signal. Waving her phone about a bit, she wasn't prepared for what she saw across the bar. It was Alexander, and he wasn't alone. Who was he with? And what was he doing in what was, after all, a pretty seedy pub in Soho?

A large column partially blocked her view of the section of the long, narrow pub where she'd spotted him, so she sidled over to a frosted-glass divider that set one area of the bar apart from the rest. Fortunately for Christine, she managed to find an angle whereby she could see into the nook where Alexander and his companions were sitting by using the reflection in the etched glass behind the bar. There he was. He was with a trio of men; the three of them were sitting on a leather-upholstered banquette, while Alexander was perched on a small stool facing them. He had his back to the bar, and therefore to Christine, but she recognized him immediately.

Pulling out her phone and making a meal of pretending to check for messages, she snapped a few shots of the threesome. She didn't recognize any of them, but wasn't surprised about that. They were rather large men, and she had the suspicion they would all know how to handle themselves in a tight corner. The way they were dressed didn't give her any clues about their lifestyles, other than they had what seemed to be expensive-looking leather or suede jackets on the seat beside them – not something they'd really have needed, given the warmth of the day. One of them got up and headed for the loo, quickly followed by a second.

Christine smiled inwardly at the recollection of so many jokes told by men about how women always seem to use the lavatory in pairs. A few minutes later, as they were in the little vestibule area where the men's and women's facilities led into the main body of the pub, the two men paused for what they must have thought would be a moment of private conversation.

'It's not a bad offer. But I'm not sayin' yes yet. He might sweeten it a bit.' The man's rasping voice suggested too many cigarettes over decades, and the slight slurring of his words further suggested the two pints Christine had seen him drink weren't his first of the day.

The man with whom he was almost nose-to-nose shrugged his agreement.

As they settled back into their seats, Christine watched for a while, then could see all three men had reached an agreement with Alexander. Under cover of saying a fond farewell, she saw Alexander handing an envelope to the largest of the three. They left, he sat down again, and pulled out his phone to make a call.

Christine was startled when her phone rang in her pocket. She saw the word ALEX on the screen. Instinctively pulling back behind the glass screen she answered, 'Hello. Nice to hear from you.' She tried to make her voice sound as normal as possible as she hurried across the pub toward the front door.

'I'm going to be free tonight after all,' said Alexander cheerily. 'How about I pop over to yours, or would you like to meet at our little spot on Battersea High Street? I fancy a bit of Django-style music and some sinful dessert.'

Christine panicked. Silently.

It seemed Alexander took her silence as meaningful. 'Not you – I don't mean *you* as dessert. That would be presumptuous of me. I mean dessert at the restaurant.'

Uncertain of what to say, Christine allowed her mind to whirl; she told Alexander she was just about to leave her parent's house. 'I dropped in to see Mammy and stayed on for a bit longer than I'd planned. How about I meet you at the restaurant at eight?' She hoped that would give her enough time to speak to Baz, then get back to her flat and change her clothes.

'Good plan. I'll see you there, then.'

'OK, must go.' Christine cut off the call and raced across the street to the tattoo parlor.

'You return in good time. Baz is free now,' said the tiny hostess. 'Come.'

Christine was ushered into a back room filled with bizarre furnishings, most with an air of steam-punk about them. A tall, emaciated man wearing a sleeveless vest which displayed his own, impressive body-art, and with the most elaborate arrangement of facial hair Christine had ever seen, stood beside what looked like an old barber, or dentist's chair.

He grinned. All his teeth were silver. 'Hi, I'm Baz. What can I do you for?'

'I'm here about Lizzie Llewellyn,' said Christine.

'Really? I wondered when someone would show up to ask me about her. Journalist, are you, love?'

'Private investigator.' She handed him her card.

'Cor, brilliant. Go on then – grill me!' He slapped his thigh and roared with laughter. 'Seriously, have a seat and ask me whatever you want. Miss her like crazy, I do, and I don't care who knows it. Not though anyone's asked. Who told you about me?'

'Her brother.'

Baz looked shocked. 'Nathaniel?' Christine nodded. 'Didn't know he even knew about me. Terrible what he done. Can't understand it. Why would a brother do that to his sister?'

'You think he killed her?'

'Duh! The whole world thinks he did. *Knows* he did. Found him guilty and thrown away the key, they have. Why? You working for him?'

'No.' Christine didn't want to lie.

Baz's suspicious expression softened a little. 'Who then?'

'I'm not able to say.'

He picked up one of his many stainless steel tools of the trade and started spinning it between his fingers. Christine tried to work out if he was trying to intimidate her. 'But not him, himself?'

'No.'

'OK. Shoot.'

'You and Lizzie used to live together, I understand.'

'Uh huh.'

'And I also believe you were her tattoo artist.'

'Uh huh.'

Christine glanced around the artwork plastered all over the walls. 'That's one of hers, right?' She nodded at a stark scene of girders and cranes. It stood out among the variety of tigers' heads and snakes wrapped around various forms of daggers and swords.

'Uh huh.'

'We're not going to get very far if that's all you're going to say,' snapped Christine.

'I'm answering you, aren't I?'

'True. Have you seen Lizzie in the past couple of years?'

'How could I. She's dead.'

'How do you know that?'

'Look, love, detective or not, this is all rubbish. She's dead. Her brother killed her, or haven't you heard?'

'What if I suggested to you Lizzie isn't dead at all, but that she set up her brother so it looked like he killed her, then she disappeared?'

Baz put down the tool he'd been fondling and sat on a leather-topped stool beside the massive chair. He twirled the stool around, much as a child would do, spinning and smiling. His eyes grew narrow as he used his feet to stop turning. 'Is that what she's gone and done?'

'If she had, would you have any idea where she might hide out?'

Baz gave the question some thought. 'Having thought she was dead until about two minutes ago, no. But if she were to be anywhere, she'd still be making art, of that I'm certain. Obsessive is a word people bandy about these days until it's almost lost its meaning. They should have saved it up for Lizzie. Always creating, and always one for the overload, she was. Reading, headphones on, drawing over a magnifying glass all at the same time. And eating. Always eating. Like a fruit bat was Lizzie. Never without a couple of apples, an orange – something all the time. Like living in a fruit shop it was, when she was at my place.'

'Nothing else?' Christine felt defeated.

'What else do you want? I knew she hated her brother, but who wouldn't? Told me any chance he had, he slagged her off something rotten. Always talking about how her stuff was rubbish, but his was great. And that mother of hers? Undermined her every chance she got, Lizzie said. Always standing next to Nathaniel when he was pulling the cover off some great big ugly thing he'd made, but for Lizzie? Didn't even turn up at her big exhibition in London, she didn't.'

'The exhibition Jeremy Edgerton gave of Lizzie's work?'

'Yeah, that's it.'

'Her mother wasn't invited.'

Baz rolled his eyes. 'Whatever the reason, she wasn't there. Biggest night of Lizzie's career, and no one from the family there at all. Hurt her a lot, that did. I could tell. I was with her. We hadn't been together long then. Truth be told, we were only really together for a couple of months in any case. But after that exhibition? Disappeared for days, she did.' He looked at Christine with a curious gleam in his eyes. 'Yeah, disappeared for days.'

Christine recognized what she believed to be the light of recollection in the man's eyes. 'What have you just remembered, Baz?'

'It might be nothing,' he replied, his voice guarded.

'Try me.'

She could tell he was thinking about his words before he spoke them aloud. 'Came back to my place, upstairs, here, after about a week, she did. Told me she'd been to St David's. In Wales. Said she needed to be as far west as she could get. Said "West was Best." No idea what she meant.'

'St David's the place, or St David's the cathedral?'

'Same place, innit? Always going on about that part of the world. Narberth, Haverfordwest, Solva. Never been to any of them, me, but the names stick. Funny names.'

'Thanks.'

'That it? I've got a bloke coming in for a big job on his back pretty soon.'

'Just one more thing; why did you and Lizzie break up?'

Baz's face creased into a broad, rueful grin. 'You met her, outside. Tammy works here now, so we can be together all the time. We both knew it was right the minute we clapped eyes on each other. Lizzie – well, she walked in when she shouldn't have.'

'Ah. Any fireworks?'

Baz laughed aloud. 'Fireworks? Yeah, you could say that. Really breathe fire, don't they, them Welsh dragons? Well, Lizzie did, in any case. Anything not nailed down was smashed against the walls within a couple of minutes of her finding us *in flagrante delicto*, let's just say that. We hid under the bedclothes till she started grabbing all her gear and stuffing it into a bag. I won't tell you what she called us, because I'm not sure I can recall every specific term she used, but the overall sentiment was she'd never forgive either of us, and she wanted us both to suffer for our sins in every way imaginable – and then some. She left about an hour later, and the next thing I heard she'd disappeared, then they were doing her brother for killing her.

Having seen Lizzie in full dragon-mode, I remember thinking the poor bloke might have had good cause to do her in.'

Christine could tell Baz was getting a bit twitchy, and Tammy stuck her head through the door to announce Big Dave had arrived.

'We done?' asked Baz.

'Yes. Thanks.'

'So what do you reckon – she isn't dead after all? Just hidin'?'

'We'll see. Do you think she'd do that? That she'd be capable of it?'

Baz rose and stuck his hand toward Christine. 'Say hi from me if you find her. Or maybe not. Nah – on second thoughts, don't even mention my name.'

Christine left and headed along Greek Street toward the car park in Chinatown.

THIRTY-THREE

Henry Twyst regarded his sister Clementine with impatience. Nurse Thomas was beside his sibling, watching over her charge, but Clemmie was managing to walk rather well with merely the aid of a cane. He was relieved to see it, and hoped she'd be out of his hair before too long.

'There you are,' he said loudly as his sister took a seat in the drawing room. 'You're a little more mobile today, I see. Good.'

Stephanie greeted her sister-in-law with a kiss on the cheek. 'I think you're looking better all-round, Clemmie. Don't you think she's looking better, Nurse Thomas?'

'I've been sitting in the sun for a while each day,' replied Clemmie. 'It's rather pleasant. Of course, with skin like mine one does have to take great care to not overdo it.'

'Yes,' said Henry, 'one wouldn't want to lose that vampiric pallor, would one?'

'I'll have my G and T with lime, not lemon, please,' called Clemmie.

'Me too, please, Henry,' added Stephanie, and Henry prepared the pre-dinner drinks with good humor.

'For you, Nurse Thomas?'

'A plain tonic water, thank you, Your Grace.'

Soon the foursome were settled around the massive hearth, where, instead of a crackling fire they all stared at a well-buffed seventeenth-century brass coal-scuttle filled with dried wheat and poppy-heads.

'Thank you for sparing time to talk about this before dinner, Clemmie,' opened Henry. 'As you know, we'll be celebrating Mother's eightieth birthday under the public's gaze at the fete soon, though of course we'll have a private celebration on her real birthday. I thought we'd save up the proper gift-giving until then, but Stephanie has suggested it behoves both you and I to say a few words about our mother over the microphone. You know the sort of thing – address the assembled masses.'

Clemmie shifted uncomfortably in her chair. 'I hate speaking in public. You know that, Henry. You're not too keen on it yourself, as I recall. You completely fluffed that bit at your own wedding, remember?'

Henry recalled the sweaty palms, jelly knees and the un-laughing crowd only too well. 'I know, I know, but one has learned over the years that it's expected of one. And I do see my wife's point—' he smiled at Stephanie – 'she makes a good one. Mother deserves to be praised in public and it should be we, her children, who do it.'

Henry was pleased when Stephanie threw an encouraging smile toward his sister, but Clemmie was pouting. 'I wouldn't know what to say. Besides, Mother hates that sort of thing too. She'd be expected to produce some sort of a response, surely.'

Henry was grateful when Stephanie waded in with: 'Of course, I don't know all about your life with your mother as a child, but Henry has mentioned how the three of you would ride horses together and take long walks with the dogs. You know, before the two of you went off to school, and when you came home during the holidays. Maybe you could talk about that? About how she gave you a love of the countryside. The people who live around here might also recall you walking through the village. The older ones, in any case.'

'I used to hate those walks,' said Clemmie petulantly, 'and I don't love the countryside. I can't wait to get back up to London.'

'You used to enjoy painting *en plein* when you were here on the estate, Clemmie,' said Henry. 'I recall our preferred styles were somewhat at odds with each other, but I know for a fact you found inspiration here. That must have a thread back to Mother somehow.'

Clemmie was at least giving the matter some thought, which relieved Henry. 'It's true,' she said, almost grudgingly, 'when you

and I first arrived at the commune outside Arles, I recall my style
was heavily influenced by some of the members of the Cambrian
Academy. Of course, I was quickly able to rid myself of such paro-
chial influences, and fell happily into the bosom of the masters at
the commune.'

Henry bit his tongue. He knew only too well how even the most
scandalous interpretation of his sister's last statement would be correct.

'I found my own muse quickly, and followed it where it led. I
could have been a unique female voice in the world of art, you
know, Nurse Thomas,' observed Clemmie.

'I like that Lizzie Llewellyn myself – you know, the one who
was killed by her horrible brother,' pronounced the nurse, to the
surprise of all in the room. 'I'm pleased to hear they're taking down
that monstrosity he built that they plonked in the middle of Castle
Gardens, in Swansea.'

Stephanie smiled. 'If you're a lover of all things Llewellyn, you
might like to join us here before the fete, Nurse Thomas. We have
a group of experts coming in from London to look at, and hopefully
authenticate, a collection of miniatures by Lizzie, that were discovered
in some books in Hay.'

Henry was taken aback by how Nurse Thomas changed, right in
front of their eyes. She actually blushed. 'Oh, thank you, Your Grace,
but I don't know if I could. I love her stuff, yes, and I've seen a
good bit of it over the years – but to be with people whose job it
is to understand everything about it? I don't know about that.'

'You never think twice before telling me off, so why on earth
would you be nervous to meet such people?' snapped Clemmie. 'I
dare say none of them is the offspring of a duke even if they have
the odd "Sir" with them. You're quite at home here in the stately
pile; make the most of it. You could even attend *sans* uniform, then
they'd think you were one of us.'

Nurse Thomas looked scandalized. 'Now that wouldn't be proper,
Your Ladyship. That would be like lying to their faces, that would.'

Henry felt compelled to respond, 'No different than Mother
gadding about the place in that disguise of hers earlier this week,
I wouldn't have said. That was great fun, wasn't it? I say, I know
we wanted to have this chat without her being here, but has anyone
seen Mother about the place recently? It seems she's rather gone
to ground. I told the MacDonald woman I couldn't track Mother
down, and she said she'd look into it. Never told me what's what,

though. Any of you any the wiser?' Shrugs greeted his queries. 'Oh well, I'll give her a tinkle later on. Now – can we please make some plans about who will say what, for how long, and when? I expect that's all you need to know for now, isn't it, dear?'

Stephanie agreed it would be enough to be going on with, 'Tudor Evans was voted by the committee as the person who should speak about the dowager's role in the community through the decades.' Henry saw his wife wince as she spoke.

'Was it a difficult decision, dear?' he asked as soothingly as possible.

Stephanie forced a smile. 'We had to have a secret ballot to choose whether he or Marjorie Pritchard should do it. It was a tie; it shouldn't have been possible, but it was a meeting when Mr Probert was ill, so we had an even number around the table. It meant I had to cast the deciding vote. I'll be honest, I didn't know what to do for the best – whatever I said I was going to displease half the people in the room.'

'But you voted for Tudor Evans in any case?' asked Henry.

Stephanie blushed. 'I tossed a coin.'

'Best thing for it,' commented Nurse Thomas.

Stephanie rallied. 'What it means is that you can focus on speaking about your mother as your mother, rather than in her role as duchess, dowager or local benefactor. I'm sure Tudor will do a good job of covering all that side of things. And I have a plan for a few surprise guests up my sleeve too.'

THIRTY-FOUR

Friday 27th June

Christine padded around the kitchen of her Battersea flat making coffee as quietly as possible. She didn't want to wake Alexander. She opened the door to her tiny balcony and stepped out into the cool morning air, the buzz of traffic on the road in the background, her thoughts filling her head with a dizzying set of conundrums.

Neither she nor Alexander had mentioned his meeting in Soho the previous evening, and she'd been unable to talk to him about the Llewellyn case, so conflicted was she about her thinking. Instead they'd 'enjoyed' small talk and dinner, then had drifted to sleep in each others' arms, as though all was right with the world, when Christine knew everything was very wrong.

'I brought my own,' said Alexander as he joined Christine on the balcony with a mug of coffee. 'Penny for them?'

'It's this case,' lied Christine. She hurriedly tidied away her concerns about the type of men to whom she'd seen Alexander hand what was undoubtedly an envelope full of cash the previous evening.

'Tell me about it. Maybe I can help.'

Staring him down, Christine asked, 'Do you understand hate, Alexander?'

He placed his mug on the wrought-iron tabletop. 'That's a big question for so early in the morning. Why do you ask?'

'I'm trying to work out if a sister could hate her brother so much she'd fake her own death just so he'd be convicted of her murder, or if a brother could hate his sister so much he'd actually kill her.'

Alexander sipped his coffee. 'Which one of them loves their mother the most?'

Christine nodded. 'That's what I'm trying to work out, too.'

'When you do, I think you'll have your answer.'

'You're right.'

'As always. You left out "as always" at the end of that statement.' Alexander threw Christine his most winning smile.

Did I? she thought as she sipped her own coffee, smiling and winking.

Alexander let it pass. 'So, what will you do about it?'

'I have to make some phone calls, then get on the road to Wales.'

'How can I help?'

'Let me get on with it alone?'

'You mean leave?'

'Do you mind?'

'I always mind leaving you. It's easier when I know we have a plan to be together again.'

'I have to do this alone.'

'You'll call me? We'll make a date?'

'I will. We shall.'

Alexander leaned forward and kissed the top of Christine's head. 'I'll be gone in five minutes.'

'Thanks.'

THIRTY-FIVE

Carol lay in the bath and lazily drizzled hot water from a sponge over her belly. Her body would never be the same again, she knew that much, but at least it had done something useful – it had created Albert. She'd been a 'chubby little girl,' then a 'youngster with big bones' and had finally grown into 'a substantial woman.' She knew pretty much every euphemism for 'overweight' that existed.

Hauling herself out of the indulgent early-morning soak she'd been able to enjoy because of David's work schedule, she told herself she was living the life she'd dreamed of having; a loving husband, a healthy son, a wonderful home in rural Wales and, to top it all, a form of employment that not only allowed her to use her brain and skills, but also to do good for other people.

She perked up a bit as she massaged the stretch marks on her belly with some oil Annie's mother Eustelle had sent from London, claiming it would work wonders. Carol suspected it was no more than scented coconut oil, but she did as instructed and dutifully rubbed it for a few minutes, then wiped it off with a cotton cloth. Eustelle had been most insistent about the cloth being cotton.

By the time she presented herself, pink and glowing, in the kitchen, the place was empty. David had written a message on the kitchen's blackboard to say he and Albert were off for a walk along the riverbank to see the ducks at the millpond, and Carol noted Bunty had installed herself beside the Aga, her favorite spot. She tidied around a little, but realized she had some work to do, and would need to pull on some tidy clothes and be ready for a Skype meeting at 10 a.m. with her colleagues. By the time Mavis called, she was raring to go. Annie and Mavis were at the office with McFli and Gertie, while Carol squished her feet in her slippers under her own kitchen table and Christine was using the speakerphone in her vehicle.

Mavis called the meeting to order and invited Carol to speak.

She began, 'Thanks to some excellent work by Althea yesterday, I have been able to establish that Honoria Estella Sophronia Davies died on January 12th this year. Her will is being held at the probate registry in Cardiff. I've ordered a copy online and it should be with us in no more than ten working days.'

'Why can't they just email it when you ask for it, like everything else in the world these days?' asked Annie. 'You can order it online, why don't it just show up right away?'

'Procedures,' replied Carol.

'Just another way for people to get all puffed up about their self-importance,' said Annie. 'Ah well, we'll have it soon enough, I s'pose. Then we can find out if she did leave everything to the Cruickshanks and we can be sure Bryn and Val really own the books that are going to be worth a fortune. Right?'

Mavis agreed. 'It's a pity we couldn't have found out about "Daisy's" real names earlier and therefore have had that information before the meeting at the Chellingworth fete. Might it speed things along if someone popped into the office in Cardiff and had a wee word with the good people who work there, do you think?'

All the eyes on her screen – including those of the two dogs in the distant barn – focused on Carol. She shrugged. 'I can't imagine it would make any difference at all. But if someone wants to volunteer to go there, then I don't see that it can do any harm.'

'Do you want me to swing by there on my way back from London?' asked Christine. 'If you text me the address I could be there in a couple of hours. Is it right in the middle of Cardiff? The traffic could be a bit of a challenge on a Friday.'

'It's at the Magistrates' Court there. I'll dig out the exact address and get it to you. Thanks for that,' said Carol.

'Good for you, Chrissy, or should we call you Mobile Unit One?' mugged Annie.

'I feel a bit like it,' said Christine heavily. 'I've put a few miles on this beast in the past couple of weeks, that's for sure. Anyway, it's all worth it to help people. Speaking of which, kudos to Althea. I've gathered from various messages she went undercover at the old folks' home and dug up some useful information. Good for her. What's she up to now? Coming back to the fold today?'

'She told me in a text she was planning an early night last night,' said Carol, 'and today she's going to be rehearsing for her bit at tonight's performance at the home. By the way, we're all invited, and I think we should all go to support her. It could be quite amusing to see Althea, as Gladys Pugh, reciting Dylan Thomas's *Fern Hill*.'

'Ha! OK – I'll try to make it,' said Christine.

'Bringing Alexander?' asked Annie as though butter wouldn't melt in her mouth.

'No,' replied Christine simply.

'I hope Althea treats herself to a wee lie-in,' commented Mavis. 'She did a very good job yesterday, whatever misgivings I might have had, so she's due a bit of a rest. I have an appointment with one of the partners at the legal firm in Brecon where that slippery Mr William Williams works today, but I should be back in plenty of time to collect you, Annie, to take you along. Unless you'd rather have Carol give you a lift? What time does it all start, Carol?'

'The concert party starts at six, but there's tea beforehand, from four onwards. We could all get there for about four thirty, how would that suit? See how your meeting goes, Mavis, and we can decide later who'll give Annie a lift, OK?'

Everyone agreed.

'There we are then,' pronounced Mavis. 'I'm tied up today, and Christine's also spoken for, so what will you be filling your day with, Annie, my dear, and you, Carol?'

'Before we get too bogged down, I want us to make a group judgement call,' said Christine. 'Carol, have you brought Mavis and Annie up to date with all our findings about Lizzie Llewellyn?'

Carol replied, 'I've sent the package of information I gathered after we spoke yesterday. Everyone should have the photos of the building Lizzie couldn't have drawn if she died when she's supposed to have done. Is there anything else?'

Christine told her colleagues about her meeting with Baz the tattoo artist. She didn't mention the reason she hadn't typed everything up the previous evening was because she'd been having a strained dinner-date with Alexander.

Mavis was the first to speak. 'I know we're all now thinking there's a much greater chance that Nathaniel Llewellyn did not, in fact, kill his sister at the time he was supposed to have done, but I must say, Christine, this further insight into the girl's character does make me wonder if she's got it in her to have planned the whole charade just to be cruel.'

'Seems like she'd have to be completely barking mad to do it,' said Annie. 'Vindictiveness on steroids.'

Mavis responded, 'I think we should now consider calling on the

police in the matter of the Lizzie Llewellyn case. Would you no'
agree, ladies?'

Carol held her breath before she answered, counting to five. 'I
see why you say that, but I don't know what we've really got to
give them, Mavis. I know we've got the miniature that is supposedly
by Lizzie's hand of a building that didn't look exactly the way she's
drawn it until after she was presumed to be dead. And she seems
to be a person with a wicked temper. But listen to what I just said
– "supposedly," "presumed" and "seems." I know you're the one
who's presented our cases to the local constabulary in the past,
Mavis, and maybe they'd give our suppositions a bit more weight
than others would. But this case doesn't fall within their jurisdiction.
You'd have to deal with the people at HQ in Bridgend, I think. Or
maybe the CID people in Swansea? I'm not sure. Let me check on
that.'

'Hold your horses,' said Annie. 'I don't think we go to the police
ourselves with what we've got right now. Why don't we ask Althea
and all her top-brass connections to get hold of someone with enough
fruit salad on their lapels that anyone below them will listen to us.'

Mavis and Carol stared at each other through cameras and screens.
'She's not wrong, Mavis,' said Carol at last, with a heavy sigh.

'Good thinking, Annie,' said Christine.

'Aye, you're right. Well said, Annie.' Mavis patted Annie on the
shoulder. 'So I'll phone Althea and get her involved in this case
too. But, before I do that, let's get our ducks in a row, and make
the strongest case we can so we're ready to present it as soon as
we have the chance. Let's begin. Carol – you're good at this, why
not outline what we've got?'

'Right-o, here we go. We have the miniature of the Great Hall
in Swansea; even though it's not been formally attributed to Lizzie,
that process is as good as done. If, as that drawing suggests, she
wasn't dead when everyone thought she was, the next step is for
us to explain away all the evidence presented in court that "proved"
she was dead. That amounts to two key elements – the blood at the
scene, and the testimony of Mrs Wynne Thomas that she saw
Nathaniel.'

Mavis spoke up, 'As a medical professional I would say the
pathologist's report, and testimony, could go either way. On the
stand she admitted it was possible for a person to lose that much
blood and survive, and I agree. What I'd add is that to do it points

to a cold-hearted planner – someone who would be prepared to risk themselves to carry out a plot that would, possibly, result in their death.'

'From what I've been hearing about Lizzie, I'd say she might be that determined, that obsessed with causing her brother to suffer,' said Christine. 'Any idea about the exact logistics, Mavis?'

Mavis sighed. 'If I were to do it I'd have a container handy, and would allow for two or three rounds of bloodletting to gather the amount I desired. There didn't seem to be agreement on exactly how much blood was found at the scene, but the estimates were in the realm of one to two pints. One pint is what they take when you donate blood, and, if Lizzie were capable of doing it, a needle and tube into the correct spot on her arm would allow her to collect a pint, then take a rest, drink fluids and recover, then repeat the process for another half pint, then another. She'd have been very weak, at least, possibly dizzy and a little disoriented.'

'Would she have been able to drive, do you think?' asked Annie. 'Not being able to do it meself, I'm not sure how many of your wits you'd need about you to manage it.'

'I'd no' fancy it myself,' said Mavis.

'Shame,' said Annie. 'See, I'd imagined her stuffing a red wig on her head, dressin' up like her brother and sticking something into the back of his car when she knew that Thomas woman would be out and about with her dog – and she'd have known that 'cos she used to live there after all – and setting him up that way.'

'She could have done so between each drawing of blood,' said Mavis, hesitantly. 'Take one, rest up, drive around, then return and take more. She could have made sure to put some blood, and some of her own hair and skin cells, in the back of his car at the same time.'

'Good idea, Mavis,' said Carol. 'Then there's only one problem left – how on earth did she get away from the place after she'd done it all, without being seen.'

'How'd she get there in the first place?' asked Annie 'Car? Train? Did her brother pick her up somewhere?'

Carol replied, 'There was nothing about that in the trial documents.'

'There was in the papers Ollie gave me,' said Christine. 'Nathaniel picked her up at Swansea railway station. She didn't have a car.'

'So back to Carol's question – how'd she get away?' said Annie.

'It was early summer when she went – about the same time of year as it is now,' said Christine. 'When Alexander and I were there, we saw a lot of people wandering about with backpacks, in walking shoes. She might have just walked away, dressed to look like a hiker. Anyone know what the buses are like in those parts?'

Carol said, 'Hang on a minute, I'm looking online now. There you are – yes, they're pretty regular, though not frequent, from the main road at the bottom of the hill where the cottage is located. They go to the bus station in Swansea, or else to Mumbles. She could have done that – then just taken herself off to anywhere from Swansea either on a bus, or a train.'

'I'm guessing the cops never looked, did they?' asked Annie.

Carol shook her head, 'Nothing came up about it at the trial – but then you wouldn't expect it to because it was a murder trial. Did your mate Ollie make anything of this angle in his defense of Nathaniel, Christine? It doesn't look as though he brought the matter up in court at all.'

'I noticed that, too, but he said if he'd tried to raise the idea in front of the judge of Lizzie not being dead, it would have been shot down. The Crown Prosecution Service did a good job of pushing the murder agenda, and he had nothing to go on, because, as you quite rightly assumed, no enquiries were made at the time she vanished. Certainly he wasn't able to find any CCTV footage showing anyone who looked remotely like Lizzie at any transport hub in the days following her disappearance.'

'Well, until we find the lassie, if we do, we'll have to leave it at a good set of assumptions then,' said Mavis. 'I hope to have the chance to ask her how she did it face to face, one day. What else is there we have to tackle, Carol?'

'If we've worked out how she could have done it, I suppose we're left with why she'd do it,' she replied glumly.

'Mad as a box of frogs,' said Annie bluntly, 'and had it in for her brother.'

'Hated Nathaniel's success, and wanted to bring him down,' said Christine.

'Wanted to make her brother lose everything, and suffer,' said Carol.

'She broke her mother's heart,' said Mavis, 'she must have wanted to do that too.'

'Well, she's done all that, and more,' said Annie. 'It seems we've agreed she's not short of motives. So what remains is – where the 'eck is she?'

'If we knew that, we'd have cracked it,' said Mavis. 'I keep thinking back to what Christine told us Baz said about Lizzie running off before. If she really thought "West is Best" might she be hiding out in some hamlet on the west coast of Wales, somewhere? Carol – is there anything you can do about searching through that sort of thing? How, in this day and age, can a person truly disappear? Is it even possible?'

Carol gave the matter a brief moment of thought. She needed no longer. 'It's funny you should ask. I asked myself the same question after we spoke last night.'

'And what did you come up with?' asked Annie.

'Well,' began Carol, 'it's not too difficult so long as you're prepared to either forego some of the things we take for granted in life, or you have the cash to be able to work around those challenges.'

'We're all listening, give us a tutorial,' said Mavis.

Carol settled back in her chair. 'First there's your name: you only need your real name if you're going to be asked for ID, and there are only certain times in life you need ID, so, frankly, you can call yourself whatever you want until you need to be able to prove it. Hence – you either avoid the need to prove it, or you buy the means by which to be able to do that. Avoidance is cheap, but inconvenient. It means you can't have a bank account, a drivers' license, a credit card or own a vehicle – unless you're prepared to buy a vehicle illegally and then drive it illegally, which is a matter of choice. Cash will be king. You'll have to rent accommodation that doesn't need references, you'll also have to be able to earn an income from a job that doesn't need references. You'll exist by using pay-as-you-go mobile phones. You'll be known by whatever name you choose but, of course, you'll have to avoid being tagged or whatever, by that name, on any social media by anyone you get to know, so you probably won't mix with others much, and you won't, in all probability, have many close friends.'

'She could have changed her appearance so much none of her old friends would recognize her,' offered Annie. 'Maybe that's easier than avoiding all the phone cameras everyone's got these days. And she'd have to do that in any case, wouldn't she, just in case she ran into someone who knew her – you know, by accident?'

'Quite right, Annie,' agreed Carol. 'It would be a lonely life, and you'd be forever wondering if the person who looked at you in the street with a glimmer of recognition knows you by name A, or name B, so it's not just about her not looking like Lizzie anymore, she'd probably change her physical appearance often so she'd be unrecognizable if she unavoidably bumped into someone from her previous life or lives.'

'And you'd keep moving, because I'm sure it gets very tiring to pretend to the same people all the time,' said Mavis. 'You might grow to like them and not want to lie to their faces every day.'

'But you'd be free, and alive,' said Christine.

'You would be,' agreed Carol. 'And if you had a good lump of cash to start with you'd be able to maybe purchase false ID – though you'd also need contacts to make that possible, and they aren't as easy to come by as Annie's LA private-eye-world of gumshoes and crazy broads might lead one to think.'

'I bet Alexander would be able to arrange it in about five minutes,' said Annie, laughing.

'You're right, he probably could,' replied Christine, her voice flat.

Mavis interjected, 'So there's a possibility, if she took all these precautions, that Lizzie Llewellyn could have disappeared a couple of years ago, and has been lying low all this time, watching her brother and mother squirm. That's what you're saying, Carol.'

'That's what I'm saying. Though I'll add, I might see her doing that until her brother was convicted, but since then? That's so cold. So harsh.'

'But hang on,' said Annie, 'if that's what she did do, you know, set up the crime scene, disappear, hide out – all to bring down her brother – what sort of trouble would she be in if she turned up again? She might have thought it was a good idea at the time, but how can she get out of it now?'

'You make a good point, Annie. Having wasted so much police time, surely she'd be open to charges being made against her,' said Mavis.

'Absolutely,' replied Carol. 'The minute she's found, she's going to be in a lot of trouble, and I don't mean just because of how her mother and brother will react toward her. What she's done is criminal in itself.'

'Might she be able to plead some sort of mental breakdown?' asked Christine.

'That would depend on her legal and medical representation,' replied Carol. She paused. 'It might even be true, I suppose, that she did indeed suffer some sort of breakdown, during which she hatched this elaborate plan. Her only other possible endgame would be to always live on the run, in hiding.'

'So all we have to do is work out where she's hiding right now?' asked Annie.

'Ach, I'm no' so sure about that. I think we need to sit down with someone who's going to listen to us, who can then hand this over to a police service that has the ability to carry out a proper hunt for the woman.'

'They need to find a woman in her thirties, with lots of tattoos, who can't help but create art, has a job that pays cash, that's maybe in the St David's area, and has allowed her to be in Swansea within the past couple of years. She'll have been renting cheap rooms and keeping herself to herself,' said Christine.

'And she's been near Picton Castle, too,' said Carol, 'that was in one of the miniatures too. They had some sort of zorbing festival there – big plastic balls people roll around in. I noticed that one especially, and I finally worked out which castle was in the background.'

'That's out west, too, isn't it?' asked Christine.

'Yes, not far from Haverfordwest, so sort of near St David's,' replied the Welshwoman, proudly.

'It might all be enough for the police to get started with,' said Mavis thoughtfully. 'If we can get the right person to hear us out.'

'Why don't you phone Althea and get a name from her?' asked Christine. 'I have to hang up now; I'm nearly at the Leigh Delamere services, and I need a nature break. I'll meet you all at Mountain Ash House as soon as I can get there, after I've done my best to pry the last will and testament of "Daisy" Davies out of the authorities. See you later. Bye.'

After Christine had left the meeting, the three remaining women agreed who would do what for the rest of the day, and went about their business.

THIRTY-SIX

The return of David and Albert from their walk came about ten minutes after Carol's meeting wound up, so she was able to spend some time with her husband and son hearing all about how active the ducks had been, and how Albert had seemed to be fascinated by them. With nap time on the horizon, Carol knew she had to grasp the chance to get all her files in order so they'd be ready to present to the authorities, if only Althea could come up with the name of someone who'd give the women the chance to do so.

She was surprised when Annie arrived at her front door, bearing gifts of lemon tarts and dragging Gertie behind her. Bunty and Gertie had met on two previous occasions, neither of which had seemed to impress Bunty at all. Upon the arrival of the rambunctious puppy, knowing she wanted her son to sleep, Carol suggested to Annie the two of them took a turn around the village green, and munched the lemon tarts as they went.

Of the four women, Annie and Carol had known each other the longest, so Carol was able to draw Annie out on the topic of Tudor Evans more fully than when they were in the company of the others. She hoped he and Annie would take some sort of step beyond dining and walking their dogs together, but Carol sensed Annie was still wondering if Tudor was a man she could rely upon.

'Never needed a man, me,' said Annie, licking her lips after her third tart. 'I'm getting a bit long in the tooth for romance, and Tude? He's a nice bloke, steady and all that, but not going to sweep me off me feet, is he?'

'He seems to be really interested in you, Annie,' said Carol. 'And I can tell you like him a lot,' she added with a smile. 'I know the difference between you having a hot flush and getting all excited because you're due to spend time with him, even if you don't seem to.'

Annie nudged her friend with her bony elbow, managed to trip over Gertie's lead, and ended up flat on her backside on the grass verge opposite the Lamb and Flag pub. Carol had just managed to untangle her chum when Tudor joined them, pink in the face and looking panicked.

'Are you alright? I saw you go flying and I was in the middle of serving a round of beers from the tap – I couldn't leave the bar. Sorry, I'd have been here sooner if I could have been.'

Annie brushed herself down while Carol hung onto Gertie's lead. 'I'm fine, Tude, no worries. It'll take more than a little slip onto this—' she patted her rear end – 'to cause me any problems. Couldn't be better padded, could it?'

Tudor seemed pleased Annie was alright and said, 'Perfect amount of padding, I'd have said,' then blushed, and rushed back to his pub.

'I rest my case,' said Carol, handing the lead back to Annie. 'Daft as a brush about you, he is. You're neither of you getting any younger – go for it, girl.'

'Hmm,' was Annie's only reply. 'So come on then, let's talk shop for a minute. Do you think the cops will listen to us? Got a bit of a colorful track record with them, haven't we?'

'True enough,' replied Carol, looking at her phone, 'which is why having access to Althea's contacts could be useful. It's a tricky situation, that's for sure. I wonder where Lizzie is. The more I think about it, the more certain I am she planned this whole thing and is living a secret life somewhere.'

'We haven't been able to connect her to those books that Daisy Dickens once owned at all, have we?' said Annie. 'I meant to bring it up at the meeting, but I forgot, and then I got a bit sidetracked. I should make more notes.'

'Aw, come on, Annie – you're not half as disorganized as you'd like us all to think. I know you don't care for meetings much, but you made some really good points in that last one. And you've made another now. You're right, we've worked out who Daisy Dickens became, and that she owned the books in which Lizzie drew those miniatures – but how did the lives of those two women intersect?'

Annie paused. 'I've had a thought. Do you think the Cruickshanks are the sort of people who'd pay staff cash in hand? That would be a great place for Lizzie to hide out, don't you think? She could be earning money and living there, and no one would be any the wiser.'

Carol's mouth fell open. 'Brilliant idea, Annie! Good job. You know, you could be right. I didn't get the impression Lizzie was the sort of person who'd be happy to cook, or clean and look after the elderly, but it's a good idea. We should look into that. I tell you what, there's a program I can use that would show me what Lizzie would look like with different hair and make-up, that sort of thing. I've used it to work out what different haircuts might look like on me before going to the hairdressers.' She grinned. 'I don't know why I bother, because I always get the same thing done. I could play around with that a bit, then make some print-outs for us all to have on hand when we go to Mountain Ash House this afternoon.'

'Great idea, Car – glad to be of service,' mugged Annie.

'You always are, and don't you forget it. I know how deeply you were hurt when those creeps in the City made you redundant after all those years of loyal service – don't ever, *ever*, think you're not appreciated nowadays. You are. If only you'd open that hard shell a little bit, and let everyone know you as I do, they'd see you for the pussycat you really are.'

'Safer if everyone thinks I'm a tiger,' said Annie as she headed back to her cottage. 'Give us a ring if you're the one picking me up later?'

'Will do,' replied Carol, heading back to her home and the computer she was hoping could come up with another tool she and her colleagues could use to help solve their case.

THIRTY-SEVEN

Mavis convened an emergency telephone meeting at three that afternoon; Christine was in her car in a car park in Cardiff, Carol at her home-desk, Annie at a table outside the Lamb and Flag pub – having enjoyed a late lunch with Tudor – and Mavis herself perched sideways on the seat of her Mini in Brecon.

'Thank you all for this – I needed to speak to you all as a matter of some urgency,' began Mavis.

'Shoot,' said Annie, safe in the knowledge Mavis couldn't stare her down.

'Aye – I will that, and I know who I might be taking aim at,' snarled Mavis. 'But enough of this. I have just concluded a most worrying appointment with Miss Eunice Phillips, a partner at

Phillips, Bennett, Wilson and Jones here in Brecon. I raised my concerns with her about their young William Williams's meeting with Althea at Mountain Ash House yesterday, and she was worried enough – and diligent enough – to carry out some immediate checks. Because of the nature of their business, and the confidentiality they owe their clients, she hasnae been able to share any specifics with me, but her demeanor and general comments have led me to believe the young Williams chappie has been acting beyond the law, representing himself as a qualified professional, and giving advice he has no business giving. She confirmed that "quite a few" residents of Mountain Ash House have used her firm to prepare wills in which they leave everything to the Mountain Ash House Trust, about which Carol was able to discover nothing – which in itself is cause for concern.'

'Has she said any more than that?' asked Carol. 'Anything about Williams possibly working with Fred Cruickshank?'

'I wouldnae expect her to do so, and she didn't. As I have called this meeting with you, she is in the process of doing the same with her partners. I've left her in quite a state. I also warned her I felt it was time for us to go to the police with our findings and suspicions about the probable scam being run at Mountain Ash House.'

'How'd she react to that?' asked Annie.

'She turned pale, and said she understood why we'd do it.'

'I've got Daisy Davies' will in my hand,' said Christine.

'Really? They gave you a copy right there and then, just because you turned up?' Carol was amazed.

Christine coughed politely before saying, 'Old school tie, again, I'm pleased to say. Daddy's on this occasion. He knew someone, who knew someone, and here I am with Daisy's will.'

'Thank your father for his help,' said Mavis.

'Sure now, me Daddy doesn't need any thanks – he's just happy to have the chance to help out his little girl,' mugged Christine. 'Even happier to use "the ties that bind the world" as he always likes to call them.'

'He's got a point,' said Annie. 'So did she leave the lot to them at the old folks' home, fair and square?'

'Given what Mavis has just told us about William Williams, I can't be sure about "fair and square," but she certainly made out her will clearly enough: a few specific bequests, but the residue to the MAH Trust, to be used as the trustees see fit.'

'Fred Cruickshank lining his own pockets, then,' said Mavis. 'That'll be helpful, thank you, Christine, though if there's a police investigation, or even a legal, ethical one, into the way Mr William Williams has conducted himself, and therefore if he brought undue pressure to bear upon those writing said wills, it might be a very long time indeed before we're able to prove whether Sarah Cruickshank had legal ownership of those books when she "donated" them to the Crooks & Cooks bookshop.'

'Poor Val,' said Carol.

'And poor us, too,' said Mavis, 'because we're looking at a long wait to be paid for our services.'

'So, what next?' asked Annie.

'I've no' been able to reach Althea on her mobile phone today. Granted, she's done her bit for us, and I know she told you, Carol, she'd be rehearsing for tonight, but I am somewhat concerned. Especially if there's really a case against the Cruickshanks, which there seems to be. If it's alright with you, I'd like to head off to Mountain Ash House from here, and maybe get there even before the tea begins. I'd like to see Althea and bring her up to speed – and make sure she's ready to leave with us after the evening's performance. Could you bring Annie along, please, Carol? And you meet us there, Christine?'

The plans were agreed and the call ended.

THIRTY-EIGHT

C arol collected Annie from the Lamb and Flag, where Gertie had been deposited to play with Rosie for the rest of the afternoon and evening.

Annie looked through the copies Carol had produced of Lizzie Llewellyn's face sporting different hairstyles. 'Could be anyone, really, couldn't she? Just a thin face, pale eyes, and then – well, whatever she wants to make herself look like. I can't say these hairdos make that much difference, do they?'

'Funny thing, hair,' said Carol as she pumped the brakes yet again in the busy traffic. 'I've never been able to do anything with mine. It's curly – that's it. I swear when I was young everyone thought I was constantly having it permed.'

'You could straighten it, if you wanted,' said Annie. 'At least you've got hair. Look at me. No more than a fuzz, is mine. Gets to be about an inch long and it just breaks. Eustelle – Mum – got lovely hair, she has. I wish mine was like hers. But I've got hair just like me dad's, more's the pity.'

'It suits you, though. You've got the right-shaped head for it.'

'Ta, doll. I do get to wear some wigs and that, when I'm under-cover. That's always fun. Though I have to admit it's a bit of a fiddle-faddle. I s'pose I should be grateful all I have to do is wash this in the shower, then rub it dry.'

'Yeah, mine too – just wash it and leave it, because there's no point doing anything else and, with Albert around now, I'm not likely to have the time to do anything fancy with it, even if I had the inclination.'

'So do you think we'll find her there? Lizzie, I mean. Do you think she'll look like one of these pictures and be hiding at the old folks' home, in plain sight?'

'Christine mentioned seeing only one member of staff at Mountain Ash House, and she described her as short and round. I don't think Lizzie could manage to look short and round, because, even if she put on weight, she'd still be quite tall.'

'But it makes sense she's at least been there, even if she's not there now.'

'It does.'

'There's no other way she could have got her hands on Daisy's books, right? I mean, if she didn't do those drawings in them there, then where? The books have only been with Daisy and at the book-shop in Hay, right?'

Carol swore – which surprised Annie, who was the one everyone said had a penchant for turning the air blue – and pulled off the road, the car crunching and juddering to a standstill in a gateway to a field.

'You're right, Annie!' she shouted.

'Yeah, I know I am. What's up, Car? You feelin' alright?'

'No. No, I'm not. I'm feeling completely and utterly stupid, Annie. Tall, thin, can't stop drawing, lives on cash, been to West Wales and now this area. Moves around a lot. Keeps herself to herself.' She slammed her hand on the steering wheel. 'It's Sam.'

'Who's Sam?'

'The girl who works at Crooks & Cooks! I've got it all wrong.

Lizzie isn't hiding at Mountain Ash House posing as a cleaner, or a carer, she's hiding out at Val and Bryn's bookshop, and that's where she did those drawings in those books – she found them on Bryn's shelves and "doodled" on them. She never met, or knew, Daisy Dickens/Drayton/Davies. She just got her hands on the books.'

'And she's working there now?'

Carol started the engine and looked for a break in the traffic. 'Yes. At least she's supposed to be.' She nudged out into the stream of cars, causing horns to be hooted, then headed back in the direction of Hay-on-Wye.

'So this Sam is covered in tattoos, is she? And you never thought to mention that?' Annie grabbed at the handle of the door to stop herself slithering about on the seat as Carol drove as fast as she dared, and the other traffic allowed.

'I don't know, I suppose she must have. The only time I saw her she was wearing one of those hoodie things, on a perfectly lovely summer's day. But I know she has a lot of piercings and I also know those two things often go together – a love of tattoos and piercings. It's all about using the body as a canvas for expression.'

'But she doesn't look enough like any of these renditions you printed out for the penny to have dropped?'

Carol blushed as she drove. 'No. Sam had jet black hair, a fringe, and a bun on top of her head. I didn't do one like that. If I had, you're right, I might have put two and two together.'

'So we're doing what now? Racing to Hay to apprehend her on our own? I think I should at least tell Mavis what we're up to. She might have a thing or two to say about this.'

'No, don't phone Mavis, phone Val. Ask her if Sam's at work – don't say anything else, just that. Go on, quick.'

Annie did as she'd been asked. 'It's Sam's day off,' she announced, relaying Val's response as she held the phone to her ear.

'Friday's her day off? Why? Isn't that a busy day? She was there when I visited last Friday.'

Val had heard Carol's question in the car and Annie passed her reply on, 'Val says there aren't a lot of coach trips on a Friday – the roads are too bad – so, for them, it's a quiet day. Sam came in on her day off last week because Bryn had to go up to Chellingworth Hall that morning, as wasn't sure how long he'd be gone.'

Carol shook her head as she hit her horn, to no effect, because they were on a single-lane road.

'Ask Val if she knows where Sam lives, and write it down.'

Annie followed her instructions. 'Val's asking why you need to see Sam so urgently.' She rolled her eyes as she spoke, even though she knew Carol wasn't looking at her.

'Just a couple of questions about Sarah Cruickshank,' Carol shouted. 'Oh yes, and has she got any tattoos?'

Annie said, 'Val says she has no idea, she's never seen any, but Sam's always bundled up. Seems to be eternally cold.'

'OK, thanks for that, Val,' shouted Carol. 'Nothing to be concerned about. No worries, thanks. Hang up now, Annie,' she said.

'Cheers, then,' concluded Annie, and held onto her phone after she'd disconnected. 'So? Mave next?'

'Hang on a minute, don't bother her yet. Let her go and see Althea, whose contacts might be useful for this part of this case, too. Besides, Mavis is across-country from us, so we'll let her do that, and we'll do this.'

'Do what? Turn up at this Sam's place and confront her? Having heard what a temper she's got, and thinking about what she's capable of, I can't say I like the sound of that. Not that I'm not good at handling myself in a tight corner, but . . . Oh, I dunno, Car, sounds like we might be biting off a bit more than we should be trying to chew. And what if it's not her, in any case?'

'Well, then, we'll just ask Sam to show us her arms, and leave it at that.'

'Yeah, 'cos why wouldn't a person show up at your front door and ask you to do that, right?'

Annie folded her arms, then unfolded them again as Carol cornered at speed.

THIRTY-NINE

Mavis arrived at Mountain Ash House just as several other cars were making their way along the winding driveway, bringing guests, she had no doubt, for the tea which was due to begin soon. She'd taken longer to make the journey than she'd hoped, and was doing her best to control the heightening anxiety she was feeling at not having been able to reach Althea on her phone.

She approached the front door where two uniformed schoolgirls were already selling tickets for the tea and the evening's event, and handing out photocopied sheets with song lyrics on one side and a running order on the other.

'One, please. Do you have a concession for those of us over sixty?'

The girls looked down at Mavis. 'Over sixty-fives only,' said the taller of the two. 'Are you old enough?'

Mavis smiled sweetly. 'Not quite, and thank you for recognizing that fact. Here you are,' she handed over the necessary cash. 'Now, where do I go, please?'

The shorter and wider of the two girls replied, 'The evening performance will begin at six o'clock in the main lounge area. Seating for that is on a first-come, first-served basis. Please don't move the chairs about. Until then, there's tea and entertainment, plus a cash bar, serving non-alcoholic drinks, around the back. Go all the way through here . . .' She waved a welcoming arm.

'And the facilities?' asked Mavis quietly.

Both girls giggled. 'The loos are inside on the right, behind the stairs,' said the taller of the two. 'There might be a queue.'

'And where might I find Mr or Mrs Cruickshank?'

'Out the back,' chorused the girls.

'Most helpful,' said Mavis, and attended to her natural require-ments, thereby allowing herself to focus on the matter of tracking down Althea.

Unable to see what she knew would be a blonde-wigged Althea anywhere about, Mavis headed for the woman she recognized as Sarah Cruickshank, who was serving lemonade from a large punch-bowl with a ladle.

'You must be the lady of the house, Mrs Cruickshank,' said Mavis. 'I'm Mavis MacDonald, a friend of one of your residents – or, I should say, a possible resident. Mrs Gladys Pugh invited me along. Have you seen her about?'

Sarah Cruickshank paused, the ladle in mid-air, dribbling lemonade on the plastic tablecloth. 'Oh yes, Mrs Pugh. What a lovely person. I do so hope she's been enjoying her time here. She's made herself at home, that much I can tell you.' She looked around, a blank expression on her face. 'Come to think of it, I don't recall having seen her about today.' She returned her attention to Mavis. 'There's been such a lot for me to do to get ready for this concert, you see, so I dare say I wouldn't have done. Maybe one of our residents will know where she is. You're welcome to ask about.'

Mavis was not pleased with the response, but thanked the woman politely. As she'd been speaking, Mavis had been sizing her up; was this a woman who could happily talk people into leaving all their worldly goods to her for her own benefit? Mavis wasn't sure.

Taking her lemonade and moving slowly among the knots of people standing and chatting merrily in the afternoon sunshine, Mavis tried to not allow the feeling of dread in her stomach to affect her focus. She made a beeline for anyone with blondish hair, only to be disappointed every time. After about ten minutes, and unable to locate Althea, she asked a woman with a white face, a black top-knot wig and chopsticks in her hair if she'd seen Gladys Pugh anywhere.

'Gladys?' The woman looked around. 'I don't think she was planning to wear any sort of costume that might disguise her – some of us are, as you can see – but I can't spot her. Do you know her?'

'Yes, I do. She invited me. I believe she needed a hand with her final preparation for this evening's performance and I volunteered to let her do a run through for me, but I can't find her anywhere.'

The top-knotted head tilted. 'Isn't that nice of you. I'm Maisie, by the way, and I've spent a fair bit of time with Gladys. Lovely woman. She'll fit right in here. I haven't seen her today, come to think of it. It's been a bit of a busy one, what with one thing and another. So much to get sorted out, you know. She might be in her room. Have you tried there?'

'Where would that be?' asked Mavis.

Maisie pointed to the window of a room on the top floor, at the back of the house. 'There's her room, see, up there.' She waved toward the rear of the house. 'That's probably where she is. Last-minute nerves, maybe. I shouldn't worry, I'm sure she'll be fine. You could phone her. Use the house phone inside – it goes through to all our rooms. Just dial her room number.'

'And what might that be?'

Maisie gave it some thought, 'I'd have said fourteen or fifteen – I think those are the numbers for the guest rooms. You could try them both.'

'Aye, thank you, I'll do that.' Mavis moved into the rear lounge of the house and did exactly as had been suggested. There was no response from either number. She weighed her options, and made a decision.

Mavis reckoned she'd be less noticeable if she didn't rush about, so walked slowly up the staircase past the signs announcing she was entering a Residents Only area. Once she'd reached the correct floor, she walked along the narrow, wood-block hallway until a window overlooking the festivities at the rear of the property showed her that either the room on the right or the left must be Althea's. Each room had a doorbell, though neither bore a name. She pressed the button of the room on her right and heard a bell ring inside the room. She waited. No response. She rang again. Maybe Althea was napping? Still nothing. She repeated the process for the room on her left, with the same result.

Glancing along the corridor to make sure no one was there, she tried both doors. They were both locked. The Yale mechanism on each was the sort that could be easily defeated by using a plastic card to slip the lock open, but she didn't want to do any breaking and entering. Yet. She weighed her options, again. She rang the bell marked 'Thomas' for the room next along the corridor on the right-hand side. No answer. She worked her way along the entire corridor. Not one person responded. Her training in criminal insights told her the place was ripe for the invasion of thieves; the inadequate locks, the fact not one person was there and the ease with which she'd made her way to the landing concerned her greatly. When all this was over she'd have a word with the Cruickshanks about security matters, but she knew that wasn't her concern at the moment.

She returned to the window overlooking the garden, and peered about. Might she be able to spot something from above? All she needed to see was one, small, blonde-wigged woman, tottering about on legs that were very nearly eighty years old and she'd be happy. But there was no such person.

She looked at her watch; where on earth were Carol and Annie? It was a time when more women might have made the job easier. Then she wondered what they could do that she couldn't, and realized she had to take action herself. Creeping back along the corridor to make sure no one was coming up the stairs – no one was – she finally pulled out an old credit card she no longer used, and slipped the lock on the door to the guest room on the right. It took a couple of minutes, but she managed it.

Once inside, it was clear to Mavis the room wasn't in use; there was nothing on the bedside table, the wardrobe was empty, and the toilet paper in the empty bathroom had been folded to a point. She closed the door, and moved across the hallway, listening for footsteps before she repeated her trick with the card. This time, the room was much more promising; a glass of water beside the bed, a collection of beige ladies' clothes in the wardrobe and, in the bathroom – oh joy – a navy blue and gold box. Floris Special No 127 Eau de Toilette. Althea's perfume, as worn by both Winston Churchill and Eva Peron. Mavis knew the dowager had worn the same fragrance for over fifty years, her beloved Chelly having given it to her as a gift on their first dinner-date, and she wouldn't go anywhere without it. It was a sure sign Mavis was in Althea's room. The question was, where the devil was the woman herself?

Mavis started as she heard a sound outside in the corridor. She spun around, pleased she'd closed the door behind her upon her entry. Was that someone opening the door? It might be Althea . . . or not. Something in the pit of Mavis's stomach told her not to fling open the door hoping to see her friend, but to hide. Her only option was under the bed, which was where she lay as she watched a pair of man's shoes walk around the room. She heard him pull open the wardrobe, drop something she assumed was Althea's suitcase on the bed, and proceed to stuff everything from the room into it, in what Mavis assumed was a haphazard manner, so roughly did the bed bounce above her head.

She breathed as quietly as she could as the man went about his business. He paced back and forth between the bed and the bathroom, then, finally, he was gone. Mavis remained where she was for a few minutes, until she was sure the coast was clear. Then pulled herself out of her hiding place, a little dusty, but no worse for wear. The room in which she stood now looked as devoid of life as the one across the hallway. She peered into the bathroom; no, the man hadn't folded the toilet paper into a point.

She perched on the end of the bed. She had a very bad feeling about Althea, and it seemed she was going to have to make some difficult decisions alone.

FORTY

Carol parked on the double yellow lines outside the small, stone-built house high on a hillside in Hay-on-Wye, and leapt out. Annie joined her. They both hammered at the door and were grumpily greeted by an elderly man wearing a turquoise shell-suit that looked as though it had dropped through a time-portal from the 1980s. 'Hello then, and who are—' was all he managed before Carol interrupted.

'It's an emergency. Is Sam here?'

'I expect so,' he mumbled. 'Know her, do you?'

'I know the woman she works for, Val Jenkins, down at the Crooks & Cooks bookshop.'

'Oh yeah,' replied the man slowly. 'Nice girl, Val. Knows her father, I do.'

'Well, they are the reason I'm here. We're here,' said Carol acknowledging Annie's presence. 'I know it's her day off, and I need to see her. Is she here?'

'Back room downstairs, is hers,' said the man. 'Go on through. Give it a knock yourself.'

Carol shot along the hallway and knocked on the door. 'Keep it calm,' called Annie at her friend's back.

The threesome waited, until it was clear there was going to be no response.

'Could you let us in?' asked Carol as politely as she could, given how desperate she was feeling.

'Oh hang about now, I don't know about that. Pays rent for this, she does. Privacy is her right, I'd have said.'

Carol and Annie exchanged a meaningful look, and Annie launched in with: 'Mr . . . um, what was it?' she asked sweetly.

'Daniels,' replied the man.

'Mr Daniels, the reason we've come here is because we are private investigators, working on behalf of the Jenkins family. They are very concerned about Sam. They think she might . . . you know . . .' Annie allowed her facial expression and a finger drawn across her throat finish the sentence.

Mr Daniels' eyes grew round. 'You don't mean she'd do herself some harm?' Annie nodded. 'Under our roof, you mean?' Again Annie nodded. 'Oh, we can't be having that. No indeed.' The man walked to the bottom of the stairs and called, 'Margaret? Margaret? Have you got the spare key for the back room, love? Bring it down, will you. Quick as you like.'

'Just a tick,' came the reply. A couple of minutes later a woman wearing a suit similar to that of her husband, but with the addition of a scarlet chiffon scarf tied around her head, which was a mass of curlers, appeared and handed her husband a key. 'What's up, and who are you, then?'

'Private detectives, they are. And they reckon Sam is going to do herself in, in our house. What do you think of that then, Margaret?'

Margaret Daniels looked from Carol to Annie, and back again, 'Well, we can't have that, can we? Better go in and see if she's alright.'

This time four people crowded outside the door to Sam's room. Having unlocked the door, Mr Daniels stood back and said, 'There you go then.' He swallowed. 'I'll let you professionals go first,' and stood aside.

The room was a mess; the wardrobe doors hung open, the drawers from the chest were empty and strewn on the floor. 'Gone,' said Carol as she strode in, Annie just half a step behind her.

'Any idea where she might be?' asked Annie. 'Mr Daniels? Mrs Daniels? Did Sam say she was leaving?'

Two heads peered into the room. 'Not a dickie bird,' replied Mrs Daniels.

'When did either of you last see her?'

Blank looks. 'When she came in from work yesterday,' said Mr Daniels eventually. 'Ran into her at the front door, I did.'

'So she might have quite a head start. Maybe overnight.' Carol waved her arm at the walls. 'Definitely Lizzie, I'd have said.'

Four pairs of eyes peered at the dozens of miniatures, each drawn on a large sheet of paper.

'Has she stuck drawing pins all over my walls?' shouted Mrs Daniels. 'I'll have her for that, I will. I told her no pins.'

Carol flopped onto the edge of the bed. 'Oh no,' she said, her head in her hands, 'we're too late.'

Margaret Daniels moved toward Carol's juddering body and patted her back. 'There, there. I might be able to smooth them all out with a bit of thinned-down wallpaper paste on a sponge. No need to cry, lovely girl.'

'Car, come and have a look at this,' said Annie stepping out of the tiny bathroom that led off the room.

Both Carol and Margaret peered into the space.

'Is that blood?' screamed Margaret, covering her face with both hands in horror.

Carol sighed. 'Red hair dye, I'd have said. Don't panic.'

'Panic? *Panic?*' replied Margaret. 'Well, I'm glad it's not blood, of course, but how on earth am I going to get that out of those towels? Ruined, they are.'

'Carol,' said Annie, 'I think that's your phone, ringing in your bag.'

Carol answered the call. 'Yes? What? Now? No – we're in Hay at the moment. It's a long story. She's what? Oh no! Right-o, we're on our way. We'll see you there as soon as possible.' She pushed her phone into her handbag and looked at Annie, tears streaming down her face. 'That was Mavis. Althea's in trouble. At least, she's completely disappeared. We've got to get to the old folks' home. Now.'

'You mean you're leaving?' asked the Daniels couple, as a duet.

Carol nodded. 'Yes. We're going to have to hand this over to the police now. I advise you to lock the door, and don't touch anything. I'll try to let you know what's happening. Thank you, and I'm sorry for all your trouble.'

As Carol and Annie took their leave, Carol wiped tears from her face with the back of her hand. 'Flamin' hormones. You'd think I'd be like a normal human being by now, wouldn't you?'

Annie hugged her friend. 'Never had kids, don't know. Though all of this is really upsetting, so I understand why you'd be on edge. What did Mave say, exactly?' Carol told her as the two set off. 'Gordon Bennett, I hope Althea's alright. Where the 'eck can she be? Seems like we're up to our neck in women who keep disappearing.'

'Goodness knows. Look, I'm going to focus on the driving – but I need to talk things through with you, and you can make some phone calls, too. First of all – get hold of Val and put her on speakerphone.'

Annie punched numbers.

'Hello, Val Jenkins speaking.'

'Hello Val, Annie and Carol here,' shouted Carol. 'Just a quick one for you – do you happen to know if Sam can drive?'

'I do. She can drive, but hasn't got a car.'

'Do you think she might know how to steal one?'

'What a strange question. I've no idea. Why on earth would she want to do that?'

'Never mind, probably a stupid idea. Have you, or your father, talked to her about the fact we are looking into either the artist who drew the miniatures, or the Lizzie Llewellyn case, by any chance?'

'Well, I know I haven't, but Dad might have done. No reason not to. And I'm pretty sure she could have overheard us discussing whether we're going to sell the miniatures or not when they've been authenticated.' Val paused. 'It got a bit heated at one point. A bit loud too, probably.'

Annie and Carol shared an eye roll. 'Right then – so this is where we are with it, Val,' said Annie. 'We're pretty certain your assistant Sam is Lizzie Llewellyn in disguise, and she's done a runner.'

Val said, 'But that makes no sense. Lizzie Llewellyn is dead. Her brother's in prison for having killed her. Everyone knows that.'

'We're pretty sure now that's not the case,' said Annie. 'I haven't got time to go into it now – but this is what we need to know . . . has Sam mentioned anyone or anywhere you think she'd run to if she was in trouble?'

Silence. 'No. She's never mentioned anyone, or anything that matters to her. Ever. I know she came here from Haverfordwest, and that's about it. I could ask Dad to phone the bloke there she used to work for, if you think that might help.'

'It could do, but before you do that, maybe you could text the address to this phone, so we have it to be able to pass it onto the police,' replied Carol.

'The police? Why the . . . oh, yes, I see. Well, if what you say is true, what a terrible thing for her to have done. And you mean to tell me Lizzie Llewellyn was sitting downstairs from me all that time and I had no idea. Well . . . what can I do to help?'

'Nothing I can think of, thanks,' replied Carol miserably.

'We should phone Mave,' said Annie urgently.

'First of all, let's think this through,' replied Carol. 'If Lizzie is making a run for it from Hay-on-Wye to St David's – and I'm going with that because it's where she ran off to before, and we know she moved here from Haverfordwest so it sounds like that's her comfort zone – how would she do it?'

'I know there are trains running from Hereford to Haverfordwest, 'cos I've seen them when I've been going to Cardiff or Swansea,' replied Annie. 'How you'd get from Hay to Hereford?'

'Buses,' said Val, her voice echoing. 'They're not too bad at both ends of such a trip. Better than pinching a car, I'd say, and much more likely if she's trying to stay under the radar.'

'You're right,' said Carol. 'So, public transport, and maybe she set off last evening. She could be in St David's already.'

'But what you were saying yesterday, about someone trying to hide – wouldn't it be dangerous for her to go back to the same place? Wouldn't she be more likely to be spotted? Even if she's changed her hair color, someone might recognize her,' said Annie.

'That sayin' about there being "nowt so queer as folk," well, it's true,' said Val with certainty, 'and they also do some stupid things when they're under stress. She could just head back where she feels safe.'

'Hey, Car – why don't we ask Chrissy to head off out that way, rather than coming back here?' suggested Annie.

'Good idea,' replied Carol. 'Listen, Val, I know you'd like to help, but I think you'd better let us lead on this now. We'll do our best to get the police onto it, and we'll keep you in the picture. Thanks for all your help.'

'You're welcome,' replied Val from her shop, and disconnected.

'I can't stop driving – and we've got to get to Mavis to help find Althea as quickly as we can. That's what has to be our first priority for now, Annie. Could you phone Christine and ask her to head off for Haverfordwest and all parts west of that, then can you phone the police and tell them what's going on?'

'Who shall I phone? Locals hereabouts? CID in Swansea, or Brecon, or wherever? What's it best to do?'

Carol replied, 'Tell you what, phone Christine, then phone Stephanie and ask her the name of the top-ranking police officer she's met face to face since she became a duchess. Let's work it through that way. If we can't call on Christine's school tie, and Althea's contacts aren't available to us, it's the best way I can think of to go about this.'

'Good thinking, Batman,' said Annie. 'Your faithful Dobbin is all over it like a rash.'

'Less Dobbin, and more Robin,' said Carol as she leaned on her horn to encourage two cyclists to consider not riding abreast on the road.

FORTY-ONE

B y the time Carol and Annie arrived at Mountain Ash House, the car park was almost completely full and couples and small groups were hurrying toward the front door of the imposing building.

'Looks like this concert thing is pretty popular,' said Annie as she extracted herself from the car.

'I've got to be honest and say I'd never have guessed it,' said Carol as she joined her friend in the queue waiting to pay for their tickets.

'The show begins in five minutes,' announced one of the schoolgirls taking entry fees in her loudest voice. 'Seating is still available,' she added.

'Two please, and where might we find Mrs Cruickshank?' asked Carol.

'Carol, Annie – at last,' said a frazzled-looking Mavis as she spotted them enter. 'Come with me, quick.'

'Mave – sorry, doll, I have to go to the loo first,' said Annie. 'Me eyes are crossed.'

'Ach, go on with you, it's through there,' said Mavis roughly. 'And be quick about it. You too, Carol? Aye, well I'll wait here then.'

The threesome reunited and hurried to the garden. 'The show's just about to begin, ladies,' called Sarah Cruickshank as she ushered some stragglers toward the lounge. 'Aren't you going to join us?'

'Ah, just the person,' replied Mavis, swooping on the woman and grabbing her by the arm. 'You're coming with us.'

'But the show . . .?' wailed Mrs Cruickshank over her shoulder.

'It'll go on without you. It'll have to. We need a word,' said Mavis. Her colleagues took their cue from her and soon all four women were standing beneath a tree with the first strains of a piece of piano music wafting on the summer air.

'Mrs Gladys Pugh – where is she?' demanded Mavis.

'Didn't you find her?' asked Sarah Cruickshank innocently.

'No, I did not. Tell me, does your husband wear brown shoes, with yellow laces?'

The Cruickshank woman looked puzzled. 'He does. It's his little way of having a bit of fun. Why?'

Annie and Carol were both wondering the same thing.

'In my search for Gladys Pugh, I found myself in her room earlier on, and, while I was there a man wearing such shoes entered said room, and bundled all of Mrs Pugh's belongings into a suitcase and took them away.'

The look on Sarah's face was one of complete bewilderment. 'How did you get into her room? And why do you only describe my husband's shoes?' She stared at Annie and Carol. 'What's going on?' She turned toward the house and shouted, 'Fred! Fred! Come here, will you.'

'When did you last see your husband?' asked Mavis, menacingly.

Sarah was panicking. 'I don't know, about three o'clock? Four-ish? I've been very busy and people have been coming and going for hours.'

Mavis's voice grew alarmingly quiet, 'Mrs Gladys Pugh has completely disappeared, Sarah – I hope you don't mind me calling you that. Now that's not like her. In fact, I can tell you for certain she would not have disappeared without telling us where she was going. And her disappearance is made even more suspicious by the fact your husband cleared out her room this afternoon, wouldn't you say?'

'Fred? Fred!' Sarah's voice was almost a scream.

A short, round woman appeared in the open doors to the rear lounge. 'Are you alright, Mrs Cruickshank?' she called.

'No – I'm not, come here, Amy.' Sarah beckoned to the woman, and tried to pull away from Mavis's vice-like grip. Mavis wasn't having any of it.

'Have you seen Fred . . . Mr Cruickshank?' asked Mavis. 'His wife is keen to see him.'

Amy gave the matter some thought. 'Last place I saw him was down by the laundry room, in the basement a couple of hours ago.'

'What's he doing there? Today?' asked Sarah.

All four women looked at Amy, awaiting her answer. She shrugged. 'I dunno. Beats me. Maybe he had a special load of laundry to do? He had a big bag with him.'

Mavis spun Sarah around to face her. 'Where's this laundry room? Take us there now, you hear me?'

Sarah nodded, her eyes round with fright, and she dismissed Amy, telling her to return to the concert. She led the three women through a pair of doors set underneath the main staircase, and down some stone steps to a large, whitewashed area. 'That's the laundry room, over there,' she said, pointing.

Finally, Mavis let go of the woman's arm, and she, with Annie and Carol right behind her, rushed to the door. 'It's locked,' snarled Mavis. 'Where's the key?'

'It's never locked,' replied Sarah. She joined the women and tried the door herself. 'You're right, it is. Now why's that?'

'Shut up!' said Althea, holding up her hand as though about to strike the woman.

All four of them sucked in their breath and listened.

'There's someone in there – I can hear a muffled thumping sound, and squeaks,' said Annie. She raised her voice, 'If that's you, Althea – don't worry, we're right here. Get away from the door, we're going to break it down.'

Carol looked at the door in question and said, 'I don't think we're going to be able to do that, Annie. It's big and old and the lock's probably a corker. Sarah – where would the key be?'

Sarah looked flummoxed. 'In the office?' She didn't seem at all certain.

Mavis bit her lip then said, quite gently, 'And where's that exactly?' Sarah pointed upwards, her hand trembling. 'Good girl,' said Mavis, followed by, 'Annie, go.'

Annie took off up the stairs and returned moments later, panting, with a bunch of keys in her hand.

'Which one is it?' asked Mavis. Sarah pointed at a big, old, iron mortise key. 'Thank you. Carol, would you be so kind?'

Carol unlocked the door, and they entered another open, white-washed area, this one housing two large washing machines and four dryers. The muffled cries they'd heard from beyond the door were clearer now, though there was no one to be seen.

'The big cupboard,' shouted Annie, springing across the room.

Pulling open the double doors of the ceiling height, built-in cupboard, the four women were met with the sight of Althea, lying on her back bound hand and foot, with tape over her mouth.

Sarah Cruickshank let out a little cry of horror, as Carol and

Annie lifted Althea to a sitting position, under Mavis's detailed instructions. 'Get some water for her to drink, now,' she barked at Sarah, 'and let me get that tape off her mouth. Stand back, Annie – this is a job for a woman with nursing experience. Ready, Althea?' Althea's eyes opened wide with fright, then Mavis yanked off the tape as fast as she could. 'Now just stay still a moment, dear, it'll soon be over. Carol – take photographs, quick as you can.'

'Oh Mavis, no,' cried Althea. 'Just get me out of here.'

'You'll be glad later on we did it, it's evidence, dear,' replied Mavis as Carol snapped away. 'Did that Fred Cruickshank do this to you,' she asked, as she helped Annie and Carol to untie the dowager's bindings.

Althea burst into tears as she replied, 'Yes he did. He really frightened me, Mavis. I thought . . . Oh, I don't know what I thought. But it's been a terrible night.'

'You've been here all night?' asked Sarah, standing with a glass of water in her hand. 'And you say Fred did this? I can't . . . why would . . . I don't understand. What's going on? Will someone tell me what's going on, please?'

As Althea sat on a chair, Annie helped her rub her ankles and wrists while Carol was phoning the local constabulary.

'You poor thing, Althea, we've all been so worried about you. I can imagine what's been going through your mind,' said Annie, 'having been kidnapped myself, I know how bleak it can feel.'

'Aye,' agreed Mavis, 'this must have been a terrible time for you, my dear. You and I can have a cuppa and talk it all through when you're feeling up to it.'

'When I'm feeling up to it? I'm up to it now. That hateful man. He treated me like so much rubbish, he did, and thought he could get away with it. You see, when you're young and lovely, everyone notices you. They certainly noticed me – I was known to be quite vivacious in my youth and from then on I was a duchess, so of course, everyone took notice of me. They didn't all like me, and I know for a fact some were quite critical of me behind my back, but everyone knew I existed. Being this Gladys Pugh for a few days has shown me how elderly women are invisible to almost everyone. Fred Cruickshank made it very clear to me he didn't see me as a person; he just saw a wrinkled face, a beige two-piece and a bad wig. He saw a thing, not a person. And a thing that could make trouble for him because I asked that William Williams some questions he didn't like. That's what started all this, Mavis – it's that young man who set Fred on me, I know that for a fact. They're as bad as each other.'

'Aye, and they'll both have to answer for it,' replied Mavis.

'It's terrible, to be seen as a thing,' continued Althea, the words spilling out of her. 'It's never dawned on me before that's what happens in the real world. I've spoken to a few of the ladies here about it and they all agree with me, but they say they've got used to it. As they've become wives, mothers, grandmothers and widows they've just become less and less visible. It's dreadful to think what society is losing. All that wisdom. All that knowledge. And you know what, it's not just because we're old, it's because we're women. I've never had any time for those feminist types, but I might look into what they say a bit more deeply now. It can't all be about burning bras. Can it?'

Carol smiled. 'Maybe the bra-burning thing was just a gimmick, a good way to get the attention of the men who ran the media back then. Of course it's still mainly men who run the media today, so maybe they didn't take as much notice as they should have done. But it's funny you should say that. I've been wondering if I'll ever have a life beyond being Albert's mam and David's wife. I used to be Carol, now I'm not anymore. It's a bit weird.'

'I was always accorded attention because of my role and my rank,' said Mavis. 'But I know you're right – without my uniform, I seem to dissolve into the background.'

'I wish I could do that,' said Annie. 'Dissolve a bit. It's all well and good being a tall black woman in London, but hereabouts? Let's just say I'm trying to grow an extra-thick layer of skin and not slouch all the time. But I know what you mean.'

'What can we do about it?' said Althea. 'Women are important. They get things done. They make life run smoothly. Why aren't we recognized for it?'

Carol tried not to laugh aloud. 'I think you might have hit upon an age-old question, Althea. I'm not sure there are any easy answers or solutions.'

'Men!' said Althea.

'There, there, now dear, don't take on so,' said Mavis in her most soothing tones. 'There's a time and place for everything, and maybe trying to sort out the gender bias in the world is no' the topic for right now, eh? Besides, I need to have a serious chat with Sarah over there. Will you be alright gathering yourself, while I take her away to the office?'

'Go, I'll be fine.'

FORTY-TWO

Mavis escorted Sarah to the upstairs office, sat her down and said, 'We understand you have been depositing books at bookshops in Hay-on-Wye as a way to get rid of them, would that be correct?'

Sarah's expression changed from one of apprehension to surprise. 'Well, yes, though what business that is of yours, I've no idea. Besides, now isn't really the time for that – is it? I don't understand what's going on here.'

'Now *is* the time. Explain your actions,' snapped Mavis.

Sarah Cruickshank was clearly taken aback. 'I've been giving away books to bookshops so they can sell them. What's the problem with that? Everyone wants something for nothing, don't they?'

'Maybe you and your husband do, but the fact remains the people in whose shops you left those books need to be sure they were yours to give, so they know they aren't selling on stolen goods.'

'Stolen goods? What? I've never heard anything like it. This is nothing to do with *anything*. Why was that woman locked up in my laundry room? And why would she say my Fred did that to her? Why would Mrs Pugh say that?'

'Her name's not Gladys Pugh, it's Althea Twyst. And she has no reason to lie. The police will be here presently. If we can locate Mr Cruickshank he can explain his actions at that time, though I have to say I suspect he's long gone by now.' Mavis consulted her watch. 'Aye, he's had a couple o' hours' head start.'

'Long gone? Why would Fred be long gone? He hasn't done anything wrong.'

'Other than kidnapping a dowager duchess and confining her against her will, as well as running a swindling scam of your residents, no, he hasn't done anything wrong at all,' snapped Mavis.

Sarah stood, shaking with what Mavis judged to be anger. 'I don't know who you lot are, but you're bonkers, the lot of you. I'm glad the police are on their way, because I'll have a few things to tell them about you lot, I will. Wait – who did you say that woman downstairs is? Althea Twyst? The old duchess? What was she doing, going about the place in disguise? This is more than a bit fishy, is this.'

Sarah's terror having subsided into anger, Mavis went in for the kill. 'Tell me about the books you've been leaving about the place, Sarah – that'll help us get to the bottom of it all.'

Sarah's expression suggested it would do no such thing, but she grumpily replied, 'Proper antique places don't buy books these days, and with Hay-on-Wye on our doorstep I thought for sure someone there would want the books. Our residents only bring books here with them that have meant a lot to them, see, so most of them are really old. Family books – from the times when families had books. I walked my feet off to start with, going to bookshop after bookshop asking if anyone wanted to buy them. Turned their noses up at the lot of them they all did. There was something not right with the binding, or it wasn't the right edition or some such. Flat out turned me away they all did. So what could I do with them all? You can't take books to the dump. They aren't something you just dispose of like so much rubbish. A book means something, it does. Someone wrote it, printed it, bound it – not to mention the ones who read them, held them and maybe cried into them. I love books I do, they've all had a life – like a person. I've kept as many as possible over the years, but I haven't got time to read them all and . . . well, there are just too many for me to keep them all. So I decided to set them free – give them to places that could find them good homes.'

'So you're happy for the bookshop owners to sell them on as their own?'

Making an expansive gesture, Sarah replied smiling, 'Yes. Whatever. Set them free in the world, that's what I say. I give them away to people who love books. They can do what they want with them – they're theirs now.'

'Thank you, Mrs Cruickshank. Is that what you did with the books left to you by Daisy Davies in her will?'

'Daisy?' The woman was puzzled again. 'No, not hers. They all went to the shops before she died, they did. Asked us to do it especially because she wanted a bit more space in her room. Nothing to do with us, they weren't. They were hers to give. I just transported them for her.'

'Music to my ears, Sarah. Thanks for that. That's a very signifi-cant piece of information. Now, tell me, do you know your husband sells a good many antiques about the place?'

'Fred?' Sarah sounded surprised. 'Well, I don't know about that. I might have seen him go off to the markets with the odd pot or two now and again.'

'What happens when someone dies and leaves you everything? One of your residents?' asked Mavis.

'Us? Why would they leave us anything? They might leave some-thing to the MAH Trust, but then a lorry comes and takes all their stuff away, and the trust liquidates it.'

'And who is "the trust" exactly?'

Sarah examined her fingernails. 'That's Fred's area, not mine. I'm too busy with this place. He sorts all that. Why? What are you saying?'

Mavis told Sarah about William Williams, her husband, and their suspected scheme. By the time the police arrived, Sarah was in floods of tears, terrified about facing a difficult interview and heartbroken her husband had clearly left the premises hours earlier, knowing the entire scheme was about to come crashing down around his ears. Mavis agreed to stay with the woman to explain to the police she was certain only Fred Cruickshank had been involved in the shady dealings that had been going on at the home.

The arrival of a police car itself wasn't noticed by most of the people enjoying the concert party, and Althea waved off all attempts to prevent her from standing at the back of the lounge to be able to take in the performance of three elderly women dressed in highly stylized Japanese garb wiggling onto the little stage giggling like schoolgirls, then excused herself. The applause increased when a young man also dressed in a kimono took his seat at the upright piano beside the stage and began playing the introduction to 'Three Little Maids.' When Mavis joined Annie and Carol she hissed, 'Where's Althea?'

'Gone to the loo,' replied Annie.

'Then who's that, down there at the front, by the stage?' asked Mavis.

'Gordon Bennett, what's she up to now?' whispered Annie loudly enough that a few people turned to shush her.

After Megs, Mabel and Maisie had curtsied many times, and

finally tottered away, Althea mounted the stage dressed, once again, as Gladys Pugh. The crowd settled.

'I was due to recite *Fern Hill*, by Dylan Thomas,' announced Althea in Gladys's accent, 'but I haven't had the time I'd like to rehearse it properly, and I do so want to do it well that I hope it's alright with everyone if I read it, rather than reciting it from memory.' A ripple of applause ran through the room.

Carol was glad she already had a handful of tissues, because she knew she was going to need them. 'Have you ever heard this, or read it?' she whispered to Annie.

Annie mouthed back, 'Nah, not my cup of tea.'

'It's about the poet remembering the times when he visited his aunt's farm when he was a boy and didn't realize how few times in life we get to feel truly free and happy. By the end he's talking about how old age is catching up with him, and he realizes he's facing his own mortality. It's quite something.' Annie shrugged, and they gave their attention to Althea's small figure.

When Althea had finished her performance – for it was so much more than a simple reading – nothing happened at all for a good five seconds or so, and Carol knew she'd been right; she could hear the odd sob in the audience before rapturous applause broke out, and Althea blushed as she took her standing ovation with grace and good humor.

Mavis rushed through the crowd to help the dowager off the little platform, and Carol could see even she had been crying.

'Give us one of them hankies,' said Annie quietly. 'Quick, before Mave sees me.'

Annie took a wad of tissue from her friend and they were both looking quite composed by the time Althea met them in the doorway, accepting many thanks and congratulations from audience members along the way.

'Time to go now, I think,' said Mavis as the women regrouped at the back of the room. Althea nodded.

A pale-faced Sarah Cruickshank joined them at the front door. 'I'll never be able to forgive my husband, and I don't expect you to forgive me, Gladys. I mean, Your Grace. He never told me what he'd been up to. I never knew anything about it, honest I didn't,' she blubbed.

'Quite often, people aren't what they appear to be on the surface,' said Mavis, and the women took their leave.

FORTY-THREE

Saturday 5th July

The day of the Chellingworth Summer Fete was just about as perfect a day as could be hoped for in Wales, in early July. The sky was pale cobalt with a smattering of fluffy white clouds, the air was freshened by a light breeze and the afternoon temperatures were forecast to be good, but not uncomfortably hot.

The snowy marquees dotting the emerald grass had been erected and furnished over the preceding days, so all that remained on Saturday morning was for them to be filled with whatever was appropriate to their particular role. In one, tables were decked with cakes to be judged, floral arrangements were made ready to be assessed and even photographic displays by schoolchildren were set up to be admired. Bryn Jenkins and his fellow members of the Hay Booksellers' Association brought their wares and displayed them to the best of their considerable abilities in another. Marjorie Pritchard appeared in full gypsy paraphernalia to take up her spot in the fortune-telling tent and graciously complimented young Sharon Jones, who ran the Post Office and general store in Anwen, on her oversight of the production of hundreds of sandwiches, the preparation of several tea urns and gallons of cold drinks in the largest marquee of all.

The fairground-style entertainments were fully furnished with stuffed toys, pellet guns were checked for accuracy when targeting metal ducks and the coconut shy was presented with tickets that could be redeemed in the refreshment tent as prizes. The gates were due to open at eleven thirty, and an hour before the appointed time it seemed as though everything was on track to allow for a successful event.

A tour of the significant artworks housed at Chellingworth Hall was led by Henry and Stephanie, accompanied by the WISE women, Nurse Thomas – wearing what she insisted upon calling 'mufti' – and the group of men from London Jeremy Edgerton had assembled.

Gwen Llewellyn had sent the piece of artwork deemed necessary for an attribution of Lizzie's work to be made in the Bentley supplied by the Twysts, but she herself had remained in Gower, with her son, who'd been released from prison immediately following the apprehension of his sister the previous Saturday. By using Stephanie's name, Annie had managed to speak to a high-ranking police officer while she and Carol had been speeding to Mountain Ash House, who'd told one of his juniors to hear her out. Luckily, the officer in question had been possessed of more than three functioning brain cells and a good deal of ambition, so he'd taken the information Annie had given him and had put it to good use. Lizzie Llewellyn had been picked up at a small B&B in St. David's where she'd given a false name but still had the red hair she'd acquired before leaving Hay-on-Wye.

After the tour of Chellingworth Hall, as the group enjoyed a specially prepared American-style brunch, Jeremy Edgerton and his colleagues happily gave their unanimous decision that the miniatures the WISE women had been investigating were indeed by the hand of Lizzie Llewellyn and signed various documents attesting the same. A rough estimate of their value was suggested as running to at least dozens of thousands of pounds, so long as an exhibition and accompanying book were to be undertaken and produced. Both Val and Bryn Jenkins agreed, on the spot, that the eventual sale of the miniatures was what they wanted. The fact Lizzie Llewellyn was 'no longer dead' didn't, in the opinion of Jeremy and his colleagues, diminish the potential value of the works. Indeed, he went so far as to suggest that the publicity her case was likely to garner might even edge prices upwards, rather than down.

Once the meeting disbanded, the attendees all went their separate ways to enjoy the festivities of the day.

As Althea and Henry left the stage, having officially opened the fete, the dowager spotted a gaggle of residents from Mountain Ash House meandering toward the refreshment tent.

'Come along, Henry, there are some people I'd like you to meet. Hang on a minute—' she rummaged in her capacious handbag – 'ah, there it is! I'd hoped I'd have the chance to wear it again.'

'Good heavens, what are you doing, Mother? Are you actually going to put that thing on your head?' Henry eyed the rather sorry-looking wig with horror.

'Indeed I am – and you be a good boy and play along with me for a few minutes, alright?'

'Mother, I don't think . . .' began the duke, but he scampered after his mother who was striding out, pulling the wig onto her head.

'Yoo-hoo, Maisie,' called Althea.

The group of women stopped and turned, several faces smiling in recognition.

'Lovely to see you again, Gladys,' said Maisie as the women met on a path. 'Despite everything that's been going on at Mountain Ash House – and I can tell you all about that when you have a minute or two . . . maybe over a cuppa in the tea tent – everyone's been talking about the lovely job you did at the concert last week. We were all very sorry to see you go.'

Althea was especially gratified to spot the caustic Sylvia Trumbell in the group. Althea flashed the woman a coy smile and pulled off her wig, causing a stir of even greater confusion. 'I'm sorry I had to deceive you all, just a little. You see, I was working undercover for an enquiries agency, so I had to play a part. I'm not Gladys Pugh, I'm Althea Twyst. This is my son Henry, the eighteenth duke.'

As consternation changed to recognition and general mirth, hugging ensued among the group as invitations for tea at the Dower House were extended. Althea even reached out and shook the dreadful Trumbell woman by the hand, pulling her close and whispering, 'I was a classically trained dancer doing a bit of hoofing on the West End stage when I met the duke. He was the love of my life.' The blush she saw color the woman's cheeks was a very singular delight for Althea.

Carol met up with David and Albert, and the three of them had a fine time at all the stalls, then sat beneath the shady trees. The photographs Carol took would be the perfect mementos of a wonderful family day, the first time they'd used the large picnic basket she and David had been given as a wedding present. She couldn't help but wonder how many more times she, David and Albert would attend the Chellingworth Summer Fete. She hoped it, along with many of the other annual events in and around Anwen-by-Wye, would become staples in their family life. She felt she was living in a lifestyle magazine as she flattened the checked tablecloth on the springy, verdant grass and delighted in the view of the marquees and Chellingworth Hall's magnificent façade in the summer sun.

'Love you this much,' she said waving her arms around her, looking at her husband.

'I know exactly what you mean,' he replied as Albert squirmed in his portable car seat and pulled on his toes.

Annie tracked down Tudor in the beer tent, where he had several barrels of ale and crates full of bottles on offer, and was being helped to serve by many willing hands. He told her he was pleased to see her because Rosie and Gertie needed more attention than he could give them. Annie took the puppies off to play, then the three of them collapsed in the shade, where Tudor found them. Annie was delighted to see he was carrying a bucket filled with cold bottles, and thrilled when he presented her with a few pork pies wrapped in a tea towel. The final flourish came when he pulled a couple of packets of hot sauce out of his pocket.

'I hope it's the right sort, it was the best I could do,' he said as he presented them to her.

Annie grinned. 'Eustelle would throw a fit, but it's me you're talking about – any hot sauce is better than no hot sauce.'

Christine met Alexander in the parking area, and they wandered the attractions together. She declined having her palm read by Gypsy Pritchard, and laughed when Alexander told her he knew her future in any case.

'You're a very clever man then, because I don't know it myself,' said Christine lightly.

'Maybe I am. But I won't say any more until I know your answer will be yes.'

Standing close in the swirling throng Christine challenged him. 'How do you know I won't say yes now?' She grinned wickedly.

Alexander held both her arms and pulled her to him. 'Did you enjoy your fizzy water in that pub in Soho, by the way?'

Christine flushed. 'What do you mean?'

'I know you saw me in that pub. Why didn't you mention it?'

Christine decided to make a clean breast of it. 'I knew something fishy was going on and I wasn't sure I wanted to get to the bottom of it.'

'Are you now?'

'You mean do I want to solve what Annie would undoubtedly call The Case of the Dodgy Developer? I'm still not certain. I saw you hand an envelope of what I assume was cash to a trio of highly suspicious-looking men. If you'd like to tell me why that was, then on your own head be it.' She stared him down.

'I can't change overnight, Christine, but I *am* making real alterations to the way I do business. Instead of fighting fire with fire, I've been trying a new tactic – new for me anyway – I put the fire out. What you saw was me buying off a competing developer. He wanted some houses I had my eye on, and I decided I'd try to talk him into stopping the campaign of terror he was waging against the residents, rather than . . . well, doing anything less savory.'

'So you did something different. For you. Good. Did it work?'

'It worked.'

'I'm glad.'

'Me too. And surprised.'

'How did you spot me?' Christine thought she'd done a good job of remaining out of sight in the pub.

Alexander smiled. 'Oh my darling – I know how you breath, how you move and how you smell. I couldn't miss all that. I could feel you in the room.'

'Really?'

'Yes. And I could see your reflection in the facets of the glass paneling I was facing. That helped.'

They hugged.

'Just give me time, Christine? I can't change overnight, but I can do it. We both need to learn to trust each other, don't you think?'

Christine nodded.

'So, with that sorted,' said Alexander after a few moments of thoughtful silence, 'how about I buy you a beer? Or a bun?'

'I've got a better idea,' replied Christine playfully, 'how about you try to knock a few coconuts off their perches and win some tickets we can redeem for a cuppa or two? More sporting all round, wouldn't you say?'

Mavis took tea in the refreshment tent with Bryn Jenkins, and was a little irritated by his underwhelming response to the conclusion of their case. She was pleased when Val joined them and showed only too well how overjoyed she was at the day's news. As the daughter rattled off how the money could change their lives, the father sat looking into his cup of tea as though the world was about to end.

'Come on, Dad, it'll change both our futures. No more living under the same roof. I'll be able to get my own place again now.'

'The chapel needs a new roof. That's where *all* the money will go,' he said.

Mavis was shocked. 'But I thought you and Val owned the business jointly? Isn't that what you said?'

'We do,' replied Val. 'Half of whatever we get for those miniatures is mine by rights, Dad.' The young woman looked distraught. 'I've been hoping it would happen, and now it has. If you want to give your half to the chapel, then you do that. I'll do what I want with my half.'

'You'll do as your father tells you,' snapped Bryn.

Mavis saw the pain in his daughter's eyes, then saw the tears well up. She wondered if she should leave them alone because she was pretty sure a storm was about to break in front of her, but she was too late.

Val Jenkins stood and looked down at her father's bowed head. 'Sorry, Dad, it's time. I've done my dutiful daughter bit, and I'll carry on doing it until we can liquidate our assets, then I'm off.' She paused to draw breath and gave her attention to Mavis. 'Thanks for all the work you've done for us, Mavis. Your invoices will be paid by our joint business. Your efforts have freed me. I'll never know how to show you how grateful I am for that. Without exaggerating – you've saved my life. I'm going to have a pint to celebrate. Bye, Dad.'

As she left, Bryn lifted his head and said, 'Terrible thing, alcohol. It can ruin a person, like her. I happen to know she goes to the pub several times a week, whatever she might say about evening classes and so forth.'

Mavis weighed her response carefully. She stood and picked up her shoulder bag. Before leaving she said, 'Goodbye, Bryn. I'm sure we'll be able to conclude our business swiftly, and without having to meet again.'

At 3 p.m. on the dot, Althea, Henry, Stephanie and Clementine gathered on the little stage, and Tudor leapt into action as the master of ceremonies. His voice boomed out across the estate and the large crowd gathered in spots where they could get a good view of the proceedings.

Henry and Clementine did a pretty good job of speaking to the assembled masses about how their mother had inspired them throughout their formative years and into their adult lives, then it was Stephanie's turn to take the microphone.

The duchess thanked everyone who'd worked so hard to make the event such a success and presented a check to the local children's charity which was raising funds for its literacy outreach. Then she called upon Tudor to speak, at some length as it all turned out, about how influential Althea had been in the local, and wider Welsh community. Applause rang out on several occasions, then he called for quiet, and Stephanie took center stage again.

'I know we can sometimes take a person for granted, especially when we are able to forget they are, actually, a person . . . not just a title. Althea Twyst is my mother-in-law, and she is a wonderful woman. She has welcomed me into the family with warmth, humor and humility, and I was in little doubt that the best birthday present she could ever have would be what's about to happen. Ladies and gentlemen . . .'

The recorded strains of the Welsh national anthem were piped through the loudspeaker system and anyone who was sitting, stood. As throngs of people dotted across the grounds in front of Chellingworth Hall joined in the signing of '*Mae hen wlad fy nhadau,*' a procession of men, women and children filed onto the stage behind Althea and the rest of the Twyst family. As the rousing end of the anthem rang around the picturesque estate, and Welsh flags fluttered proudly in the summer breeze, Stephanie took Althea by the hand and drew her toward the microphone.

'Your Grace – Althea – your work in the community has changed the life of every person you see on this stage today. These people are just some of those who have benefitted from your fundraising efforts for fighting cancer, local literacy groups, book supplies for hospitals, youth groups with their focus on sports, the arts and music, activity groups for the elderly and many more. They all wanted to come today to thank you.'

Applause and shouts of support brought tears to the dowager's eyes. She stepped forward and took the microphone.

'They don't need to say thank you to me, I should be the one saying thank you to them. Having a reason to get up in the morning is all I ask for, and I know today, more than ever, the best reason to get up and get going is to help someone in some way. Thanks to my friends at the WISE Enquiries Agency for letting me work with them to do that, and thanks to all the groups represented here – and those who aren't – for allowing me to lend a helping hand.'

A rousing chorus of 'Happy Birthday' was led by Henry while his mother greeted everyone, individually, on the stage.

As they moved away, Henry whispered to his wife, 'Mother seems to be genuinely happy. I'm delighted – and it's in large part due to all your wonderful arrangements and hard work. Thank you so much, my dear. I only hope her birthday next year doesn't prove to be something of an anti-climax after this one.'

Stephanie smiled up at her husband. 'I don't think it will be, Henry dear. It'll be the first birthday she'll celebrate as a grand-mother. That's pretty special, isn't it? Do you think she'll like that?'

Henry stood stock still among the swirling group. 'Do you mean . . .?' His wife nodded, and squeezed his hand. 'Is that why you've been a bit off color?' She nodded again. 'Bless my soul,' was all Henry could manage.